Praise for the
Crossword Mystery series

ANATOMY OF A CROSSWORD

"This is a delight for both amateur sleuths and crossword puzzle aficionados. Blanc provides a breezy mystery set against a realistic entertainment industry background."
                                                              —*Booklist*

CORPUS DE CROSSWORD

"Another dandy puzzler."   —*Publishers Weekly*

"The well-drawn characters in *Corpus de Crossword* are people we all know . . . The mood roller-coasters from pathos to laugh-out-loud funny, and the plot twists and turns before it delivers the final punch."   —*I Love a Mystery*

"Mystery fans that like a light, small-town regional mystery are going to have a lot of fun reading *Corpus de Crossword*. The two protagonists make a great investigative team in the tradition of Nick and Nora, and their connubial bliss lightens the mood when they hit a bump in the investigation. Nero Blanc is a master when it comes to constructing puzzling mysteries."   —*BookBrowser*

A CROSSWORD TO DIE FOR

"Nero Blanc serves up six actual puzzles and one solid mystery . . . Surprising revelations and ten-dollar words abound as another body turns up, a mysterious French woman causes problems, and the couple begins to receive hints via puzzles faxed from Belize."   —*Publishers Weekly*

"A Nero Blanc mystery is always fun to read . . . The story line itself is complex, entertaining, and thoroughly thought-provoking, a mystery lover's delight as well as a crossword puzzle fan's pleasure. This book, in fact this series, is highly recommended."   —*BookBrowser*

continued . . .

THE CROSSWORD CONNECTION

"Unique entertainment."　　—*Bucks County (PA) Courier Times*

"Another neat whodunit, along with some clever crosswords . . . Blanc builds the suspense slowly and surely, challenging the reader with a dandy puzzler." —*Publishers Weekly*

"An enjoyable interactive who-done-it."
　　　　　　　　　　　　　　—*Painted Rock Reviews*

"The third Crossword mystery retains the uniqueness of its two predecessors . . . The story line is fresh with the puzzles serving as an intricate part of the amateur sleuth inquiry."
　　　　　　　　　　　　　　　　　　—*BookBrowser*

TWO DOWN

"A snappy, well plotted story that combines the best elements of the puzzle mystery and the village mystery . . . *Two Down* works well as an homage to Agatha Christie and Ngaio Marsh as the solid plot never strays from its course and features a surprising yet plausible ending . . . *Two Down* is the perfect solution across and down."
　　　　　　　　　　　　　—*Fort Lauderdale Sun-Sentinel*

"[An] engaging crossword mystery . . . The [six puzzles] are an interactive touch that add to the problem solving fun."
　　　　　　　　　　　　　　　　—*Publishers Weekly*

"As entertaining as the series debut . . . The story line is smooth . . . Readers who enjoy a different type of who-done-it, starring two likable characters and six puzzles, will fully relish Mr. Blanc's latest across and down novel."
　　　　　　　　　　　　　　　　　　—*BookBrowser*

THE CROSSWORD MURDER

"At last puzzle fans have their revenge . . . super sleuthing and solving for puzzle lovers and mystery fans."

—Charles Preston, Puzzle Editor, *USA Today*

"A puzzle lover's delight . . . A touch of suspense, a pinch of romance, and a whole lot of clever word clues . . . Blanc has concocted a story sure to appeal to crossword addicts and mystery lovers alike. What's a three-letter word for this book? F-U-N."

—Earlene Fowler

"Addicts of crossword puzzles will relish *The Crossword Murder*."

—*Chicago Sun-Times*

"An eccentric cast of characters keep the pot boiling with well-paced breaks for puzzle solving . . . Good summer entertainment."

—*Philadelphia City Paper*

A CROSSWORDER'S HOLIDAY

A lethal short story collection with crosswords included— and a bonus recipe!

"If crosswords are your puzzle of choice, you'll be delighted to meet [Nero Blanc]."

—*The Mystery Reader*

"Wonderful . . . Each story is a delightful mix of mystery and fun . . . Even if you're not a puzzle fan, the characters are so likable, you will have trouble putting this book down."

—*Romantic Times*

"A cleverly designed holiday anthology that crossword puzzle fans and mystery buffs will enjoy."

—*BookBrowser*

And don't miss

A CROSSWORDER'S GIFT

Five short stories for a long winter's night— with puzzles included!

DEATH
ON THE
DIAGONAL

NERO BLANC

BERKLEY PRIME CRIME, NEW YORK

THE BERKLEY PUBLISHING GROUP
Published by the Penguin Group
Penguin Group (USA) Inc.
375 Hudson Street, New York, New York 10014, USA
Penguin Group (Canada), 90 Eglinton Avenue East, Suite 700, Toronto, Ontario M4P 2Y3, Canada
(a division of Pearson Penguin Canada Inc.)
Penguin Books Ltd., 80 Strand, London WC2R 0RL, England
Penguin Group Ireland, 25 St. Stephen's Green, Dublin 2, Ireland (a division of Penguin Books Ltd.)
Penguin Group (Australia), 250 Camberwell Road, Camberwell, Victoria 3124, Australia
(a division of Pearson Australia Group Pty. Ltd.)
Penguin Books India Pvt. Ltd., 11 Community Centre, Panchsheel Park, New Delhi—110 017, India
Penguin Group (NZ), Cnr. Airborne and Rosedale Roads, Albany, Auckland 1310, New Zealand
(a division of Pearson New Zealand Ltd.)
Penguin Books (South Africa) (Pty.) Ltd., 24 Sturdee Avenue, Rosebank, Johannesburg 2196, South Africa

Penguin Books Ltd., Registered Offices: 80 Strand, London WC2R 0RL, England

DEATH ON THE DIAGONAL

This is an original publication of The Berkley Publishing Group.

This is a work of fiction. Names, characters, places, and incidents either are the product of the authors' imagination or are used fictitiously, and any resemblance to actual persons, living or dead, business establishments, events, or locales is entirely coincidental. The publisher does not have any control over and does not assume any responsibility for author or third-party websites or their content.

First edition: July 2006

Berkley Prime Crime trade paperback ISBN: 0-425-20998-9

An application to register this book for cataloging has been submitted to the Library of Congress.

PRINTED IN THE UNITED STATES OF AMERICA

10 9 8 7 6 5 4 3 2 1

A Letter from Nero Blanc

Dear Friends,

Connecting writers to readers requires a special talent, and we'd like to acknowledge the many people whose savvy, humor, and insight—not to mention business acumen—have made our mysteries a success story. Each of you deserves an Author's Appreciation Award. Lacking a suitable lexical offering, we'll simply list you and extend a multitude of kudos from two very grateful authors.

Thank you to: Mary Alice and Richard of Mystery Lovers Bookshop; Jim at The Mystery Company; Sharon at Books & Company; Barbara and The Poisoned Pen; Creatures 'n Crooks and Lelia; Bonnie and Joe of The Black Orchid Bookshop; Augie of Centuries & Sleuths; Bruce and Turn the Page; Mystery Loves Company's Kathy; The Mystery Bookstore's Sheldon; Ed and Jean at M is for Mystery; Partners & Crime and Marshall; Richard at Head House Books; Joanne at Murder on the Beach; Booked for Murder's Mary Helen; Tom of Murder Ink; Bridge Street Books' Suzanne; Debbie at Mechanicsburg Mystery Bookshop; Angie of Voices and Visions; The Book Garden and Esther; Barry of Book'em Mysteries; Katie of Village Books; Kate at Kate's Mystery Books; the many kind folks at Chester County Books, The Bookworm, and Baker Books; and, last but not least, Nancy of The Virginia Festival of the Book.

Getting to know you has been a delight,
Cordelia and Steve

CHAPTER

1

Although his name might suggest otherwise, Moon-dog was a proven champion. He was an eight-year-old gelding, a commanding seventeen-hand Dutch Warmblood and a world-class jumper, with enough blue ribbons to fashion a debutante's satin ball gown. He had been foaled and trained at Glen-Rosalynne Farms in Louisville, Kentucky, then sold to an Oscar-winning film director with a three-hundred-acre ranch overlooking the Pacific Ocean in Santa Barbara, California. The film director had jumped Moon-dog—shooting schedules permitting—in every major competition from coast to coast for a solid year before he'd suddenly grown tired of the entire equestrian thing and decided to scrap one toy for another and try his hand at offshore sailing instead. He sold Moon-dog for $100,000—about a quarter of the price of the boat—to an investment banker in Newcastle,

Massachusetts, a medium-sized city just to the west of Cape Cod across Buzzards Bay.

The banker bought the animal for his sixteen-year-old daughter because her primary equitation horse, a gray Thoroughbred mare by the unlikely name of Willow-whisp, had yet to finish above second—meaning the beast had yet to win the banker's daughter a single blue ribbon. Not one! And this despite Daddy paying a trainer one hundred bucks a day, rain or shine, show or no show. Naturally the situation was both galling to the banker and a source of extreme exasperation to his daughter, Tiffany.

Both mounts, Moon-dog and Willow-whisp, were now boarded at King Wenstarin Farms, a show and breeding stable fifteen miles outside of Newcastle. It was a top-drawer place, as befitted the pricey animals residing there, but the lower stable in which the gelding and mare were housed had one disturbing complication on this particular early October evening, and that was the unmistakable presence of smoke.

Moon-dog was the first to smell it. In fact, he'd heard the unusual noises that had initially triggered the problematic situation, watched the culprit flee the scene, and so knew precisely how the predicament had begun. The only thing the animal didn't know was how to unlatch the gate to his stall—or how the story would end.

Horses do not react well to smoke. As with most mammals, humans being one notable exception, their internal mechanisms take them rapidly to the logical conclusion: Fire! Danger! Death! This intelligent insight creates in them a burning desire to put large distances between themselves and the smoke as quickly as possible. Moon-dog first snorted and then began anxiously pawing at the straw that covered the dirt floor of his roomy box stall. The acrid smoke tickled at his flaring nostrils. He whinnied and backed solidly into the wooden gate that barred his exit. The iron hinges creaked, and the steel latch jumped, but both held the gate in place. It would be only two minutes before Moon-dog would begin to do some serious damage to the stall and to himself.

The large round clock positioned in the center of the immaculate wall that rose above the stable's entry read 7:06 P.M., when Moon-dog began his nervous pacing and the building's equally gleaming windows revealed a deep-blue sky and a bright full moon hanging low and orange as it turned the autumnal leaves a molten silvery red. The color eerily replicated the light from the fire that was now brewing in the tack room located at the west end of the stable. Known as the "small" stable, the space had room for only sixteen stalls, eight of which were presently occupied.

Moon-dog's antics swiftly attracted the attention of the other seven equine residents. Willow-whisp, three other mares, and three additional geldings trusted the chestnut-colored Warmblood, like baby ducks trust their mothers; and if the big guy wanted out, so did they. After fifteen additional seconds, all eight horses were rearing and bucking in their stalls, their eyes huge and terrified, and their whinnies panicked, while the smoke grew thicker and the brightness of the tack room fire illuminated the stable's center aisle from one end to the other.

"Fire! Fire at the lower stable! We need some help down here!"

Orlando Polk, the barn manager, seemed to appear from nowhere as he shouted the warning up the hill toward the

Big House and the horse farm's owner, Todd Collins. Polk rightly surmised that the tack room's telephone and intercom system had most likely been reduced to melted balls of plastic, and he also realized that trying to call the local firehouse, five miles away at best, would be a futile exercise. The barn would be ash long before the boys in helmets and waterproof gear could possibly arrive.

Orlando had been working at King Wenstarin Farms for six years. He was forty-two years old and had been around horses his entire life. He was proud to say he was one hundred percent Pequot Indian. He kept his raven black hair tied in a ponytail that reached halfway to his slim and sinewy waist, and his nose for smoke was as good, if not better, than Moon-dog's. He was already cursing himself under his breath for not having smelled the fumes sooner. But even if he had, he couldn't have stopped the blaze; it was spreading far too quickly, and he had a good idea why. Unlike Moon-dog, however, Orlando had heard no strange noises or spotted anything out of the ordinary. He shook off questions of how the fire had begun and concentrated, instead, on logistics. He realized that if the horses weren't freed soon they would claw at the sides of their stalls, pointlessly attempting to climb their way out and tearing their pricey flesh, or worse, fracturing their fragile bones.

With this assessment in mind, he ran up the aisle to the double barn doors at the stable's east side, shoving them open and outward and latching them in place before heading toward the structure's west end. A less-seasoned horseman might have made the mistake of freeing the horses from their stalls before opening the doors, thereby creating pandemonium and probably getting trampled to death in the process, but Orlando prided himself on remaining calm in times of crisis. At least where horses were concerned.

As he raced back to open the west-facing doors, he passed the tack room, which was now completely engulfed in flame. The air in the building had turned as thick and dark as mud, but fortunately the stalls directly opposite the blaze were empty. No animal could have remained that close to the fire without killing itself out of fear. Polk pulled his shirt over his nose and mouth and forged his way to the western doors, but before he could reach them, they seemed to swing open on their own. He then saw the farm's owner, Todd Collins, yanking them back and securing the latches.

Collins was seventy-four years old with a lean and angular six-foot-three-inch frame, a full head of wavy white hair, and an ample, matching mustache. He'd made millions in the importation of Irish whiskey to the United States, and his passion was horseflesh, especially the elegant creatures trained in the hunter-seat equitation discipline. A limp that was the result of a riding spill four years earlier sometimes made strangers imagine Collins was a frail man, but they were wrong. Todd Collins was weak neither in body nor mind.

Orlando gaped at his boss, the fire now reflecting vividly in Collins's craggy face and making him look as if he'd just stepped directly from the gates of Hell. Polk swore again, but too softly to be heard, while his boss's irate eyes bore into him.

From Todd Collins's point of view, it appeared as though Orlando had done nothing to try to save the horses or extinguish the blaze. At first sight, his barn manager seemed to be standing in the smoke dumbfounded, like a lost child.

"Dammit, man, get these horses out of here. What are you waiting for? An invitation? Get those stalls open. Force them out the other end. If any head this way stay with them; drive them through the smoke and up toward the Big House lawn."

Orlando stood frozen for a second too long, and Collins grabbed his shoulders and shoved him toward the far end of the stable.

"You work the right side stalls; I'll do the left," Collins barked.

Orlando stumbled slightly, but then sprang into action, hurrying his supple dancer's body from stall to stall, releasing the horses then swatting them hard on their rumps to direct them away from the tack room and toward the open east end of the barn. Collins duplicated the action on the other side of the stable until all eight animals had been safely driven from the building. The older man then turned to his manager and shouted, "Get to that sprinkler valve and turn it on. I don't care if we flood the entire state of Massachusetts. I'm going to drive these babies down to B paddock. If the stable goes up in smoke, they'll panic where they are now. We need to give them some distance."

"Right, boss." Orlando Polk turned and headed back into the burning barn, while Collins unlatched the gate at the far end of the paddock and began moving the horses farther from the blaze.

By the time the manager reentered the stable, the entire building had filled with smoke. He pulled his shirttails up to cover his mouth and nose and worked his way back toward the tack room. The main sprinkler valve was located on the wall a few feet away from the room, but fortunately the fire had moved up rather than out and hadn't yet reached the valve. The system was old and had been shut down only the prior week because of leakage over a few of the stalls—which had resulted in a work order but no actual repair as yet. By the time he reached the valve, he was choking and coughing uncontrollably. The smoke clogged his lungs, and his eyes felt as though they were burning up. Tears coursed down his cheeks as he reached for the round handle of the valve.

But the moment he got his hands on the metal ring, a sharp pain shot through the back of his head. In the split second that Orlando remained conscious and aware of his surroundings, he heard a pinging noise he couldn't quite identify and assumed it was produced by whatever had slammed into the back of his head. Then his thoughts returned to the sprinkler valve, and he was able to twist it open even while his body began crumpling to the dirt floor where it remained, inert as a rag, as water cascaded from the ceiling.

After securing the horses in B paddock, Todd Collins hurried back to the lower stable. When he reached the east entrance, he found his trainer, Jack Curry, standing near the barn door, and noticeably out of breath. Jack was another large man, but only in his mid-forties and more solidly built than his boss. Curry loved to affect any posture and attitude that remotely resembled John Wayne. Stance, swagger, speech, laconic grin, penetrating scowl: Jack had each characteristic memorized, and his private impersonation brought results. People instinctively respected and trusted Jack Curry. In Todd's opinion, the trainer was a class act; "the best damn horseman on the East Coast," who also happened to have once been married to Todd's eldest daughter, Fiona—the emphasis being on ex. In her father's estimation "Jack was, and continues to be, the only man capable of steadying such a high-strung filly. And look at her now," he'd add with a rueful shake of his white mane. "I swear, a brood mare has got more sense than that woman."

"I ran up the moment I saw the flames, Mr. C," Jack now told his boss in his typically easy drawl. He coughed, then spit emphatically into the dirt. "How'd this damn thing get started?"

"No telling." Todd glanced into the barn. "Good . . . Orlando was able to get the sprinklers going. Have you seen him?"

"No, sir. I thought he was off today."

"No, no, he's around. He helped me get the horses out, then went back in to monkey with that blasted sprinkler system." Todd peered into the steamy, belching murk. "He must still be inside." Collins moved toward the stable entrance, but the trainer grabbed his arm.

"I wouldn't go in there, Mr. C. There's no guarantee those sprinklers are gonna do their job. They're old as the hills. Those pipes fail, or break along the line, the place'll go up like a haystack. Orlando probably scooted out the other end. He's no hero." The final comment held a note of cowboy disdain, as if the barn manager could never hope to compete with someone whose stock in trade was saving damsels in distress and rescuing wagon trains that were under savage attack.

Todd pulled his arm free. "I don't like it. If Orlando were outside, he would have come down to check on the horses. I say he's still in there. We've got to get him out." With that, Todd's tall frame limped decisively into the stable.

Jack watched his former father-in-law disappear in the smoke and shook his head. "Crazy old coot; gonna get us both killed over some lousy greaseball." He pulled a handkerchief from his rear pocket, pushed it into a neighboring horse trough, rang it out, covered his nose, and ran inside.

Jack had no idea whether the sprinkler system was going to win its battle or not. The crackling and sighing of burning wood appeared to be getting louder with every step he made, as though the barn were getting ready to collapse around him. He couldn't help second-guessing the wisdom of entering the structure. "Mr. C," he shouted through the swirling smoke, "where the hell are you?"

"Over by the valve. Polk's been knocked unconscious. Get over here and give me a hand."

Coughing and blinking back acid tears, Jack worked his way over to the valve, where he found Todd crouched over Orlando's prone body. "Is he alive?"

"I don't know. Let's get him out of here."

"This place is gonna come down on top of us, Mr. C. Any second." Jack ducked to the side as a bale of burning hay thudded down from the loft above, hissing when it hit the water on the ground.

"I don't think so," the old man shouted back. "I think it's going to hold. Let's get Orlando out of here pronto, though. I don't want to push our luck any more than we already have."

Jack bent down and slid his arms under Polk's shoulders and lifted his chest, while Todd took hold of his feet.

"Ready?" Jack said.

"You betcha."

They stood in unison, hefting the limp form and moving gingerly toward the east end of the stable. A loud and continual hissing sound now prevailed in the barn, and the smoke was heavy with steam and the smell of charred wood and ruined saddle leather.

Exiting the stable they heard the muffled sirens of approaching fire engines. After they set the body down in a grassy patch, Todd straightened and looked at Jack. "Did you call the damn fire department?"

"No."

Todd kicked at the dirt with his good leg. "Damn . . . It must have been Ryan. Why can't she listen?"

"Something wrong with the fire department, Mr. C.?"

Collins knelt down and checked Orlando's pulse. "I like to keep situations like this in-house."

CHAPTER

2

Contrary to the sleepy atmosphere that presently prevailed at Newcastle's *morning* newspaper, the *Herald,* the offices of its *afternoon* rival, the *Evening Crier,* were rife with scurrying and worried feet, with furrowed eyebrows, grim expressions, and the kind of terse remarks that can't help but sound insulting even under the most benign of moments—which "deadline" at a daily city newspaper definitely was not.

Although the dreaded moment was nearly four hours away, the *Crier's* editors, reporters, columnists, and advertising account executives knew full well that the time could evaporate in the blink of an eye; and most were secretly envying the *Herald* employees as they did almost each and every day. Not that the folks at the *Herald* didn't go through the same hysteria on a regular basis; it's just that for them it rolled around at nine at night, not nine in the morning.

Annabella Graham stepped off the elevator on the third

floor of the *Crier* building and into this tense melee, just as she had every Friday for the past seven years: equipped with a manila envelope tucked under her arm. Belle, as she preferred to be addressed after suffering too many puns of the *anna-gram* variety, was the crossword puzzle editor at the *Evening Crier.* She was thirty-three years old, bouncy, and lithe, with quizzical gray eyes, blond hair the color and consistency of dandelion down, and a radiant smile that revealed how little she cared about her looks. She was also smart.

Preferring to create her week's offering of puzzles in the quiet and comforting atmosphere of her home, rather than at the *Crier*'s offices, Fridays were one of the few times the other employees got a glimpse of their Belle.

On the weeks when she opted to deliver the seven puzzles *after* deadline's witching hour, most of her coworkers stopped by to chat, inquiring chummily about her husband, Rosco, a local private eye, or their two dogs, Kit and Gabby. But when she chose to arrive in the morning, as she had today, very few greeted the resident "brainiac" with more than a preoccupied nod. They were a mercurial crowd whose personalities switched back and forth, depending on where the big and little hands sat on the clock; and they had hard news to attend to. Word games might be popular with readers— very popular, actually—but to those who wrote the leading stories, Belle's contributions couldn't compete with lethal twenty-vehicle pileups on the interstate, or corporate malfeasance, or government lies, or domestic violence, or celebrity scandals, or war dead, or starvation in Africa, or any of the other fun articles that made the front page.

Belle had never much liked spending time at the *Crier*. It wasn't the people she objected to; they were an entertaining bunch once you got them away from work, and she and Rosco enjoyed socializing with them. Instead, it was the building's architecture that she found off-putting. It was postmodern gone to seed, like an inner-city high school after a long and wearying week. A pale, dirty brown was the color of choice—which some politely called "greige" or even "sepia," while others chose earthier and less flattering epithets: words that don't normally appear in family newspapers.

Belle proceeded down the dingy hall, dodging the various messengers and copyboys, until she reached her own cubicle-sized office, where she opened the door into the stark and unlovely space. A chipped laminate desk, an office chair that listed to one side, and a bookcase (mostly empty) stared forlornly back at her. Atop the desk sat a small collection of pencils, a few sheets of quarter-inch graph paper that had been there so long they were almost as brown as the walls, a blotter pad, and an in-out box. It was there that Belle placed the manila envelope containing a week's worth of crosswords accompanied by their solutions. After that major effort, she was free to go home—a simple and predictable ritual, albeit a little odd. As long as the interoffice mail boy found the package, there at seven o'clock on Friday evening (word games for the next week being exempt from the demon deadline), everyone was happy.

Belle fiddled with the envelope, repositioning it until the edges took on a military precision, then murmured a quiet, "Well, that's that. Enough thrills and chills for one week. It's off to the the dog park for me."

"Oh, nay, nay, nay, say it isn't so, my dear *Bellisima*. One can't vacate the dank underbelly of the venerable *Evening Crier* simply because something as trivial as the sun may be shining in the bright universe beyond. You don't see any of the other moles running for daylight, do you?"

She turned to find Bartholomew Kerr, the *Crier*'s diminutive gossip columnist standing in her doorway, the greenish glow of the fluorescent overhead lighting casting an olive patina over his nearly bald pate and on his upturned face with its oversized black glasses. Depending on circumstances, Bartholomew either resembled a scrawny baby bird or a housefly searching out a tasty bread crumb.

Despite his oddball appearance and his florid, and often pretentious, speech, Kerr was one of Belle's dearest friends at the newspaper. He prided himself in knowing everyone in the city of Newcastle, and what they were up to and when— that is, everyone whose name could be recognized when reproduced in boldface type in his "Biz-y-Buzz" column.

"Good morning, Bartholomew," Belle responded with a glowing smile. "Does it seem unusually hectic around here today, or is it my imagination?"

Kerr strolled into Belle's office and perched his tiny frame on the corner of her desk. Only the tips of his suede loafers touched the linoleum floor. "Ah, alas, trouble ventures into the illustrious realm of high society. Why on earth do you think I've ventured into this fetid arena before eleven o'clock? I gather you haven't heard about the fire?"

"Fire?"

Kerr released a cherubic chuckle. "Oh, my dear Bella. Please say that word one more time for me, will you? It has such an angelic and innocent ring when floating from your lips. Although from the fever in your eye, I might question whether you're a devoted pyromaniac."

"What fire, Bartholomew? I haven't heard anything about it."

"Tsk, tsk . . . that's why the intestines of our *Evening Crier* are working overtime. The *Herald* went to bed too early and missed the story, so we have ourselves a good old-fashioned scoop. Apparently, someone torched one of the horse barns out at King Wenstarin Farms."

"That's horrible. Were any animals killed?"

Kerr threw up his hands in mock horror. "I'm sorry, I have misspoken myself. There is no evidence—as yet—that this was a torch job. That's only my catty presumption. Although since the Family Collins is insured to the nines by the Dartmouth Group, I suppose it won't be long before a certain crossword-puzzle editor's hubby, one Rosco Polycrates by name, is called in to . . . *look things over*, shall we say? We all know your dear boy is this burg's favored PI when it comes to ferreting out insurance fraud, don't we, now?"

Belle stomped her foot on the floor. "Bartholomew, stop, please. Did any horses die?"

"Ah, the kindhearted demoiselle. Women do love their prancing steeds, don't they? I believe most men would first ask if any of the human race had been injured."

Belle raised an eyebrow. "That's certainly a chauvinistic statement."

"But true, nonetheless. I've been taking a little survey around the dungeon this morning, and I've found that on first hearing of the blaze, women ask only about the four-footed beasts; with men, it breaks down to about fifty-fifty."

"I'd say that only proves that women are focused on one thing, and that men are all over the place."

"You're speaking metaphorically, I take it? I wouldn't care to make any off-color references to the stud business. Well, at any rate, to answer your question: All valiant members of the *Equus caballus* family escaped without harm. However, the barn manager lies in a comatose state in ICU at Newcastle Memorial. If it turns out to be a torch job, and our dear fellow drifts into the hereafter, then we'll have ourselves a dirty little murder among Newcastle's hoity-toity. Won't that keep 'Biz-y-Buzz' abuzzing?"

Belle sat in her chair and put her feet up on the end of the desk farthest from Kerr. Then she became aware that her jeans were beginning to fray at the cuff and wondered how long it would take Bartholomew to begin drawing comparisons to the Little Match Girl. She stifled a self-conscious groan. Shopping for clothes had never been one of her favorite pastimes; there were too many choices; blue was "in," then it wasn't; skirts were pencil thin, then flouncy; ditto with blouses and jackets and dresses: Who knew what to choose when designers and manufacturers seemed in such a state of flux?

"You're certain King Wenstarin Farms is insured by the Dartmouth Group?" she asked as she edged her feet back off the desk and hid them under her chair.

"Oh, please, dear girl, there is nothing I don't know when it comes to Newcastle's idle rich. Of course Papa Collins—that would be Todd—has worked hard for his filthy lucre, as did his father before him . . . although one might say that importing Irish whiskey during the early twenties at the height of the Volstead Act was frowned upon by some, most notably the FBI and that dear dead man, J. Edgar Hoover."

Belle bolted up straight in her seat. "You mean Collins's

dad was a bootlegger? King Wenstarin Irish Whiskey? That was bootlegged?"

Kerr rolled his eyes. "I think I like the way you pronounced that nasty word more than I liked the way you said *fire*. Yes, *mia Bella,* old man Collins was not in the most legitimate of trades. Where have you spent your life, my child? Everyone knows King Wenstarin started out as illegal hooch and that both of Todd Collins's uncles evaporated from the face of the earth when they tried to expand their market share by moving their *product* from Boston to New York. Of course that was before Todd was born. After Prohibition, Collins *père,* the only member of the family not to have been Tommy-gunned out of the picture, managed to turn the business into a legitimate importer of 'fine' spirits. Then Todd took over King Wenstarin and turned it into the multimillion-dollar corporation it is today."

Belle sighed. *"Multimillion dollar . . .* I like the ring of that. I wish Rosco and I could work our bank account in that direction."

"Be careful what you wish for, dear child. Todd's offspring are not to be admired or imitated. The three are nothing but a bunch of dilettantes. All they know about money is how to spend it, and spend it, and spend it. The eldest daughter, that would be the oft-married Fiona, used to pal around with your former competitor, Thompson Briephs, so I imagine your friend Sara might provide some pithy insights into the woman."

Belle nodded. Thompson Briephs had been the crossword editor at the *Herald* before he was murdered a few years back. It was the case that had introduced Belle to the man who would become her husband, and had also cemented a lasting friendship with Thompson's octogenarian mother, Sara Crane Briephs, a woman Belle had come to view as her surrogate grandmother.

"Wait," she said, suddenly crinkling her brow, "You mean Fiona Collins and Thompson Briephs were an item? Before he died?"

"Well, dear girl, he wouldn't have made much of an *item,* as you put it, *after* he was dead and gone, now would he? The Collins tots are a wild bunch, but I think necrophilia might be pushing the envelope, even for them."

"Is their mother still around?"

"*Around?* Yes, but discarded long ago. You know how such familial relationships work in the moneyed set, my angel. Toddie has his millions, then reaches the fine old age of fifty-plus and starts shopping for a trophy wife. Long-suffering mother of his offspring is unceremoniously shown the exit, and Miss Twentysomething moves into the Big House instead. That first little bride took Mr. Todd for a pretty penny and skedaddled to Miami's South Beach and a stable of Cuban houseboys—or so I hear. Todd is now on wifey number three, a comely lass named Ryan. Of course, even she will fade in time. It's now two years or so post-white-gown-and-lace-veil. So I've been told that at the age of thirty-seven, she's interviewing only the best of cosmetic surgeons." Kerr clasped the palms of his hands to his cheeks. "I'm sorry. Was that naughty of me? Oh, well . . . But then again, Toddie-pie is presently seventy-four. Perchance he has lost his wandering eye and will keep Mistress Ryan for the duration. Only time will tell."

"It's kind of odd," Belle said as she pointed to the manila envelope in her out-box, "but one of the puzzles I drew up for next week has a horse theme. Not show horses like the ones at King Wenstarin Farms, but race horses. I had a wonderful time researching the names . . . famous Kentucky Derby winners and champions who went on to take the Triple Crown. For instance, Omaha, who won it in 1935. Nowadays, the clue would be the city or the famous beach, but back then—"

"Tsk, tsk, tsk," Kerr interrupted as he waved a cautionary index finger at Belle. "I'd be careful there if I were you, *Bellisima*. If some *evildoer,* to borrow a term, is out to wreak havoc on King Wenstarin, and the horse trade in general, you certainly don't want to join the throng. Guilt by association? It wouldn't be the first time you've gotten your tush mixed up with the wrong crowd because of those infernal puzzles of yours."

"I hardly think whoever was responsible for last night's fire would notice one of my puzzles."

"Well, to quote Wilfred Owen, 'All a poet can do is warn.' "

"He was referring to war, Bartholomew, not crosswords," Belle said with a chuckle.

"Yes, but don't forget he died when he was only twenty-five."

"Which I've already passed." Belle laughed again. "I'm not concerned. The puzzle I constructed has nothing to do with arson—either real or imagined—or Mr. Collins's family."

Kerr leapt off Belle's desk. "Oh, please, don't get me gabbing about Clan Collins again. I have work to attend to."

Belle smiled. Getting Bartholomew "gabbing" was never a trick; stopping him, however, was quite another story.

Across

1. Gardner creation
6. Toss
11. Sixth sense; abbr.
14. Derby winner of 1905
15. Spanish queen
16. My ___
17. Cut-ups
18. Suggest
19. SM, MED, ___
20. Police radio call; abbr.
21. 1973 winner
24. Upper NYC thoroughfare
25. Sizzle
26. Black Sea port
27. Attach
30. Hair raiser?
31. Big name in insurance
33. Int. commerce grp.
35. A Winkler
39. Milking aid
40. Manhattan campus; abbr.
41. Harlot of Jericho
42. D.C. naval facility
43. Poetic evening
44. Kansas City university
45. U2 or ELO
47. Roofer
49. San Fernando Valley town
52. Pats' old org.
53. Grass court org.
56. 1977 winner
59. Tire need
60. Stooge
61. Easter in Italy, e.g.
62. Certain manual
64. Ike's WWII turf
65. Actor, Davis
66. 1935 winner
67. "Ask ___ . . ."
68. Scratches
69. Songster, Leo

Down

1. Certain parrot
2. Wide open
3. 1919 winner
4. ___ Rosebud, 1914 Derby winner
5. Stack role
6. Adjective for 21-Across, et al.
7. A Winkler
8. Overrun with
9. ___ many; over the top
10. 1937 winner
11. Winning jockey, 1931 Preakness
12. Long tales
13. Michelangelo masterpiece
22. Little lizard
23. Try it again
28. Circling
29. 1930 winner
30. 1943 winner
31. Tempe campus; abbr.
32. UFO crew
34. Lanyard
36. 1941 winner
37. Baron tack-on
38. Hoopster's org.
46. Even so
48. Chill
49. City on the Ruhr
50. "Cool!"
51. 1949 Preakness winner
52. Spite in Spinazzola
54. Church offering
55. Like the crowd at the track
57. Old gas sign
58. "___ Afraid of Virginia Woolf?"
63. Tumor; suffix

OFF TO THE RACES

CHAPTER

3

While Bartholomew Kerr entertained Belle with his protracted monologue on the virtues, or lack thereof, of Todd Collins's three adult children, Fiona, Heather, and Chip; Rosco Polycrates, Belle's husband, was entering his office just off Fifth Street in Newcastle's downtown business district. At thirty-eight, Rosco still had the build of a natural athlete, as well as a full head of black hair that he'd inherited from his Greek ancestors—all fishermen with a passion for the sea, a trait that had unfortunately bypassed the third-generation Greek-American version. A boat-averse Polycrates was not only a source of perplexity to his large, extended family, it was also an anomaly in a city whose residents shared an abiding love of all things nautical. Rosco's older sister often referred to him as "The Dramamine Kid."

But his lack of enthusiasm for cold salt spray, choppy waves, and bobbing vessels battling the briny wasn't his only unusual characteristic. A former cop who'd spent eight years working Homicide with the Newcastle Police Department before opening his own detective agency, his other peculiarity was that he didn't like carrying a gun, and never had—a decision that had annoyed NPD's captain for some reason. The captain had also frowned upon Rosco's unorthodox approach to his investigations, although that might have been because his sometimes quirky methods brought unexpected results.

Now in its sixth year, the Polycrates Detective Agency was doing well. It had new office space in a respected part of town, an impressive roster of former clients, and a reputation for thorough and honest work; ironically, a large percentage of which was marine-related insurance fraud. And all this with just a single employee, one Rosco Polycrates. Although he'd once made the fateful mistake of referring to Belle as a *subcontractor* of the agency, a term she relished—and used—with typical abandon.

As Rosco settled into the chair behind his desk, he reached for the telephone and punched *1 into the auto-dialer and listened while the familiar tones skipped over the digits that would connect him to Belle's cell phone. They'd only finished breakfast and kissed good-bye an hour before, but he saw no harm in telling her once again how much he adored her. Of course, the odds of Belle actually having the mobile phone on her person, or turned on, for that matter, were slim. Rosco was accustomed to leaving messages she forgot to retrieve—or when she did retrieve them, overlooked the day and month of the voice mail. But before the call could go through, there was a knock on his door. His nine-thirty appointment was early. He disconnected the phone without reaching his real or electronic wife and said, "Yes? Come in." Although Rosco was fluent in Greek, his accent was pure Back-Bay-Boston drawl.

Walter Gudgeon appeared to be in his early to mid-seventies, five-feet-nine, a bit heavier that he should have been, or probably wanted to be, with expensively cut, dark brown hair—the kind of chestnut shade that shouted *professional dye job*. He wore tailored slacks and a sports jacket, the clothes of a man who lived a comfortable, if understated, life. Rosco stood and said, "Mr. Gudgeon, I take it?"

"Yes." Gudgeon crossed to Rosco and extended his hand. He had a strong grip, which he seemed proud of, and spoke with a very slight accent, which Rosco decided was Scottish. "It's nice to meet you. You've come highly recommended, Mr. Polycrates."

"Thanks. And please call me Rosco. Have a seat, will you?"

Gudgeon sat in the leather chair opposite Rosco's desk.

"Out of curiosity, I don't believe you mentioned how you found my agency when you made your appointment. Who was it who recommended me?"

"Actually, I don't remember who it was, now that you ask."

Gudgeon gave an uneasy smile. Rosco guessed it was nervousness at hiring a PI, though he found it a bit strange that the man couldn't remember where the *highly recommended* had come from. A good way to determine what someone *really* wanted was to learn who had led them up to your front door.

"Wasn't there a Gudgeon who ran for mayor about fifteen years ago?" Rosco asked as he opened a small notebook.

"That was my brother, Charlie. He lost in the primary.

Got beat up, down, and sideways by the boys with the Big Money."

Rosco nodded in sympathy. "Well, no doubt, he would have been better than the clown sitting in the mayor's chair now."

"I think that could also be said of my grandson's hamster."

Rosco laughed. "Well, Mr. Gudgeon—"

"Call me Walt. I'm not a formal guy and never have been."

"All right." Rosco snapped his fingers. "Walt Gudgeon . . . Of course! Those are your trucks I see all over town; Gudgeon Electrical Contracting. *Walt's Wire Wagons.*"

Walter Gudgeon looked immensely pleased. "That's right. Although I retired five years ago. My son, Young Walt, runs the show now. It's really only seven trucks, but the red and gold lettering shows off well against those bright white panels. I designed the look myself. Young Walt wanted to go with green; dumbest idea I ever heard of. Those trucks are our only advertising. They have to turns heads when you see them, or what's the use? Green; I still get a chuckle over that boneheaded concept."

Rosco was beginning to wonder just how *retired* Gudgeon was if "Young Walt" wasn't allowed to paint the fleet another color if he chose to. "What can I help you with Walt?" he asked.

Gudgeon looked down at his hands as they rested in his lap and fiddled with his thumbnail. "I'm not sure where to start with all of this, but I guess what I'd like you to do is find a missing person."

"All right." Rosco picked up a pen. "Are we talking about a friend or acquaintance from your past . . . or a family member, or—?"

"Not a family member, no." The words jumped out, and the nervous movement of Gudgeon's hands increased until he clenched them purposely together.

Rosco put down his pen and leaned slightly back in his chair. "Have you contacted the police?" It was a natural question, but he gathered the answer would be in the negative.

"No," was the hurried reply.

"Well, the police department is where most folks start when someone goes missing—"

"I don't want . . ." Gudgeon interrupted in the same jerky rhythm, "I mean, I can't . . . well, this is a private matter. That's why I'm here. You're a private eye. I need to keep this information between the two of us."

"I see." Rosco regarded his visitor; experience had taught him that silence was often a good method for gathering information. People who possessed secrets usually had a need for sharing their stories.

"It's not that I've done anything illegal . . ." Gudgeon continued, "It's just that my kids . . . well, they worry about me . . . think I'm getting old and kind of loopy . . . if they knew about . . ." The words ceased; Walt Gudgeon stared at his hands while Rosco waited. Then after a moment he added, "We can keep this just between us, can't we?"

"Of course, Walt. I wouldn't be in business if I didn't keep my clients' information confidential."

Gudgeon thought, then finally leaped ahead. "Okay, the person . . . the girl, I mean . . . her name is Dawn. Dawn Davis." Then he corrected himself. "Woman, really, not a girl. She's twenty-six or -seven. It's not what it sounds like, though, a romance of some kind, but, well, I'm sure that's how my kids will view the situation—an old guy like me . . .

Dawn's been gone for almost four weeks. At least, it was over three weeks ago when I lost track of her . . ." Again, the speech trailed off.

Rosco sat back in his chair, studying the older man. When potential clients claimed that they were innocent of illicit behavior and hadn't been involved in unfortunate romances, usually they were lying on both counts. "And you want me to find this Dawn Davis, is that it?"

"Yes. That's why I'm here." Gudgeon's voice had started to verge on the shrill. "I mean, she was so sick . . . And now she's just plain *gone*."

"Maybe you need to begin from the beginning here, Mr. Gudgeon—"

"Walt."

"Walt. I can't help you if I don't know what you're after."

"I told you. I want you to find Dawn."

"But you don't want to contact the police or have your family involved."

"That's correct. The situation needs to be kept between the two of us. Just us."

"Even though she's a sick woman, as you stated—which I'm guessing refers to a physical illness rather than a mental one? Or am I mistaken?"

"Physical."

Rosco was starting to believe he'd embarked on an endless game of twenty questions. He sighed and retrieved his notebook, but Walt spoke again before Rosco could formulate his next query.

"Her last name is Davis, like I said. I-I don't have her address, Or phone number. That's part of the problem. I don't know where to start looking. As I told you, she's twenty-six or -seven; about five-foot-four or maybe five-five, slim, good figure, attractive, with auburn hair that falls midway down her back. Curls a little bit at the ends—especially when the weather's damp."

Rosco heard the wistful tone. *No romance*, he thought, *tell me another one.*

Rosco said, "Caucasian? Hispanic? African-American?"

Gudgeon thought for a moment. "Caucasian."

"And obviously you've tried the phone book?"

"Yes."

"And no Dawn Davis, either listed or unlisted? It's not an uncommon name."

"There's three in the book. I called and hung up because it wasn't her. The vocal quality wasn't the same." Gudgeon shook his head. "You see, she always phoned me. She said she . . ." His voice faded away again.

"You know what, Mr. Gudgeon . . . I mean, Walt," Rosco set his pen down on the desk and leaned in toward his visitor. "Why don't you describe your relationship to Ms. Davis? No notes on my part, okay? But I have to know what I'm dealing with if I'm going to help you."

Gudgeon put his head in his hands and all but groaned. "I just want to find her, that's all. I just need to know that she's alive. That she's not in any trouble. That she came through everything all right."

Rosco didn't like playing the psychiatrist; he preferred a more direct approach. But *direct* didn't work with everyone, and it sure wasn't working at the moment. He decided to nibble away at Gudgeon's edges in the hopes of gathering more concrete data. "When did you come to this country, Walt?" he asked.

Gudgeon looked up and smiled. "I like to think I've lost the accent. Foolish thought, huh? I came over from Scotland fifty years ago. I was fifteen when we sailed into Boston Harbor."

"And you've done well for yourself." It was a statement, not a question.

"Damn straight, I have. I'm the top electrical contractor in the city."

"And your son now runs the company?"

Gudgeon chortled. "He tries to."

"Any other children?"

"Four daughters. That's enough to drive a man insane, I'll tell you that much. I don't recommend it to anyone."

"And your wife?"

"She passed away a year and a half ago." Gudgeon said this without taking a breath. The statement seemed to bear no emotional weight. Sensing that Rosco was aware of this dearth of grief, Walt followed with a quick, "She was a fine woman. Raised five solid children; may she rest in peace."

"And getting back to Dawn Davis, when did you meet her?"

"That was about two months ago. Out at the Harbor Mall . . . In the food court."

Rosco waited for more, but Gudgeon had again lapsed into silence. Rosco slid his chair back from his desk and made a show of leaving his notebook and pen untouched. "If you truly want to find Ms. Davis, you're going to have to tell me everything about her. Including her relationship to you."

Gudgeon made no reply, and so Rosco continued, "Let's start with the moment you met her. But first: Do you want a coffee or something? I can phone down to Lawson's. They'll send it right up."

"No. No, I'm fine." He inhaled deeply and let the air out slowly. Finally he said, "Okay. Back in early August I was at the mall doing my laps—"

"There's a pool at the Harbor Mall?"

"No, no, I go there every morning at eleven and do laps around the mall; on foot, for exercise. I circle the mall at a good pace for an hour, then go to the food court for lunch. I know, it's a dumb time to go. It's always jammed by then, but I like seeing all the people, the kids running around, teenage couples hanging out—especially in the summer when there's no school. I live alone now, and it gets pretty dull. Anyway, one day, I think it was a Saturday, because the court was packed and all the tables were filled, Dawn came up to me with her lunch and asked if she could share the table. Of course, I said yes. She was a polite young woman, and there weren't any empty spots. We had a nice chat; hit it off really well, actually . . . and that was that."

"That's all you saw of her?"

"No, no. A few days later I saw her again at the food court. I waved, and I asked her to join me."

"She didn't approach you; you called her over? Is that what you're saying?"

"I don't even think she saw me sitting there till I called her name. Anyway, she seemed a little out if it. Her eyes were puffy, like she'd been crying. She's got these really soft green gold eyes, but they were all pink and sore-looking. It really broke my heart. I asked her what was wrong, but she refused to talk. She said her problems were her own and she wasn't about to get a stranger involved. I pushed her for information, but she refused to say anything more. We then kind of finished our lunches in silence, but I could see that she was on the verge of tears the entire time. I gave her my phone number and told her she could call me anytime she wanted, night or day."

"And did she?"

"No. I didn't hear anything from her. But about a week later I saw her again at the food court. She still seemed in pretty bad shape when she sat down. Very pale. She didn't look healthy at all. This time I refused to let her leave until she told me what was going on. She finally broke down; she must have sobbed for five minutes before she regained enough composure to speak clearly. It seems she'd been on a kidney dialysis treatment for the last two years and was waiting for a donor kidney. The treatments had exhausted nearly all of her savings. At any rate, Newcastle Memorial had informed her that they'd found a matching donor, but that since she'd recently let her health insurance premiums lapse, and now had no way to pay for the surgery, they were going to have to move to the next person on their list. I mean, it was just a horrible situation."

"Did you offer to help out?"

Gudgeon rubbed at a small vein that protruded on the left side of his forehead. "I did, but Dawn refused. Steadfastly refused. Wouldn't even hear of such a notion. She told me the operation alone was going to cost close to $250,000. She knew there was no way she would ever be able to pay me back."

"What about family? Wasn't there anyone else Ms. Davis could turn to?"

"An ex-boyfriend was all she had, but he'd ditched her

early on in the treatment process; a completely unsupport-ive jerk from what I could tell." Gudgeon stopped and looked down at his hands, which were again resting in his lap. "I mean . . . I had the cash. It seemed stupid to have it sitting in the bank when this girl was in such trouble. By the end of the day . . . well, I was able to convince her that it was the right thing to do, for her to take the money. If the kidney was available . . . I mean, hell, it might've been a long time before another one came within reach."

"That was extremely generous of you, Walt," was Rosco's sole response. Whether the vanished Dawn Davis had pulled a fast one or not, Gudgeon had made a kind and noble gesture.

"It's just money," was the shy reply. "My kids might not agree if they knew. But you can't take it with you, can you? I mean, aren't we supposed to help people in need if we can? Everyone just wants to get rich; and they could give a hoot about their fellow man."

"You're right, the world would be a better place if other folks believed as you do, Walt," Rosco told him. The opin-ion that the gullible might also be poorer, Rosco kept to himself. "How did you give her the money? Was it a check or cash?"

"It was a wire transfer from my bank into her account."

"And you have that account number, I take it."

"No."

Rosco reached for his pad and pen. "Not a problem; your bank will have it on file. So I gather you haven't seen Ms. Davis since you gave her the money?"

Gudgeon held up his hands. "Wait, hold on there, Rosco. Dawn didn't steal this money from me, if that's what you're thinking. I saw her quite a few times after the funds were transferred. She was very insistent about telling me how she was doing: what the prognosis was and so forth, how much better she was feeling knowing she was going to be cured . . . And she kept telling me how bad she felt about taking the money. She . . . she wanted to make it up to me . . . had all sorts of payment schedules she'd made up—every one of which would have outlasted me." He stopped and smiled, and again Rosco noted the tenderness of the expression. "Anyway, the operation wasn't scheduled until a little over three weeks ago. I drove Dawn to the hospital myself. She'd had the money in her account for almost a month by then. If I was being conned, she would have skipped town long before that."

"Okay," Rosco said. "I'm just not convinced that Newcastle Memorial plays that kind of hardball in situations such as you described. Failing kidneys aren't anything to fool around with. I don't see them turning a patient away for lack of funds. There are agencies that can step in to help indigent patients."

"They had another match for that kidney," Gudgeon argued, raising his voice. "They didn't need her. They had Dawn on the ropes. They were going to go with the person who could pay. Health care's changed; it's big business now. They don't care about the little guy."

"Did you visit Ms. Davis in the hospital?"

"No. She didn't want any visitors."

"Phone her?"

"No. She had no phone in her room."

"And when exactly did she disappear?"

"That was it. I dropped her off at Newcastle Memorial, and I haven't heard from her since."

"Did you call the hospital and ask about her status?"

"Yes. They said she checked out the next day."

Rosco shook his head slowly. "I don't know much about this kind of major surgery, but leaving the hospital after twenty-four hours seems like an unlikely scenario for what you're describing."

"It seemed odd to me, too; I admit that. I tried to get more information, but they won't release details except to next of kin. I didn't want to push them any further. I didn't want to go on record as asking."

Rosco rolled his chair closer to the desk, leaned on his forearms, and leveled his gaze on Walt's. "You're sure you don't want to go to the police with this?"

"Absolutely not. I don't want my children to hear a word of this."

"If, and I'm not saying you have, but if you have been conned out of this money, there is virtually no way you will be able to reclaim a nickel if you refuse to pursue it through the legal system; I have to tell you that, Walt."

"I haven't been cheated. I'm an old man who's fallen for a young girl who needed my help. Maybe I was a fool, okay, but I only want to know that Dawn's safe and well."

"Had you been intimate with her?"

"That's nobody's damn business." Gudgeon bristled, then added an abrupt, "What's this going to cost me?"

Rosco closed his notebook and said, "Let me first see what I can find out. I'll work up a fee schedule later."

CHAPTER

4

Friday lunchtime at Lawson's Coffee Shop was without a doubt its busiest two hours of the week. It was payday for Newcastle's city employees, and the restaurant sat dead square in the center of the action. With the municipal courthouse a block away, the DA's office behind that, and the police department another block and a half distant, Lawson's was packed to the rafters at every week's end; and depending on what had "gone down" during that particular seven-day period, the atmosphere among the town's legal guardians could swing from jovial and partylike to outright glum.

The eatery was one of the few remaining single-story structures in the downtown area. Caught in a kind of fifties time warp, its decor was classic diner: lots of plate glass windows facing the street, lots of chrome dotting the long pink Formica countertop with its matching swiveling stools, and a linoleum floor that had carried so many feet in identical directions it could have doubled as the Yellow Brick Road—except that Lawson's tiles were gray and pink. Pink was the coffee shop's theme color—bubble gum, cherry, flamingo, cotton candy: Somehow they all blended together in the vinyl-upholstered banquettes and booths, in the waitresses' uniforms, and in the walls themselves.

What was remarkable was that no one questioned the choice—and hadn't for half a century. Just as none of the regular patrons would have dreamed of asking why the jukebox stations in every booth still operated on nickels, or why only artists like Johnny Mathis, Frank Sinatra, and Patsy Cline were represented. Lawson's was pre–rock-and-roll, pre-Elvis; and just forget about rap, hip-hop, or ska. Besides, the volume was turned down so low it was impossible to hear the songs over the din of clattering glasses, dishes, and silverware, and the boisterous banter between customers, waitresses, fry cooks, and dishwashers.

Rosco stepped through Lawson's etched-glass doors at twelve-thirty and couldn't help but smile. The clamor inside was actually louder than outside. Street noise had nothing on the restaurant. He was immediately greeted by Martha Leonetti, senior waitress, self-styled top dog, and wiseacre supreme. She and the eatery were more or less the same age, proof of which was the blond beehive hairdo Martha had sported for the thirty-plus years she'd been employed there.

As was her wont, she slapped Rosco on the butt and said, "Hiya, cute buns, where's that little wife of yours? You two are like those black-and-white magnetic Scottie dogs; can't pry 'em apart with a spatula or dynamite. Makes me worry when I don't see you and Belle together."

Rosco glanced at his watch. "She's meeting me at . . . well . . . twelve-thirty. I gather she's not here yet."

Martha winked. "Would I have patted your tush if your missus were sitting at table number two? I don't think so. But your ex-partner is down at the corner booth with Dr. J . . . Big barn fire out at Collins's last night, but I guess you heard all about it. The whole thing sounds fishy, if you ask me. When the rich can't get richer legally, they can always rake their insurance companies over the coals . . . or get into politics. That's where the real money is."

Rosco chortled. "Everything sounds fishy to you, Martha. But who knows? You've been right before. I'll join Al and Abe. If Belle shows up, send her over, will you?"

"You betcha, buttercup."

Rosco worked his way down the restaurant's center aisle, dodging waitresses and greeting former coworkers: plain-clothes and uniformed officers alike. There wasn't an empty table. At the far booth sat his former partner, Lieutenant Al Lever. With Al was the police department's chief forensic investigator, Abe Jones. The two men couldn't have been more dissimilar. While Al was decidedly middle-aged, balding, and overweight, with a smoker's cough that followed him everywhere, Jones had the appearance of a movie star in his youthful prime. He was African-American, the son of an Episcopal priest who'd named him Absalom, after Absalom Jones, in the hopes that Abe would follow in his vocation. But Abe had gone the science route, and his father had had the good sense not to push the issue. Besides, Abe was well known as having a keen eye for a pretty lady, something that doesn't always play out well in the priesthood.

"Heya, Poly-crates, what's shakin'?" Al said as Rosco slid

into the booth. The butchering of his ex-partner's last name was something Lever had been doing since the day they'd met. Rosco had realized long ago that it wasn't likely to stop any time soon.

"Not much," was Rosco's offhanded reply. Despite the fact that he and Al were as close as two friends could be and that they often continued to collaborate, Rosco wasn't disposed to discuss his recent conversation with Walter Gudgeon.

The denial brought on a hearty laugh from Jones. "Oh, right, how many times have we heard 'Not much' from this guy, only to find out he's been hired by some high-profile, bigwig muckity-muck to look into the nefarious shenanigans of a capricious consort."

Rosco chuckled and held up his hands in a gesture of innocence. "No. Really. It's been a slow day over at the Polycrates Agency. As a matter of fact it's been a slow week. It seems nobody's cheating on anybody lately. What's the world coming to?"

Abe shook his head, grinning with the perfect smile that melted his women friends' hearts. "Sometimes I wonder."

"Can we keep this conversation on a more elevated plane, you two?" Lever said before he was attacked by a sudden coughing fit. "Dang allergies," he added as he caught his breath.

"A downright shame you're being bothered like that, Big Al," was Jone's laconic reply. "I would have thought they'd leave you alone by October. Pollen count being down and all."

"The *Camels* must be kicking it up," Rosco tossed in.

"Yuk . . . yuk . . ." Al wheezed.

"I guess it's a year-round kind of affliction," Rosco added.

"Just keep it up, guys," Al told them. "You get to be my age and show up with mysterious maladies, you'll be laughing out of the other side of your mouths."

"*Mysterious maladies*—is that a nickname for filter tips?" Rosco asked.

"Har har." But Lever laughed in spite of himself while Rosco changed the subject.

"I gather the department's had a busy morning out at King Wenstarin Farms."

"A nonstory on that one," Al offered. "It's all cooled off, no pun intended. The fire marshal has ruled a 'nonsuspicious blaze.' The way he pieced it together—with help from old man Collins—is that the barn manager, one Orlando Polk, must have accidentally knocked over a countertop space heater, which in turn tipped over an open bottle of booze, and the combination caused the tack room to light up like a bonfire at a Boy Scout jamboree. Seems like Collins had been after the guy to clean up his act."

"Have either one of you been out there for a look-see?" Rosco asked.

They said, "Nope," in unison, but it was Lever who continued. "What for? *Nonsuspicious* means exactly what it says. If Todd Collins is insisting the fire was an accident, who are we to argue? It's up to him or his insurer to get the ball rolling on any investigation. Apparently, Collins also told the marshal that this Polk guy was a hard drinker, which was another big problem. Kind of ironic; a guy makes millions on booze, then his barn burns up because the same stuff fans the flames. But it seems Polk was sober enough last night to help his boss get the horses out of danger, then he went back into the building, where a falling timber or something whacked him in the back of the head and knocked him out cold. It was Collins who risked his hide to save Polk—who was then rushed off to

Newcastle Memorial. But who knows? When the poor shlub regains consciousness, he may have a different story."

"What if he doesn't make it?"

It was Abe who answered. "The doctors are giving him an eighty percent shot at pulling through."

"Hey, Poly-Crates, don't start giving me more work than I already have. I don't need no more dead people right now." Lever coughed again and reached for his cigarettes. Both Rosco and Abe shook their heads, while Abe picked up the *No Smoking* sign on the table and perched it atop Al's coffee cup.

"Oh, you guys are cute. Anybody ever tell you that?" Lever coughed for a third time, but left his cigarettes in his pocket. "Anyway, until the fire marshal sends up a red flag, or someone dies, neither me or the good doctor here are going anywhere near King Wenstarin Farms. Which is fine by me."

Martha arrived with two cholesterol-laden platters of cheeseburgers and French fries, then plopped a cup of coffee in front of Rosco. "What'll it be, doll face?" she asked.

"I'll wait for Belle." Rosco reached over and snagged one of Lever's fries. The lieutenant tried to slap his hand away, but Rosco proved too quick for him.

"I'll bring a couple of extra orders of fries," Martha said, "I wouldn't want to see anyone get hurt, or have one of you boys starve to death on me." She glanced down at Al's well-endowed stomach, gave her eyebrows a sarcastic twitch, and walked off.

Lever groaned. "She's worse that my wife. I don't know why I come in here."

"Any idea who insured the Collins farm?" Rosco asked.

Lever laughed. "You're beginning to sound like an ambulance chaser, Poly-crates. Things *must* be slow over at the agency. Maybe you'd like to come back onto the force? Have

yourself a steady paycheck, and all the other thrilling benefits that come from working for our beloved city."

"The Dartmouth Group covers Wenstarin," Abe said.
"You've worked for them, haven't you?"

"Yep. They're a tight bunch. Clint Mize is their chief adjuster now. Left his job with Shore Line about a year ago.
Dartmouth doesn't pay out their claims lightly—or will-
ingly. They're going to need something a lot more specific
than a *maybe* accident involving a heater and a bottle of fire-
water before they get out their checkbook."

Abe smiled and looked past Al and Rosco. "Here comes
the *Belle of the Ball* now." The other two turned and watched
as Belle walked the length of the restaurant and slid into the
booth next to Abe. Two young police officers ogled her as
she passed, but when they realized she was joining Lever,
Jones, and Rosco, they made feeble attempts to make it appear as if they'd been looking for a waitress.

After Belle kissed Rosco and all exchanged greetings, Al
said, "You're early."

Belle looked at her watch. "Actually I'm ten minutes late.
Sorry. Friday traffic."

"No, no, no, I judge these things by using my wife, Helen, as a barometer. Any woman who's less than half an hour
late is early in my book."

Belle laughed and looked at Rosco. "How'd things go
with the potential client this morning?"

"Ah-ha!" Abe said, "Mister 'Not Much' has something
shakin' and refuses to share it with his trusted friends."

"Hey, you know how it is, Abe," Lever added. "These PIs
squeeze us for the inside dope right and left, but share and
share alike isn't in their playbook."

"Sorry guys, client privileges," Rosco responded. "Don't try to tell me you don't have information you can't divulge."

"You can tell us though, Rosco," Belle complained. "It's not like we're going to blab it all over town."

"What're we blabbing all over town?" Martha set a cup of coffee in front of Belle and two extra orders of fries in the center of the table. "Is there something I don't know? Customers count on me to keep them informed about the city's darkest and dirtiest tales—those items that don't appear on the evening news."

"I'll have a grilled cheese sandwich with fries and coleslaw," was Rosco's evasive reply. "What about you, Belle?"

Belle looked at Martha. "Rosco's refusing to tell us who his new client is or what he—or she—wants."

"Tut, tut, tut, it's not nice to keep secrets from your wife, buttercup. It may come back to haunt you in the bedroom later on this evening." Martha winked at Rosco, then asked Belle, "What'll it be, blondie?"

"I'll have the waffles with vanilla ice cream and strawberries, syrup on the side."

"Coming right up."

Martha moved off, and Lever shook his head at Belle's lunch choice. "Do you know what I'd look like if I ate like you?" He then pointed a finger at Jones. "And don't even think of answering that question, wise-a—" Al was interrupted by the ringing of Rosco's cell phone.

Rosco glanced down at the caller ID readout and stood to leave the table. "I should take this."

"Who is it?" Belle asked.

"Clint Mize over at the Dartmouth Group."

CHAPTER

5

"Why won't you tell me?" Belle protested as she studied the meatloaf ingredients lying in a stainless-steel bowl on the kitchen countertop. Being "culinarily challenged," this was the first time she'd ventured into such haute cuisine since her first dinner with Rosco. On that occasion she'd misinterpreted the recipe, substituting hot red-pepper flakes for chopped red bell peppers. To say that the result was spicy would have been an understatement. Just to be certain history didn't repeat itself, Rosco sat on a stool nearby flipping the plastic jar of pepper flakes in his hand as he watched his wife blend together ground veal, pork, beef, chopped green and red *bell* peppers, and an assortment of nonlethal spices such as oregano and basil. The couple's two dogs, Kit and Gabby, were also showing a great deal of interest in Belle's labors. Kit, a brown and black Lab-shepherd mix, politely waited at her side, on the off-chance that some morsel might escape the bowl. Gabby, a gray terrier-poodle blend, took a more aggressive attitude, placing her front paws on the counter's edge and voicing low, guttural groans intended to solicit direct handouts.

"Gabby, get down," Belle said without much conviction. She waved her wooden spoon at the dog, but Gabby only leaped up in an attempt to grab it from her.

"Okay, Gabsters, that's enough, beat it." Rosco nudged at the determined creature with the tip of his shoe, and she proceeded to flop down on the floor beside Kit, the picture of mischief, wounded pride, and woe.

"Maybe we should have a nice, cozy fire tonight," he added, wondering if the inspiration had come from the events at King Wenstarin Farms or the jar of pepper flakes in his hand. "What do you think? First one of the season . . . a little romance to heat things up?"

"Don't change the subject," was Belle's airy reply. "Why won't you tell me who you're working for? And what you're doing? Don't you trust me?" Although the tone was half-teasing, she was dying to know. Belle was a determinedly inquisitive person, and patience had never been her strong suit.

"We've been through this, Belle. If a client asks me not to reveal their problems, I have to honor the request. It's as simple as that."

"I don't think that applies to your wife. Especially *this* wife, who is the very soul of discretion. Besides, maybe I can help. What good is a *subcontractor* if I can't throw my two cents in? I might even know your client. I mean, how big is Newcastle?"

Rosco laughed. "All the more reason why you shouldn't be involved."

"You mean I've already met this person? Hand me those pepper flakes, will you?"

"Not on your life. I'm not letting you anywhere near these. And no, you and my client have never met."

"Hmmmm . . . At the risk of repeating myself, how can you be so certain I don't know him?"

"Him? Did I say it was a he?"

"It's a woman? You're working with a woman? Rosco, you can't sit here and tell me you're secretly meeting with another," she put on a Bogart accent, "gorgeous dame, and expect me to take it lying down."

He hopped off the stool, stood behind Belle, and put his arms around her waist. But when he tried to kiss the back of her neck, she moved her head to the side. "It's not a woman. I promise," he lamented.

"I don't believe you. And if you don't tell me exactly who she is, I'm not going to share all the juicy stuff Bartholomew Kerr told me about the Collins family."

"I doubt that. You're desperate to blab. Look at your face."

"Not a word, I swear. Give me those pepper flakes, you cretin."

He reluctantly handed her the jar. "Go easy. I think one or two will be plenty." Then he crossed to the refrigerator. "Do you want a glass of wine?"

Belle nodded, then removed the cap from the jar and began shaking flakes through the perforated lid. It was clear her mind wasn't on her task. "Who is she?"

"It's not a woman." He turned to face her. "Hey, that's enough . . ."

"Ahhh . . ." she almost screamed. "Who put the lid on so loosely?"

Rosco shook his head and walked to his wife's side. He held a bottle of white wine in his hand as he looked down at the mixing bowl. The lid had dislodged, and the entire jar of pepper flakes was now sat scattered across the meatloaf's surface.

"I can't believe I did that," Belle groaned.

"We can go out for dinner."

"No, no, I can fix this. Where's the vacuum cleaner?"

"You can't vacuum a meatloaf, Belle."

"It'll work just fine. I'll use that pointy little nozzle thingamajig. It'll just suck the flakes and seeds right through the air—without even touching the food."

Rosco rolled his eyes, walked off to the hall closet, and returned a moment later carrying a small canister vacuum cleaner. He plugged it into the wall socket and opened the bottle of wine while Belle aimed the vacuum nozzle into the mixing bowl.

"There! Perfect!" she announced triumphantly when she'd finished. "I got almost all of them."

"What's your definition of 'almost'?"

"The meatloaf may still be a little spicy, but who doesn't like their food nice and zesty?"

"Nobody I know. Well, look at the bright side; we are now completely out of hot red pepper flakes. The odds of history repeating itself anytime in the near future are slim."

Rosco returned the vacuum cleaner to the closet and then poured them each a glass of wine. He handed one to Belle and lifted his in a toast. "Here's to my resourceful wife. What would I ever do without her?"

Belle gave him a long and loving kiss. When they parted she said, "That's exactly the term Bartholomew used for Ryan Collins—*resourceful.*"

"Meaning?"

"Meaning she saw a good thing in Todd and latched on to it. A typical trophy wife, but on the downward slope, according to Bartholomew. It also seems she has a classic evil-stepmother relationship with Todd's kids." Belle began to mold her creation into a loaf shape but stopped abruptly. "Oatmeal."

"Oatmeal?"

"Yes. I forgot. The recipe calls for rolled oats instead of bread crumbs, remember? Do we have any oatmeal?"

"Why would we?"

"From the last time I made this, Rosco! Maybe it's in the freezer."

"There's too much ice cream in the freezer for anything else."

"No, wait, I know where it is. There's a cardboard canister of rolled oats in the cabinet behind all that herbal tea your sister gave us last Christmas."

"No wonder I've never seen it. I wondered what happened to that tea." Rosco opened the cabinet, pushed the tea aside, retrieved the oats, and handed the box to Belle. "How fresh is this stuff?"

"It's oatmeal, Rosco. It lasts forever. They found some in King Tut's tomb."

"You're making that up."

She winked at him. "Maybe."

"Okay, clarify your meaning of *evil stepmother.*"

"How about *Cinderella*? Twenty-plus years ago, Dad dumps the real mother for bride number two, then he proceeds to axe her, and eventually brings in Ryan who happens to be younger than his natural daughters. According to

Bartholomew, the eldest Collins daughter, Fiona, is now forty-five; Heather, the next in line, is forty-one—meaning that the only sibling younger than dear step-mama is Todd's son, Chip, who's thirty-two compared to Ryan's thirty-seven. To add insult to injury, the minute she took over the house, she tossed away all photos and other memorabilia that reminded her doting hubby of the past. So, I'd say the *Cinderella* slipper definitely fits the picture—"

"Except that I thought there were step*sisters* in the story . . . Anyway, that sounds like a bit of a generalization, Belle—"

"Ever the innocent male." She kneaded the meatloaf into shape, placed it on a broiling pan, and smeared steak sauce over the top. Rosco opened the oven, and she slid it in. The dogs followed each action attentively, then sighed mightily as Rosco closed the oven door. It was as if they believed that this was the last glimpse of food they'd be permitted during their brief and tragic lifetimes. "No wonder those kids are messed up," Belle continued.

"In what way are they *messed up?*"

"Well, this is from Bartholomew again, so you have to take it with a grain of salt . . ." She stopped and looked around the kitchen.

"What?" Rosco asked.

"Did I put salt in the meatloaf?"

He shook his head. "I don't know. I wasn't watching. Don't worry about it. We can sprinkle it on later if we need to."

Belle's shoulders slumped in defeat. "Oh darn . . . I really thought I had this recipe nailed."

"Well, one less ingredient isn't bad."

"I almost forgot the oats, too, Rosco . . ."

"But you didn't."

Belle sighed again. "Maybe cooking is a skill that can't be learned. Maybe it's a gene you have to be born with, like musical ability or perfect pitch or a good ear for languages."

"Or ironing and cleaning?"

"Exactly! I've never made that connection before. Some people are absolute naturals when it comes to domestic chores; they enjoy vacuuming and washing windows and scrubbing kitchen tiles, but I get bored to tears. Besides, everyone knows that dusting only attracts more dust."

"Is that science you're spouting, or the World According to Belle?"

"Smart aleck." Then Belle returned to her previous subject. "Anyway, Bartholomew told me—"

"That Ryan is hardwired to be a gold digger, that her mothering gene is severely undeveloped, and that the resulting mutant breed is ruining the Collins kids' lives."

Belle raised a caustic eyebrow as she regarded her husband. "That wasn't what I was about to say, but I've got to admit it's an intriguing concept."

Rosco chortled. "Right. And maybe those pepper flakes are genetically engineered to attack a mixing bowl in huge clumps."

Belle crossed her arms. "Should I have the feeling you're not taking me seriously?"

"Never."

"*Never* what? That you're not giving my theories the weight they deserve, or that you are?"

"Whichever choice is going to get me off the hook."

"Hmmmm."

"Actually, I'd like to hear more about Bartholomew's take on the Collins family, since I'm meeting with Clint Mize out there tomorrow. If the fire were purposely started in order to collect insurance money, most likely a family member set it. And if there are darker forces at work—sibling rivalries, for instance, or long-standing resentments, or feelings of parental betrayal—then that information also goes into the mix."

"Ah-ha!" Belle grinned. "That just goes to show how much I help with your cases. Okay . . . I'll show you mine, but only if you show me yours first."

"You're not suggesting I reveal client confidences?"

"Of course I am."

The couple strolled into the living room, a treasure trove of eclectic secondhand-store "rescues," and Belle sat on the couch, while Rosco lit the fire. When he stopped playing Boy Scout, Belle leaned forward. "Well?"

"Well, what?"

She grinned. "Don't play dumb with me, buster. You're no good at it. You may be able to pull off that dim-witted-guy stuff with some poor unsuspecting crook, but I'm on to you."

"I can't tell you what my client wanted. It's privileged information."

"I know. However, as your wife *and* a subcontractor for the Polycrates Agency, aren't I entitled to—?"

Rosco raised his hands in a gesture of mock-surrender. "Just tell me why I ever gave you that title."

"Love?"

He snuggled in beside her, followed immediately by Kit and Gabby, until the couch was full of entwined human and canine bodies. Then he proceeded to outline Walter Gudgeon's story about the vanished and needy Dawn. "I asked him point blank about their relationship," Rosco concluded, "but he wouldn't go there."

"So the answer is yes, they were intimate."

He laughed. "You don't know that for a fact."

"Sure, I do. If they hadn't been romantically involved, Gudgeon would have emphatically denied it."

"And if he *had* denied it, I guarantee your response would have been, 'I don't believe that for a second.'"

Belle thought for a moment. "You may have something there."

"Some people just get insulted when you ask the question, and they refuse to answer it; I put Gudgeon in that category."

She gave him a kiss. "Do you know what I love about you?"

"What?"

"That you can be so naive at times."

"At least 'Young Walt' won't have Dawn hanging around dictating what color his father's 'former' business's trucks get painted."

"Unless you happen to find her. . . ."

CHAPTER

6

Rosco had agreed to meet Clint Mize, the chief adjuster for the Dartmouth Insurance Group, at the main entrance to King Wenstarin Farms shortly before 10 A.M. the following morning. The weather was gorgeous, another bright, crystalline day when autumn's gilded leaves made such a magnificent photo-op contrast to the cobalt-colored sky. In time-honored tradition, the "leaf peepers" were out in force, yawing over the roads as they tried to focus both on oohing and aahing over the drop-dead scenery and staying within the pesky yellow lines. But who could criticize this entranced state? The views were almost too beautiful to be real.

Especially the rolling acreage of King Wenstarin Farms—a mile of whitewashed wooden fencing that looked as though Huck Finn had just finished work: paddocks, emerald green pastureland, immaculate stables, artistically arrayed on the sloping ground, the "Big House" all but hidden within plantings of oak and maple and yew, and a meandering drive climbing upward through an avenue of copper beeches. The leaves' deep maroon color reminded Rosco of the oxblood shoe polish he'd used on his penny loafers during college days; an appreciator of beauty he might be, but a horticulturist he was not.

Rosco had driven past the farm's main entrance many times over the years but, not being a horseman, had never considered entering. For one thing, the wooden gate could only be opened by a security guard stationed in a small but sturdy building nearby. The man's forest green uniform matched the trim on the guardhouse, while its pristine white clapboard echoed the farm's other structures—all of which provided Rosco a second reason for having avoided the place; it simply looked too rich for his blood.

He parked his red Jeep in a grassy spot not far from the gatehouse. Taking advantage of the sunny weather, he'd removed the Jeep's canvas top and door panels and left them at home, now making the vehicle resemble an out-of-place beach buggy. He was certain it wasn't the type of ride that would be normally found on the grounds of King Wenstarin Farms, unless it was pulling a load of fertilizer. He stepped from the car, approached the security guard, and handed him a business card. The man looked to be in his sixties, and his eyes seemed to bear a perpetual squint as though he'd spent a lifetime staring into a questionable distance. The King Wenstarin Farms emblem was stitched onto the right pocket of his uniform jacket. Above the left pocket was the name *Pete*.

"Good morning. My name is Rosco Polycrates. I'm meeting a Mr. Mize. He hasn't gone in yet, has he?"

"No, sir, but Mr. Collins is expecting you both. I can open up for you." Pete smiled, a brief expression, but warmer than expected.

"That's okay, I'll wait for Mize." Rosco leaned against the fence and glanced out over the pastures. "This is quite a spread. I've never visited before." He glanced up at the crystalline sky. "Have you been working here long?" he asked casually.

"Almost twenty-five years now. Seen a lot of people come and go, I can tell you that. Some of the kids who took riding lessons when I started working here are now back with their own kids. 'Course the whole business has changed a heap since then."

"How so?"

"Most of the newer riders don't do it for fun no more. It's all about competition. And who can outspend who. It's nothin' for some of these parents to buy their kids a hundred-thousand-dollar piece of horseflesh nowadays—or two or three. The only thing that matters to them is that their kids beats the neighbors' kids. That kind of attitude is bound to take its toll on the youngsters themselves; they throw hissy fits when they don't get their way, and back-talk their families and the trainers who try to teach them any kind of patience or control. And their language sure ain't sweet as clover."

"So the farm's money is made mostly from giving lessons?"

"There's that; but there's also boarding, training champion jumpers, and so forth . . . and sales, of course. But all that's really a sideline. The Collins folks don't need the cash this place generates; they just live and breathe horses. And not just any horses. They've gotta be the best of the best, as well."

Rosco sniffed at the pungent air. "To each his own. I hope their house is upwind of the stables."

Pete laughed. "You get used to it after a few years; actually grow to like it."

"I guess that was some fire the other night."

"Oh, yeah. The stable's one thing, but they lost a bundle in saddles and equipment. Real bad timing, too, with the Barrington coming up in a few weeks."

"The Barrington?"

"The Barrington Horse Show, out on the Cape? It's one of the top hunter-seat competitions in the country. Certainly the biggest in Zone One. All three of Mr. C's kids plan to ride in it. Mr. C used to compete in it, too, until he had his spill a few years back. He's got a string of ribbons from all over the country. Anyway, gonna be a little tough for the kids to compete without proper saddles." Pete laughed again, but this time the sound was edgy and hard. It gave Rosco the impression the guard had far more respect for "Mr. C" than he'd ever have for Fiona, Heather, and Chip.

"I understand the barn manager got banged up pretty bad in the blaze. Friend of yours?"

"Orlando? Not friends, no . . . I mean, I say 'hey' to him, goin' in and out of the gate. Him and his wife, Kelly. Nice folks, but private and businesslike, which is fine by me. They keep to themselves most of the time, but Orlando's *The Man* when it comes to keepin' the place in top-notch condition. Not gonna be an easy fella to replace."

"Well, he's regained consciousness, from what I hear. Hopefully he'll be back to work before long."

Pete shrugged. "If you say so." He then looked down the road at a car slowing. "This must be Mr. Mize now."

Rosco turned. "You know Clint?"

"No. But the swells who come and go through this gate all drive tanks. You know, Range Rovers, Hummers, and whatnot. Only *peasants* like me and insurance adjusters drive cars that get sensible gas mileage."

Mize parked his Toyota sedan in front of Rosco's Jeep and approached the two men. He was carrying a manila file folder. Mize was probably the same age as the security guard but short and bulldog-shaped; what little hair remained was white-white and buzzed to a stubble-length bristle. Clint Mize was an ex-Marine; he took pride in the fact that most people could guess that part of his history without being told.

"It's good to see you again, Polycrates. Been a long time." Mize shook Rosco's hand and added, "What was it?" He snapped his fingers. "That torch-job on the yacht a few years back, right? When I was with Shore Line?"

"Sounds about right."

"I'm glad you could fit this one into your schedule." That was enough small talk for Mize. "I'd like to go over the fire marshal's report with you before we go in."

"Lead on."

They walked over to Rosco's Jeep. Mize opened his folder and set it on the hood.

"Okay . . . Mr. Collins has been a grade-A client of the Dartmouth Group for a long stretch, so they're not looking to make any waves." He tapped the report with his finger. "The marshal's classifying the blaze as an accident, 'nonsuspicious,' and Dartmouth's inclined to agree. I just need to look it over and come up with a dollar figure that everyone can live with."

"So why bring me in?" Rosco asked as he scanned the report.

"S.O.P. It's going to be a hefty check, and Dartmouth's board could raise a stink if I didn't have a PI with some arson know-how look it over for me. But our CEO wants to handle this one P.D.Q. Scuttlebutt back at the office is that him and Collins are longtime buddies. And to be honest, any stalling would look bad in a high-profile deal like this." Mize put on a Waspy accent and finished with, "Of course, nobody likes it when dirty looks are exchanged between long-standing members of the Patriot Yacht Club."

"No, we certainly can't have that." Rosco chuckled, then read from the report. "So the barn manager allegedly knocked over a faulty space heater, along with a bottle of booze . . . which provides us with our primary source as well as an accelerant." He looked at Mize. "That's pretty much what I got from NPD yesterday." He flipped over the report. "I don't see evidence that anyone's talked to the barn manager, Polk, yet. I understand he's regained consciousness. Can he corroborate these facts?"

Mize shook his head. "Apparently there's a slight case of amnesia going on there. He doesn't remember how it all went down, but my guess is he's trying to save his own hide. I mean, supposedly it was his hooch that started the blaze, and his reputation for not being what you'd call a teetotaler is apparently common knowledge out here."

Rosco closed the folder. "Well, you know me, Clint; if I smell a rat, I'll go to the fire marshal with it. And the DA, too. I won't bury anything."

Mize raised his hands. "Hey, I'm with you, buddy. That's why I called you rather than some PI who's going to roll over and play dead for the fat cats. I don't like games any more than you do. I just wanted to brief you on company policy before we drove in there."

The two men returned to their vehicles, passed through the gate, and proceeded along the alley of copper beeches. After a quarter of a mile they came to a rise in the lane. When they got to the top of the hill, they could see the whole of King Wenstarin Farms stretched out below them. The Collins mansion commanded another rise. From this vantage point, the entire house was visible. Built in the early 1920s, the residence looked as though it belonged in Newport, Rhode Island, rather than on a farm in Massachusetts. Six stately pillars spanned the front elevation, creating an imposing entrance and broad portico. The remainder of the structure was mostly Georgian in design: Palladian windows, French doors on the lower level, a slate roof punctuated by six chimneys. It was clearly a comfortable and spacious home. A number of large and small ancillary cottages stood at a respectful distance; lawns of perfect grass rolled between each building.

Five stables lay below the farm residences, one of which was now half-destroyed by fire. Each barn was equipped with a paddock as well as a fenced exercise area. Within sight also were two professional-sized practice arenas; one was fully enclosed for winter use, and the other was open-air and equipped with a small grandstand. That ring was presently arranged in jumping-course mode, with fifteen obstacles set at varying heights. Four teenage girls and a boy were taking their mounts through their paces, as a trainer stood at the center barking orders alternatively to the youngsters and their horses. Three women, whom Rosco guessed to be the kids' mothers, sat in the grandstand chatting and laughing and paying little to no attention to their children's activities. To a person, the women were clad in woolens and tweeds that were intended to appear casually mismatched as if the costumes had been hastily tossed together; instead the muted colors, the buttery Italian leather, and quite obvious cashmere and silk bore the unmistakable stamp of wealth. The mothers had their backs to the burned building, and their animated conversation seemed to indicate that they either didn't notice the acrid scent of fire still lingering in the air and the muddy landscape surrounding the charred structure or that they refused to do so. *If it's not pretty,* their postures said, *it's not worth wasting our time.*

Rosco followed closely behind Clint's Toyota, and also parked by the ruined stable.

"Mr. Collins said he'd meet us down here," Mize told Rosco as they stepped from their cars. He then nodded back toward the mansion. "That must be him and the missus now."

Rosco turned and watched Todd Collins and his wife, Ryan, stroll down to meet them. Collins was exactly as he'd been described: tall, rangy, white-haired, and uncompromising, with a slight limp he seemed determined to ignore. Ryan also matched prior descriptions: a strikingly beautiful woman in her late thirties with blond hair braided into a single plait and sharp green eyes. As the couple neared, however, deeply etched lines in her face became evident, turning her expression into one of perpetual disappointment rather than ease, while the braid took on the tightly woven appearance of a show horse's tail.

Mize conducted the introductions, and Ryan responded with a testy, "I don't see why we need a private investigator.

It makes us sound like we've committed some sort of crime, and personally I find it a little insulting."

Mize's response was conciliatory but assured. "Don't think I'm being flippant when I say this, Mrs. Collins, but even though Polycrates and I are both working for the Dartmouth Group, we have cross purposes. My job is to assess damages, make certain that you get a settlement you're comfortable with, and that we get it to you in a timely fashion." He cocked his thumb toward Rosco. "My buddy here plays the bad guy. It's his job to come up with a reason Dartmouth can use for *not* paying the claim. It's S.O.P., standard operating procedure. Works the same with any large claim—fire, theft, personal liability, you name it." He smiled his brisk, no-nonsense smile. "I want to be thoroughly up front with you both, because Dartmouth has every intention of making good on this claim. So please, don't let anything Rosco asks insult you; he's only doing a job. Dartmouth's CEO has a board of directors to answer to, and if we didn't play this by the book it would only raise more questions than answers."

"Fine," was her less-than-gracious reply, "but I still don't like it. How long's this going to take?"

Rosco opened his mouth to respond, but Todd jumped in with a placating "Ryan needs to leave shortly for Logan Airport. The wife of our injured barn manager has been away in Kentucky. She's arriving in an hour, and she hasn't yet seen her husband. Ryan's taking her straight to the hospital."

Clint glanced at his watch. "You can go now if you like, Mrs. Collins." He then looked at Rosco. "Do you have anything to ask?"

Rosco pulled a small pad from his pocket. "Just one or

two quick questions, if you don't mind? Were you home when the fire broke out, Mrs. Collins?"

"What? You think I started it?"

"No, not at all; consensus seems to be that your barn manager was responsible. I only wondered if you were home, and if you might have seen or heard anything unusual prior to the onset of the blaze."

"Yes I was home, but no I didn't see or hear anything suspicious—if that's what you're getting at. Of course, I saw the stable burn. Everyone did."

"And it wasn't you who called the fire department?"

"No. Todd said I . . ." She stopped and looked at her husband, but his eyes were fixed to the charred and hulking building, and his expression gave no indication whether or not he'd heard her speak. She returned her concentration to Rosco, and gave him a small and chilly smile. "No. It wasn't me who called."

"The dispatcher said it was a woman. Do you have any idea who it might have been?"

"What difference does it make?"

"I'd just like to talk to her, that's all."

"Well, I'm afraid I can't help you." Ryan Collins glanced at her watch. "Now, if you'll excuse me, I've got to go." Then she headed back toward the main house without another word.

CHAPTER

7

Rosco, Clint, and Todd watched in silence as Ryan Collins's blue Mercedes coupe roared down the lane.

"Sorry about all that," her husband said after the car had disappeared, "this situation has been tough on her. On everyone actually. We lost a lot of good leather in that tack room. And with the Barrington coming up so soon . . . let's just say we're all extra tense."

"Fortunately there was no loss of life," was Rosco's quiet response. "Human or equine."

Todd regarded him, shifting his weight as if in pain. "You're right, of course. What was I thinking?" Then he shook his head as though Rosco's remark had finally sunk in. "We competitive riders tend to forget everything except the next show, the next event. Anything that causes even minor setbacks—damage to a lucky saddle, for instance—is a problem, and we act out accordingly. The days surrounding a major competition can be downright ugly; nerves are frayed; tempers are continually on edge. I've heard the world of professional yacht racing is the same, although I don't have any firsthand experience since most of my life has been devoted to the fickle business of getting big and contrary beasts to run and jump as if they were circus-trained poodles." Then he gave Rosco a crooked smile. "I know who you are. Are you aware of that?"

"Pardon me?"

"You've done a marvelous job of keeping your mug out of the newspapers, but I recognized your name immediately."

Mize laughed. "Yeah, that chop-shop case Rosco cracked back in March got more press than a presidential visit. Guess you had to pull some major strings to keep the paparazzi off your front door, didn't you, pal?"

"No," Todd continued, "I was referring to who he's married to. I'm a crossword puzzle addict, and I go to bed with your wife every night."

Rosco laughed while Clint said, "I'm not going near that line with a ten-foot pole." He pulled a small tape recorder from his jacket. "Getting back to business; I'm just going to poke around and make some verbal notes, Mr. Collins." He began to head toward the stable. "I'll need a list of everything that was in the tack room with a value placed on it. The policy was drawn up for a content value of three hundred thousand dollars. I assume that's going to cover it, but we're going to need to see some written appraisals or receipts. Whatever documentation you have."

"I'll have to look around," Todd replied. "Most of the saddles cost upwards of four thousand dollars. They were French Bruno Delgranges and Luc Childérics as well as English

Crosbies . . . but it's not simply a matter of replacing them. Once a rider gets his—or her—rump into something he's comfortable with, anything else feels like a wooden merry-go-round seat. Stupidly, most of the paperwork was kept in the filing cabinet right in the tack room—which wasn't fireproof."

"I think we'll be able to give you some leeway there," Mize told him. "I'm sure your supplier will have records on what you paid."

"I'd like to take a look at what's left of the tack room myself." Rosco added.

"Sure."

The three men walked through the mud and entered what was once the building's west entrance. That half of the structure had collapsed into a pile of charred beams and ruined box stalls; the threatening odor of smoke and drenched wood and ash remained, while the burned leather of the saddles and bridles emitted a ghoulish stench of scorched flesh. Apart from the pervasive smell and a few blackened patches of wood, the eastern end of the stable remained untouched. Once the sprinkler system had been activated, the fire had been stopped dead in its tracks.

Collins shook his head as he stared at the scene. "I could just shoot that damn plumber."

"As long as you had a work order for the sprinkler repair, you're in the clear as far as Dartmouth is concerned, Mr. Collins," Clint told him. "It shows intent."

"I don't give a hang about the insurance. I just hate to see the place torn up like this." Collins kicked at a number of steel bits and stirrup irons lying near his feet, all that remained of some of the ornate trimmings that were as much a part of a horse show as rider and steed.

"Maybe you could tell me what happened the other night," Rosco prompted.

Collins drew in a deep breath and released it slowly. "I had just finished watching the evening news, so I can place the time as being a bit after seven. I was in the den. The room looks out over this stable, which is damn lucky. I don't know why I happened to glance outside, but I did . . . and that's when I spotted flames kicking up through the window in the tack room. I saw the shadow of someone swatting at them with a large cloth, which I assume was a horse blanket; obviously that person was Orlando. I don't know how he could've been so stupid; we had three-quarters of a million dollars worth of horseflesh stabled in this barn, and there he was trying to put out the fire before getting the animals to safety. Anyway, I just tore out of the house, bum leg or no. All I could think about was, save the horses."

"Which you did," Clint said.

"Damn straight. I ran down here, yanked open one of the doors, and found Orlando standing there like a bump on a log. I don't know what the hell he was thinking. Anyway, we got all the stock out. Then Polk ducked back inside to activate the busted sprinklers." Collins abruptly ceased talking; his eyes moved past Rosco and Clint. "Ah, here's Jack . . . Jack Curry. He's the head trainer around here. He helped me drag Orlando out. Good thing he showed up when he did. I couldn't have done it alone."

Jack introduced himself to Clint and Rosco and finished with, "I saw you drive up. Just thought I'd swing by and throw in my two cents if you needed it."

"Sure," Rosco answered. He looked at Curry, who gazed affably back as if he hadn't a care in the world. Rosco's

suspicious nature made him wonder whether Jack had arrived in order to validate answers rather than supply them.
"Perhaps you could tell me when you first noticed the fire."

Curry pointed to one of the three largest cottages farther
up the hill. "I'm staying up in Tulip House. The minute I
saw the flames, I was out the door and on my way down
here. I didn't bother to look at the clock."

"And you didn't consider contacting the fire department."

Curry shook his head. "I'm a horseman. If my animals are
in trouble, I want to be with them. The fire department's
ten minutes away—if we're lucky. A lot can happen in ten
minutes."

Rosco turned back to Todd. "Did I understand Mrs.
Collins correctly when she began to say that you told her
not to call the fire department?"

Todd's jaw tightened, and his eyes turned slit-thin as
though he were staring at the sun. Rosco recognized the expression; it was the look of a man trying to decide whether
or not to tell the truth—or whether it was more expedient
to simply belt the person who'd asked the question.

"Yes," Todd finally offered. "I'd totally forgotten that the
sprinkler system was down. I didn't think the department
would be necessary. Plus, like Jack said, they would've never
been here in time to save the stock, and all those sirens and
noise, they would have spooked the other animals; which
they ended up doing anyway when they arrived." His mouth
remained tense as he pointed to the far end of the stable. "As
you can see, if the sprinklers are working they can handle
just about anything."

"And just so I can get a clear picture of who was where,"

Rosco continued, "Mrs. Collins was watching the news with you? So you both noticed the fire break out at the same time?"

"No," Collins answered, then paused a second too long before continuing. "Ryan had been trying out a new course in the enclosed arena. She was returning to the house when she saw the blaze and was actually running to get me at the same moment I dashed outside."

"So her horse was in this stable?"

Collins shook his head and pointed off to his left. "Ryan's equitation horses are over in A barn. This stable is mainly occupied by boarded animals."

"But this is where you keep the saddles, right?"

"Most of the competition packages, yes. But casual work-out gear is stored in other barns."

"Do you have any idea who *did* call the fire department?" Rosco asked. "As we know, it was a woman, and according to the fire marshal it came from your phone number."

Jack answered for Todd. "From what I understand, the call came from the central number—which can be accessed from the stables, from Mr. C's house, as well as from the three main cottages: Tulip, Magnolia, and Gardenia. Technically, the call could have been made from this stable, too—if someone got to the phone before it melted."

"Are the other two cottages occupied?" Rosco said.

It was Todd who responded. "My daughter Heather and her husband, Michael Palamountain, live in Magnolia; my son, Chip, has Gardenia."

Rosco glanced at his small pad and the notes he'd made from Belle's telling of Bartholomew Kerr's gossip. To confirm one of Kerr's assertions he asked, "And your other daughter, Fiona, was she here, or are she and her husband, Mr. Applegate, at their home in Florida?"

Both Todd and Jack stiffened at Rosco's question. After an uncomfortable silence, Todd said, "My daughter and Whitney Applegate are . . . Fiona was here when the fire broke out."

Rosco pointed to the mansion. "With you and Mrs. Collins?"

"No," Jack said sharply. "She resides in one of the other cottages. Temporarily, at least. What's the point of all this?"

"Nothing really, I'm just trying to narrow down who was here, in case I have any follow-up questions later." He made a note before continuing. "Now, I was under the impression that the barn manager lived here as well?"

"There's an apartment in the back half of B stable." Jack said. "Orlando and Kelly live there. Kelly's his wife."

"This is the woman Mrs. Collins is picking up at the airport?"

"Right."

Rosco jotted down the name. "As Clint explained, the Dartmouth Group hired me. I know you've got a good relationship with Dartmouth, and that Clint—and you—want to settle the claim quickly. But is there any reason for you to believe that the fire was something more than the accident it appears to be? Is there any chance this might have been arson?"

Both men shook their heads, but a voice behind Rosco said a loud and emphatic, "Absolutely."

Rosco turned to see a woman striding toward them. She had the ramrod-straight bearing of someone who'd been riding since she could walk; her prematurely gray hair was cut into a flat and unflattering bowl as if real locks were of less value than a derby or velvet-covered hunting helmet; and her clothes bore the same stamp of disdain: a stained sweatshirt and frayed jeans that would be replaced by a monogrammed shirt, hand-tailored jacket, and color-coordinated breeches when she was in the ring. She stepped forward and offered Rosco her hand. He noticed that her grip was even stronger than Jack Curry's, and that she was pleased with the fact. "I'm Heather Collins." Her voice was equally firm, the tone as plain as her appearance. She nodded a brief greeting to the others. "Jack, Daddy, Mr. Mize."

"I'm Rosco Polycrates, and I—"

"I gathered," Heather interrupted. "You're the PI."

Rosco studied her. "And you feel there's reason to suspect arson?"

"Heather," Todd interrupted, "let's not go into these conspiracy theories of yours right now." He turned back to Rosco. "My daughter is convinced that Holbrooke Farms—those are the folks who will be our major competition at next week's Barrington—are responsible for burning up our saddles."

"And why not? You haven't danced around a show ring with those creeps in a long time, Daddy. Last year they did everything they could to throw me off my game. You don't remember Judy Holbrooke telling me she was going to see me burn in Hades after I took the blue?" Heather pointed at the sodden ashes at her feet. "This is no coincidence."

Todd continued speaking to Rosco as though his daughter hadn't voiced this opinion. "Of course, she hasn't considered the fact that this mysterious arsonist from Holbrooke Farms would have to drive past a guarded and locked gate, start the fire, and then steal away without a soul seeing them."

"It could have been an inside job," Heather's hard voice stated. "Someone could have hiked in; this isn't Fort Knox. And all these people who come and go around here? A couple of hundred dollars, and they'd do anything they were told. You believe everyone has such devotion to you, Daddy. Me, I don't think they care a lick. You don't know what goes on behind your back."

"Okay, that's enough," Collins said quietly.

"I wouldn't even put it past my darling sister to have pulled this off. You'll notice she's too highfalutin to keep her saddles and tack in this barn." She glared at Jack. "What does she do, Jack, sleep with them?"

"Drop it, Heather," was his level reply. "Fiona and I aren't any of your business."

"Really? Since when did that happen? I thought the Jack-Curry-and-Daddy's-darling-daughter deal was all anyone cared about." Then she spun toward Rosco. "Do you have a business card, Mr. PI?"

Rosco handed her a card, which she stuffed unceremoniously into a back pocket of her jeans.

"Thanks. I'll call you."

Then she marched off, jaw tucked in tight, eyes fixed, and elbows jutting as though she were aiming at a very high hurdle. There was something about Heather's tirade that seemed rehearsed and premeditated to Rosco. He couldn't put his finger on what it was, but wrote it off to the fact that she'd probably been waiting to get it off her chest for some time.

"Everyone's out to get poor Heather," Jack observed with a thin-lipped smile after she was out of earshot. "Don't take her notions too seriously, Rosco. She views any bad news as a personal assault—especially when it comes to her big sister."

Rosco glanced a Todd, finding it odd that Curry felt free to criticize Collins's younger daughter in front of him.

Todd interpreted Rosco's unasked questions and gave a dismissive shrug. "Jack's known Heather for a long time. He's almost family. And like the rest of us Collinses, he calls it like he sees it. We don't mince words around here. Never have."

It was Clint Mize who broke the ensuing uneasy silence. "I'm ready to move on now, sir. If you can fax me whatever paperwork you have on lost contents, I'll get the claim in the works. I'm afraid we're only going to allow you sixty percent of the replacement value on the building, though. The east end still appears sturdy as a rock."

"You do what you have to do," was Collins's distracted response. "I'll let you know if I have any problems . . . oh, and I'll have our saddlery supplier contact you, as well." He then nodded to his former son-in-law. "Jack, I need to talk to you in private."

They excused themselves and walked up the hill toward the house.

Mize glanced at Rosco's face and laughed. "You don't like the situation, do you?"

Rosco shook his head. "I can't say I do. I'm getting some weird vibes here."

"Hey, isn't that what makes the rich different from you and me? They're *encouraged* to be eccentric. Us? We'd lose our jobs. But weird or not, Polycrates, arson ain't part of what's going down here."

"I'll feel a lot better after I get a chance to talk to the barn manager."

Mize chuckled again. "How did I know you were going to say that? Well, fish around all you want. If you come up with something, even if it's real iffy, let me know, so I can put a stall on Collins's check. Like I said earlier, that's what the Dartmouth Group pays you for. And I don't roll over and play dead for anyone."

The two men returned to their cars, and as Rosco was about to start the Jeep, Clint called back to him, "Off the subject, but did a Walter Gudgeon ever get in touch with you?"

CHAPTER

8

Maxi's "Manes on Main" didn't sound like the name of a high-class beauty parlor—which was precisely what had originally attracted Sara Crane Briephs to the place. Not for her the froufrou decor and fawning attention of its pricier competitors, or the cooing clucks of how *resplendent* her *coiffure*, or how *classic* and *timeless* her aging face. Sara was an old lady; she was proud of the fact; and at eighty-plus she didn't like pussyfooting around—not that she ever had.

Sara Briephs was New England through and through; her ancestors had helped build the city of Newcastle, and it was a history she regarded as both her legacy and duty. Thus, she liked Maxi's Manes, with its reasonable prices, with its dearth of *little extras*, like spa treatments and massages with warm aromatic oils or—heaven forbid—seaweed wraps. A weekly hair appointment was all Sara wanted and needed, and Maxi's was the shop she chose. Besides, if Sara wanted to cover herself in seaweed, she had only to lie on a beach at low tide and let the slimy stuff wash over her.

She found a parking space directly in front of the shop, a feat that would have been remarkable for anyone other than Newcastle's reigning grande dame. But wherever she rambled in her ancient and gleaming black Cadillac, empty spots magically appeared as if the years had rolled back to an era when there were fewer vehicles on the road, and when automobiles such as hers were piloted by ladies and gentlemen dressed in formal hats and gloves.

Sara could still parallel park with the best of them, which she did in a heartbeat, then set the emergency brake, removed her own kid-gloved hands from the steering wheel, daintily retrieved her purse from the passenger seat, and swung her still-athletic and taupe-stockinged legs from the car. As she stepped out she glanced at the lettering on Maxi's window and smiled as she always did. " 'Manes on Main,' " she mused aloud. "The name makes it sounds as though Belle should be bringing her monsters, Kit and Gabby, here for a wash and blow-dry." It was ten minutes before three in the afternoon; her standing appointment was at three—every Saturday, week in and week out.

But no sooner had Sara opened the door to Maxi's Manes than Fiona Collins zoomed out, nearly colliding with the elderly lady. Without slowing her pace she giggled a decidedly unapologetic, "Sorry about that. Must be the champers I had at lunch. I can't seem to see straight any longer." Fiona giggled again, then flitted up the street toward the municipal parking lot on Thirteenth Street and Winthrop.

"I trust she's not driving," Sara sniffed as she walked into the salon.

Maxi—or Maxine as she seemed to call herself on alternating days—raised a caustic eyebrow. "Well, guess again, Sara."

"Those people," was the imperious response, but the shop owner merely grinned a wide, amused smile and handed Sara a cotton wrapper.

"So, what are we doing this week, Sar . . . ? Spikes? Orange and green streaks, a touch of violet to match your doll-baby blue eyes?"

"I didn't know the Collins girls were your customers," was Sara's still-haughty reply. "I would have guessed anyone other than Bruno or Claude at Chez Claude would have been beneath their stature."

"It's only Lady Fiona, and this is only her second appearance. She runs through hairdressers like she runs through men, so I'm not counting my chickens before they come home to roost. But you know me . . . if she doesn't cause any trouble or make too many demands, or sulk or pout or whine about not looking simply *divine* at age forty-five, then she can get an appointment. If not, she's outta here. All I do is hair, no face-lifts, no cosmetic dentistry, no laser treatments, no peels, no waxes." Maxine tossed her own hair—this week a soft, strawberry blond—in a customary display of streetwise toughness. "I mean, I'm thirty-seven, and I'm a big girl. How divine am I gonna look once I reach the dreaded age of forty? Not very, is my guess. Even Bruno and Claude would have their hands full."

"For one thing, you're not big, Maxine; you're tall. And for another: forty or, for that matter, forty-five or even fifty is a mere child when compared to—"

"I know . . . I know . . . eighty-whatever." Maxi gave a hearty laugh that matched her ample frame. "So, surprise me, Sar . . . what'll it be this week?"

Sara winked at the hairdresser's reflected image in the mirror. "The usual. Shampoo and set."

"You're no fun, you know that? When I get to be an old broad like you, I'm gonna cut loose. I'll be playing with hair colors they haven't even invented yet."

"Hmmmph," Sara sniffed again, but the teasing exchange was interrupted by Fiona Collins's return.

"Silly me . . . I forgot my purse." She bumped into the reclining chair where Maxine's assistant was now preparing to shampoo Sara. "Woopsie-daisy . . ."

Sara closed her eyes and leaned her stately head back into the sink. The activity made a strong statement, as if the likes of Fiona Collins—sober or tipsy—didn't exist.

"Hey, I know you . . ." Fiona mumbled. "You're Tommy's mom . . . or were, I guess I should say, since he's no longer with us . . . Ooh, sorry . . . Foot-in-mouth disease, that's me."

Sara stiffened, but made no reply. Nor did she open her eyes.

"He was a fun guy, Tommy, a real party animal. I miss him a lot."

"So do I." Sara's voice was so firm and monotone that both Maxi and her assistant grew instantly silent. Not Fiona, however.

"I'll just bet you do. Everyone does. I'm not a mom, so I wouldn't know about maternal stuff, but Tommy was one hell of a good-time Harry . . . or Charlie or whatever . . ." As she spoke, Fiona hunted for her missing purse. "Damn! It's not here. Maybe I left it in the restaurant. I paid you, didn't I, Maxine?"

"In cash. You had a one-hundred-dollar bill in your pocket. A couple of them, in fact."

"Really?"

"You put the change in the same pocket."

Fiona checked her jacket. "Damn! So I did . . . I forgot this money was here. I'll check the restaurant and see if I left my stuff there. Well, toodles, Tommy's mom. Good to meetcha . . . again."

"His name was Thompson, not Tommy," was Sara's taut response, but Fiona was already gone.

Seated at Maxine's workstation with her white hair now dripping onto her shoulders, Sara's expression remained grim. "That awful woman," she announced between clenched teeth. "The whole lot of them. They're simply cowboys with money. The worst sort of people."

"If I had their kind of dough, you could call me a cow, and I wouldn't care," Maxi said to lighten the mood. But Sara was not to be appeased.

"Three husbands and counting, the first being that trainer the father apparently dotes on, and has rehired despite his hellacious past . . . and the third being that ne'er-do-well dilettante, Whitney Applegate, whom I've heard is still lurking in the shadows, despite the fact that his wife has rekindled her romance with spouse number one. Who, I might add, left Collins's employ under a severe cloud last time . . . gambling debts . . . suspicions of filching his mate's pin money. I imagine Fiona's heading for a very messy divorce. Well, good for her. Thank goodness she never corralled my son, that's all I can say."

"It's probably not called 'pin money,' Sar," Maxi observed, as she affixed a Velcro roller to the thinning hair and pink scalp. "Especially, if you're a Collins and your current hubby—and future ex—is Mr. Whitney Applegate, the fourth, of Palm Beach, et cetera. Pin money in their case probably means diamond brooches."

"The Collinses are a most unstable family."

"As it were," Maxine rejoined, but Sara was on a roll and not inclined to play.

"And I've heard that the father's present wife, Ryan, is the worst of the lot."

Maxi laughed. "So Lady F. was telling me. 'The Black Widow' is what Fiona calls her stepmom. I just got the whole sordid story in a single sitting: how Ryan got her hooks into dear old Dad, while she was convalescing from a riding accident that Lady F. is convinced was staged. 'Riding spill, my butt. No one even saw her fall,'" Maxine quoted. "And how self-same Dad blamed himself for Ryan's misfortune, insisted on paying all medical bills and having her recuperate at his house, how much the kids hate her—despite the fact that Fiona suspects stepmom of coming on to Chip. Which little Chip has never denied. Yep, I got it all today. Of course, she wanted to refresh her highlights, so we had extra time to gab."

"Well, nothing would surprise me," Sara stated with a patrician lift to her head. "Nor would I be astonished if the *Chip* off the Collins block weren't encouraging the woman . . . along with the string of ladies he's been reported to keep company with."

"You're bad, Sara," Maxine chortled.

"I'm merely reporting what my eyes and ears have seen and heard."

"And they say hairdressers like to gossip."

"Oh, I don't engage in gossip, Maxine," was Sara's lofty response. "As an amateur student of human behavior, I relish the opportunity to examine character. I only tend to verbalize these thoughts to determine if others are in agreement with my assessments."

Maxi raised both eyebrows as she studied her client. "You're ready for the dryer, madam."

"More to the point, you're probably ready for a little P and Q."

Brushed out, her white hair as fluffy and bright as a new cotton puff, Sara smiled into the mirror. "You make me look like a queen, Maxine."

"Well, don't let it go to your head, doll-baby."

Sara chuckled and stood, but as she did, her right foot went out from under her, and she crumpled to the floor with a startled gasp of pain. "Oh, my knee . . . my knee just . . ." Involuntary tears sprang into her blue eyes. "Oh, how silly . . . oh!"

Sara tried to rise, but Maxine grasped her shoulders, holding her in place. "Don't you move, now. You know what they say? When older people take a tumble, they've gotta sit for a bit and figure out what happened."

Despite this injunction, Sara attempted to straighten her leg, then winced in agony and slumped back down.

"I'm gonna call for an ambulance," Maxi said, finally relinquishing Sara's shoulders.

"I refuse to be carried out of here on a stretcher!"

"That's for the EMTs to decide."

"It is not, Maxi! I'll have nothing of it."

"Sara, if you broke a bone—which seems real likely—you'll leave this shop as the pros see fit. And not how your regal highness wants."

"Will you call Belle for me, at least?"

"I will, but I promise she won't agree to take you to the hospital in that little car of hers—or drive you home."

CHAPTER

9

"Bad news," the driver said as the other coconspirator slid into the passenger's seat of the car. "He brought Polycrates in on it."

"Tell me something I don't know," was the trenchant reply. Before the person behind the wheel could continue with more gloomy news, a hand was raised. "Who do you want to be tonight? Bonnie or Clyde?" It was a game they'd played before.

The driver considered the choice for almost a full minute and then answered a quiet, "Bonnie."

"Good, 'cause I'm feeling just like that hunky killer dude. I'm all revved up and rarin' to go." On the lap of the newly dubbed "Clyde" was a flat paper bag from Papyrus, an office superstore not far from their rendezvous.

"Bonnie" pushed the shift knob into first gear and pulled away from the curb. "Slide down in the seat. The less people see us together the better."

"Oh, boy, you're really getting into it. You mean like we're strangers? Like we've never been spotted together?" Despite the words of protest, the request was honored. Clyde pulled a baseball cap down over a pair of deep-set eyes. "Better?"

"This isn't a joking matter. We can't afford to have anything traced back to us."

"Look, you had to realize there was a chance he'd bring in a PI. That's the way these things work. Be thankful it's not the entire Newcastle Police Department."

The response was a distracted, "But he's not a public kind of guy. I figured he'd stay mum as long as—"

"So we have to try a little harder, Bonnie honey, be a little sneakier. What's the gripe? Besides, like I said, a private eye ain't no cop. Anyway, the whole thing's given me a great idea." Clyde depressed a button to close the car's window against the cold evening air. "Listen, I have no intention of being ferreted out either; not this late in the game."

"Neither of us can afford it." This was a statement of fact, not an opinion, and it silenced Clyde for a long and heavy moment.

"Anyway, Bonnie baby, back to my dynamite idea. This is going to take us some time—which is why I wanted to get right on it."

"Where do you want to go?"

"How about Munnatawket Beach? No one will be there this time of year; especially after dark. Any beachcombers or dog walkers will have left when the sun went down."

"Okay." They passed through three stoplights and turned onto the beach drive. Once they'd left the city limits, high beams were flipped on, and Bonnie pressed a lead foot down on the accelerator.

"Hey, take it easy. The last thing we need is a cop on our tail."

The response was an acid, "I hope you're not attempting to tell me how to drive—on top of everything else, Clyde." Despite the words of protest, their speed was reduced considerably. "So what's this big hush-hush plan?"

Clyde chortled. "Wait till we get there . . ."

Pulling into the parking lot of Munnatawket Beach fifteen minutes later, both were relieved to find the place deserted. Fluorescent streetlamps illuminated the asphalt, puddling a flickering greenish light every fifty yards or so, and windblown sand drifted up and over the recycled horizontal telephone poles that separated the lot from the beach. Where the seashore began in earnest, small dunes had formed around the mangled aluminum chairs, treadless tires, and chunks of driftwood washed in by the ocean waves. Not a trace of summer's mirth remained.

"I hate the beach when it looks like this," Bonnie observed. "It makes me think the end of the world is near; like in that old movie. What was the name of it?"

"I have no idea."

"It gave me the creeps. It had that guy in it."

"Oh, *that* movie," was the snide reply. "The black-and-white one with *that* woman?"

Clyde's obvious sarcasm eluded the person sitting behind the steering wheel. "Yeah, that's the one."

"Hell of a film."

"It gave me the creeps." Bonnie set the parking brake and stared at the gloomy darkness, "Okay, what's this brilliant plan?"

"Who's he married to?"

"Who?"

"Polycrates, Bonnie darlin', who do you think?" The words were pinched and exacerbated.

The answer took a few seconds and was formed as a half-question, half-statement. "The crossword puzzle lady at the *Evening Crier*, Annabella Graham?"

"Exactly." Clyde reached into the Papyrus bag and removed a pad of quarter-inch graph paper. "This is called 'Watch Your Target and Focus.' We make a crossword puzzle and fax it to her. Something that will grab her attention, and then get her hubby jumping to the conclusions we need him to—"

"That won't work. Fax transmissions print out the originating phone numbers. If we're trying to pass along information and remain anonymous, that's not the way to do it."

"Don't worry. I've got a solution worked out."

Bonnie sighed. "Let me see that pad of paper."

It was handed over and then examined. Graph lines were printed on both sides.

"I don't know . . . this seems really rinky-dink. Like schoolkids' stuff."

"That's part of the deal. We send *la* Graham something that looks totally unprofessional . . . like it was done by some loony-tunes ratting on a onetime buddy, or a loner nursing a grudge, or an old geezer with nothing better to do. The important thing is that we point her and Polycrates in the right direction."

"But we're hardly loners."

"*Looks like*, not *is*," was the sharp reply. "We make her and hubby dearest think this is a solo act. Then when he tries to figure out who's tipping him off, he won't be hunting for a couple." Clyde pulled a pencil from the bag and started to mark off lines. "Okay, here's what I figured out; the puzzles are fifteen squares across and fifteen down, and the words are at least three letters long—"

"How do you know that?"

"Because I'm Clyde, aren't I? I'm one hot and sexy *hombre.*"

"For today," was the quick retort. "Besides, I still don't—"

"Stuff it, sweetheart. I'm telling you this'll work. We clue him in; he makes the right move . . . bingo, case solved, bad guy's arrested, and no one knows who tipped him off. Okay, let's try song titles, how's that? These crosswords should have a theme."

"Songs . . . ?"

"Are you going deaf or what? Come on, Bonnie baby. Get with it. *Light My Fire,* as they say . . . we're trying to open *Doors* here."

Ten hours later, a puzzle was complete, and the light of a new day was just beginning to mark the sky.

CHAPTER

10

"Sara was darn lucky. That's all I can say." Belle stretched the sleeves of her favorite Irish fisherman's sweater to cover her chilly hands, then plunged her sweater-clad fists into the pockets of her down vest as she walked in almost perfectly synchronized step with her husband.

"It's probably not all you can say," Rosco rejoined, but his wife failed to notice the quip. Nor did she seem aware of the lovely morning weather or the several seagulls lofting high overhead, the coastal city's unofficial avian mascot.

"No fracture, no severely damaged ligaments. Of course, she'll be forced to keep her knee immobilized for a while and then engage in physical therapy to strengthen the muscles. But when you think about her age, Rosco . . . it could have been her hip! She could have busted her shoulder when she fell. Or she could even have been alone—without a sensible person like Maxi to take charge of the situation."

Rosco nodded, then picked up and tossed a small stick for the dogs to chase up a lane pleasantly devoid of traffic. Sunday morning was a peaceful time in the village-within-a-city that was known as Captain's Walk. An area originally populated by Newcastle's seafarers, the homes dated from the late eighteenth and early nineteenth centuries. They were small and compact dwellings by modern standards; most, like Belle and Rosco's, had street-facing porches, tiny patches of grass, a mini entry drive suitable for a single sub-compact car, and a leafy rear garden. When Newcastle was a bustling whaling port, Captain's Walk probably felt like the suburbs. Now it was a time-warp oasis within the township's hectic sprawl.

Kit retrieved the stick, and Rosco tossed it again. The shepherd-mix bounded off in renewed pursuit; Gabby, slier and wilier, waited at Rosco's side to pounce on her returning "sister" and thereby wrestle away the prize.

"You're a sneak-thief, Gab," Belle observed with a chuckle.

"Sounds a bit redundant," Rosco told his wife.

"Doesn't it? I could call her a highway robber, but I don't think this pokey little road qualifies. At least, it doesn't any longer. Maybe once upon a time in the wagon and cart days before speed limits were posted at sixty-five miles per hour." Then Belle returned to the subject of Sara Briephs's worrisome fall, while the couple—with dog companions—returned home and climbed the three stairs to the porch.

Their stroll had lasted a little over forty-five minutes, and by the time the foursome stepped through the front door all were hungry as bears. Naturally, Kit and Gabby were fed first, then Belle started brewing coffee, while Rosco opened the refrigerator and said, "What would you like for breakfast, love of my life?"

"What do we have?"

There was a long pause. Eventually he said, "Eggs . . . and leftover meatloaf."

"That's it? That's all there is in there?"

"That's it. Well, there's some mayo and a jar of capers."

"There should be English muffins. They're in the freezer next to the chocolate chocolate chip ice cream. I spotted them yesterday morning when you were out for a run."

Rosco shook his head. "I'm not even going to ask why you were after chocolate chocolate chip ice cream yesterday morning."

"I wasn't," Belle answered indignantly.

"Hmmmm," he mouthed, indicating that he didn't believe her for a minute.

"Rosco, I didn't eat chocolate chocolate chip ice cream in the morning! What do you take me for? It was the vanilla. We didn't have any yogurt or milk. What was I supposed to put on my granola? I waited for it to melt."

He laughed. "Okay, as long as you waited for it to melt. I guess that makes it justifiable."

"Hey!" Belle exclaimed excitedly, as she rummaged through one of the kitchen cabinets. "Look at this. It's a can of corned beef hash. It was in with the dog food. Did you know we had this?"

"No."

"This is super. This is going to be a real breakfast—hash, eggs, and muffins, just like you get a Lawson's."

"But without Martha's sass," he said with a smile.

However, the moment Belle began to open the can they

heard the steady beep of the fax machine emanating from her home office at the rear of the house.

"Yuck," she said. "It's Sunday. Don't people have anything better to do with their time than to send faxes?"

Rosco placed the frozen muffins on the work island. "I'll go see what it is. It's probably a land deal in Florida that we'd be absolute idiots to ignore. We may need to respond within the next twenty minutes, though, so get your credit card ready."

He walked back to the converted porch that served as Belle's office and returned empty-handed a few seconds later. "It was a crossword puzzle submission."

"Argh, that's even worse. These constructors know I only accept contributions at the *Crier*. And sending it on a Sunday? I'll bet whoever it is wouldn't like to be pestered on their day off."

"Don't let it bother you." He stepped up to her and gave her a long kiss. "We've got the whole day ahead of us. A cheery visit to our favorite recuperating invalid . . . then a romp in the countryside with the you-know-whos, culminating with a romantic fire while the sun sinks in the golden west . . . And you'll note, there's not a step-quote puzzle in sight."

Belle smiled then shook her head in perplexity. "How do these people get our fax number, anyway?"

Rosco laughed. "Here's how." He took the kitchen phone from the wall and auto-dialed the *Crier*'s main operator. When a voice responded, he said, "Yes, could you please give me Annabella Graham's fax number?" He held the phone at a distance, so Belle could hear the operator rattle off the number, then added an energetic "Thank you so much!" before hanging up.

"Hmmmm. Maybe you should consider becoming a private detective. You seem to know all the tricks."

"That's what they pay me for."

Belle placed the hash in a frying pan and lit the gas range. "I hope I can get this as crispy as Kenny does down at Lawson's. Do you think there's a trick to it?"

"Hey, if you ruin the stuff, we still have plenty of Alpo."

Belle chuckled, but her smile turned into a frown when Rosco's cell phone rang a split-second later. He walked to the counter where he'd left it and looked at the caller ID. "I should get this. It's the surgeon at Newcastle Memorial who operated on Dawn Davis. I've left him three messages since Friday. This is the first he's called back."

Belle's "Fine" was less than enthusiastic; there was no disguising her irritation at having their peaceful Sunday interrupted twice in three minutes by communiqués from the outside world.

Rosco put the phone to his ear and walked into the living room, so Belle wouldn't have to listen to the drone. When he returned two minutes later, his expression was no longer lighthearted and sunny. "Bad news, I'm afraid. I'm going to have to run over to the hospital and see this guy. It'll take me an hour, maybe two by the time I get back."

"Oh, Rosco, that's not fair," Belle protested. "We were going to have the entire day together."

"I know, but Dr. Bownes is leaving for a two-week vacation tomorrow morning."

"He can't answer your questions over the phone?"

Rosco shook his head. "Information concerning patients is confidential. He may not tell me anything, even if I see him in person. It depends on how he wants to play it."

"Well then let it wait two weeks. What difference does it make?" Even as she posed the question she realized that Rosco couldn't let his case go cold for two weeks. His wasn't a nine-to-five job and never would be. "I'm sorry," she said as she moved close to him. "I'm just disappointed, that's all."

"Me, too." He kissed her. "Here's an idea: How about we save the hash for supper and have a late lunch out after we visit Sara? That way we can have our hash and eat it, too."

"Har har . . ." But the attempt at levity fell short, and Belle cleaned the frying pan in silence, while Rosco slugged down the remnants of his coffee and spooned up dry granola.

"Think of it as trail mix," she offered.

"I'm trying . . . any vanilla ice cream left?"

"Sorry. It's chocolate chocolate chip or nothing."

"Don't say we lack for exotic cuisine."

With Rosco gone, Belle slouched disconsolately into her office. Despite the abundant sunshine streaming in through the numerous windows, the glorious red leaves of the sugar maple in the garden, and the gold yellow of the neighbor's birch tree, her attitude reflected the room's decor rather than its colorful view: black and white, with the emphasis on black.

She examined this crossword-lover's paradise with a baleful eye: the wood floor painted in black-and-white grids, the curtains and lamp shades with a similar theme, the captains chairs with mix-and-match canvas backs, the bookshelf crammed with foreign-language dictionaries as well as her beloved *OED*, and her equally revered 1911 *Encyclopaedia Britannica.* At the moment, however, word games, derivations, anagrams, and other linguistic sleights-of-pencil seemed wholly irrelevant.

Belle opened what had once been the home's back door, watching as the breeze rustled the russet leaves of the maple tree. After a moment, the draft caught the newly arrived fax and lifted it from the machine's incoming tray and blew it onto the floor. She picked up the paper and glanced at it. "Argh, look at this stupid thing. It's not even symmetrical. And the dope didn't sign it. How am I supposed to respond to something like this? I sure can't publish it."

She crumpled the paper into a small ball and tossed it into the wastebasket.

Across

1. Viper
4. Amazon feeder
7. Retreat
10. Mayday!
13. Ms. Hagen
14. Pond feature
16. Literary collection
17. Dangerous ___
18. Cards' home
19. Boy
20. Beach Boys hit
22. Home to China
23. Chevy model
24. String instrument
25. Horse follower
26. Ray Charles hit
31. Type of movie
33. Sodium hydroxide symbol
34. Corn unit
37. America hit
41. Big ___
42. When doubled, antiaircraft fire
43. Creepy
44. Friends of Distinction hit
49. Grief
50. Crew member
51. Compass reading
52. Fleetwood Mac hit
58. Grow older
59. "Come and ___!"
60. Lassos
64. Mexican Mrs.
65. Comédie des ___
66. "We'll ___ that bridge . . ."
67. That woman
68. Chicken general?
69. Passes over

Down

1. BMW rival
2. Amos Alonzo ___
3. Bread and butter, in Rome
4. "Casablanca" character
5. Large lemon
6. Empty, like a candy machine
7. Whirled
8. Shelled out
9. Spots
10. Mexican heat?
11. Radio station sign
12. Nobel Peace Prize winner
    of 1978
15. Ray Charles hit
21. Hammer and anvil
22. King topper
27. Map line; abbr.
28. Star Wars character,
    Tsavong ___
29. Bass, ball, or drag followup
30. Blacksmith at times
31. Sighs of relief
32. Actor, McClure
34. Singer, Stacey or Steve
35. French friends
36. Pee Wee or Della
38. Bettors
39. Here, to Henri
40. Computer maker
45. ___ Jima
46. Chewy candy
47. Walking sticks
48. Shaw or Winkler; abbr.
52. Cut
53. Fairy tale baddie
54. Century part
55. Mr. Preminger

SUBMISSION

56. Bends
57. Pennsylvania town
61. Hawaiian staple

62. Sixth sense; abbr.
63. Draft org.

R osco hadn't set foot in Newcastle Memorial in several years, but the moment he stepped through the main entrance a flood of memories bombarded him. Back in the days when he worked homicide for NPD, his hospital visits had not been pleasant experiences. Generally, they'd involved getting statements from dying individuals—men or women who were soon to become manslaughter victims and additional city statistics. At times, the wounded person had been a young gang member, shot or stabbed by an acquaintance; in those instances, the shadow of *omertà* often cowed the victims into silence, making them unwilling to betray one of their own, even when faced with certain death. Then there were the hit-and-run victims, the unwitting prey of robberies gone south, or innocent bystanders who hadn't a clue what had happened. More than once Rosco had stood at a bedside watching a life fade away without learn-

ing a single substantive fact that would aid a criminal investigation.

As he traversed the reception area and pushed the elevator button for the seventh floor, a slew of such details attacked him, and he forced himself to concentrate on the slip
of paper in his hand rather than recall the ever-present past.
Dr. Saul Bownes, the message read, followed by the physician's emergency beeper number; it was the only information the hospital's administration office had been willing to
relinquish. Rosco had suggested to them—or lied, depending on whose point of view one chose—that he was investigating an insurance fraud complaint against Dawn Davis in
conjunction with their institution.

The statement had sent the administrators into their
own interpretation of *omertà* mixed with a dose of panic; a
lack of transparency ensued that would have made any
gangster proud. The hospital administration was permitted to release the surgeon's name and beeper number, but
that was the extent of their latitude in such cases. Details of
the operation—anesthesia, length of stay, attending nurses,
monetary charges, or out-patient treatment—were strictly
confidential and would only be released to law enforcement
personnel equipped with a proper warrant issued by a
county judge. If Dr. Bownes opted to speak with Rosco,
without a lawyer present, that was his business. Fortunately, the physician had been willing to talk, but only on
his terms.

Rosco stepped off the elevator on the seventh floor and
proceeded to the nurses' station. Bownes had informed him
that he could spare time for an interview while he did his
rounds—and that the conversation would need to be brief.

Rosco affixed a warm smile and placed his business card on the high counter surrounding the hub of activity, but none of the personnel discussing medication protocols or peering wizardlike into computer screens took the slightest notice of him.

"I'm here to see Dr. Saul Bownes." Rosco addressed the top of the head of the woman who was closest to him.

Without glancing away from her screen, she said, "Do you have an appointment?"

"Yes."

But instead of verifying whether or not this was true—or even looking up—she stated a peremptory, "You were supposed to pick up a visitors' tag on the first floor. It should be displayed on your clothing where staff can see it." Then she added a harried, "I'll page him. You can wait in the hospitality lounge. Third door on your right."

Rosco wasn't certain how she'd determined his lack of official credentials without actually looking at him, but he answered, "They were all out," picked up his card, and proceeded to the room she'd indicated. He was relieved to see that no other visitors were taking advantage of the facility's "hospitality," which seemed to consist of stale coffee, red "juice" in plastic single-serving containers, and an empty box of jelly doughnuts.

Saul Bownes arrived five minutes later. A thin man wearing green hospital scrubs with his name embroidered in red on the right breast pocket and Newcastle Memorial's logo displayed on the left, he had a wiry and restive intensity that made his age difficult to fix. Thinning dark hair, a sallow complexion, permanent gray shadows beneath his eyes; Rosco decided the physician could have been anywhere between forty and sixty. Bownes didn't offer his hand when he entered. He simply plunked himself in a chair upholstered in institutional blue and brown plaid and opened a manila folder.

"Okay, let's make this quick," were his sole words of greeting. "Dawn Davis, what's the problem? My time is valuable."

Rosco thought, *Like mine isn't?* but didn't voice the opinion. "As I explained on the phone, there's been an unusual insurance claim submitted for Dawn Davis's procedure here at the hospital."

Before Rosco could continue Bownes said, "I signed off on that personally. That's how I work, and I do so for this very reason. I don't care to have people like *you* taking up my time; accusing me of insurance fraud."

"No one's accusing you of anything, Dr. Bownes."

"Really? Then what do you call it? All charges for her procedure were submitted by me, through the hospital, directly to Healthy Life, Ms. Davis's insurance carrier. All payments are then made directly to my practice or to the hospital. Explain to me how Ms. Davis could possibly be involved in any sort of *fraud,* as you people like to call it, if she isn't involved in the financial end whatsoever? From where I sit it looks as though you people are targeting me, and to be honest, I don't like it."

Rosco held up his hands. "No one's suggesting that you or the hospital has done anything irregular. I'm working for the Dartmouth Group, not Healthy Life." Rosco smiled inside, since this was the one part of his story that was actually fairly close to the truth. "Ms. Davis had a secondary policy with us, for which she's currently trying to seek adjustment. As you can imagine, if Healthy Life is paying for her procedure in full, then Dartmouth has no obligation to double pay."

Bownes shook his head; the dark smudges beneath his eyes seemed to grow grayer and more weary looking. "I don't buy that. Ms. Davis struck me as a very nice young woman. I don't see her as the type who'd attempt what you're describing."

Rosco shrugged. "It wouldn't be the first time a *nice* person tried something like this. Let me ask you; was she transferred to another location shortly after her procedure? I spoke with one of her relatives who tried to phone her here the day after her surgery, and he was told she'd already checked out."

"That would be correct, yes. She was kept for observation overnight, then sent home."

"I'm no doctor, and I know you're pushed for hospital beds, but that seems a little rush-rush to me for a kidney transplant."

"What, are you nuts?" Bownes barked out, nearly choking over his words. "I'm an orthopedic surgeon. Ms. Davis had arthroscopic surgery on her shoulder . . . to repair a damaged rotator cuff. I wouldn't try to replace a kidney any more than I'd try to replace the carburetor on my Porsche. Where'd you get this kidney business?"

Rosco tried to keep his face from conveying his total surprise at this information. "And there's my point," was his even response. "Your patient submitted a claim to Dartmouth Group for nearly $250,000. According to *her,* she had a kidney replaced."

Bownes flipped open his file on Dawn Davis, perusing it rapidly while his contentious face grew ever more irascible. "That makes no sense. Besides, why would you people pay out something that wasn't billed directly through a hospital?"

"The only insurance carriers Newcastle Memorial bills directly are Healthy Life and Beneficial. With other carriers, like Dartmouth, patients must submit proofs of payment for reimbursement. I'm sure you've been asked to accommodate individual's claims in that manner. The forms are fairly standard."

"Yes . . ." Bownes admitted, then shook his head slowly. "But Ms. Davis wouldn't do something like this."

"It's our belief that she did." Although Rosco had gotten a description of Dawn Davis from Walter Gudgeon he saw no harm in confirming it with the surgeon. "I was wondering if you could describe the patient for me?"

"You've never met her?"

"Not yet, no. Claims are handled over the Internet or by fax. As long as a patient's primary physician provides a clean bill of health, with no preexisting conditions—which was the case here—Dartmouth will offer health-care insurance. I believe the same holds true of all the major carriers."

Bownes went on to describe Dawn Davis exactly as Gudgeon had: twenty-six, five-foot-five, attractive, with auburn hair falling midway down her back. He mentioned two more times that he couldn't believe someone as polite and friendly as she would commit a fraud like Rosco had described, and finished with, "I have to excuse myself now. I have patients to see and a good deal more paperwork before I leave for Italy tomorrow."

"Just a couple of more things, if you don't mind." Knowing full well that the surgeon would never reveal a patient's address or phone number—information that the Dartmouth

Group, as her purported secondary provider, should already possess—Rosco opted for another strategy. "One of the reasons I haven't yet discussed the claim with Ms. Davis personally is that I'm having difficulty tracking her down. Did you prescribe physical therapy for her shoulder? I would think that would be necessary for a rotator cuff."

"Yes. Of course." The surgeon was already on his feet as he answered.

"And did you recommend a particular clinic?"

"Avon-Care on Nathaniel Hawthorne Boulevard. I send all my patients there." He briefly glanced at Dawn's file again. "Her primary policy will cover any physical therapy fees she incurs. And I know she's following the regimen, because Avon's been in contact with me." Then he walked to the door and hurried down the hall. Rosco noticed Bownes's shoes for the first time: brand-new navy blue Gucci loafers that looked decidedly out of place with the rumpled green scrubs.

Following in the surgeon's elegant if ill-mannered footsteps, Rosco decided to visit the recuperating Orlando Polk and see what information he could unearth on the genuine Dartmouth Group case. But he found himself being rebuffed by a second set of overworked nurses who, in a repeat performance, scarcely glanced at him while rattling off the latest technical jargon. *Meds* was the single term Rosco felt confident he understood from their hurried babble of speech. The "procedure" the patient was "currently engaged in" was less obvious, and open to interpretation, but the ultimate message was clear: *Try again another time.* Rosco nodded his thanks—again to no one—and rode the elevator back to the first floor.

The moment he exited through the shiny steel doors, his

cell phone rang. Rosco didn't immediately recognize the number, so he answered with a professional, "Polycrates."

"Hey, Rosco, Todd Collins here, how are you?"

"Ahh . . . Just fine. Mr. Collins. What can I do for you?"

"Well, I was just thinking that it couldn't be more beautiful out here at the farm, and the weather's due to hold for the next day or two. You city-slickers would probably pay good money to see fall foliage like we have on display right now. Of course, you had a gander at it yesterday, but I could tell business got in the way . . . so, I'm calling with a special invite for you and that wife of yours. Tomorrow. Lunch. Come early so Ryan and I can show you around—the whole royal tour. Like I said, I'd give my eyeteeth to meet *the* Belle Graham, and I think she'd appreciate the names I've given my babies."

"Babies—?" Rosco started to ask, but Collins continued talking as if there'd been no interruption.

"How's about 'Lingo,' 'Catch Phrase,' and 'Palindrome'— just for starters? I told you I was a word-game nut. All the horses I breed here have names like that. 'Sobriquet's' sire is 'Shibboleth,' and so forth . . ." Collins's monologue paused only a second in order to change tack. "Is the little lady there with you now? Go ahead, ask her—and tell her she'd be doing me the biggest favor."

"Actually, I'm not at home, Mr. Collins."

"On a day like this? You're not with your wife? You should be shot." He laughed loudly. "Ryan wouldn't let me get away with ornery behavior like that."

But before Rosco could reply, Todd added a buoyant, "See you tomorrow, okay? Let's say about ten, how's that? Oh, and wear clothes you can ride in. I'm thinking of matching your wife up with 'Eponymy.' He's a sweetheart, a gelding, and gentle as a pony."

Rosco considered the invitation for the briefest moment. "How do you feel about dogs, Mr. Collins?"

"Is that a request? 'Cause my answer is: Bring 'em. I love dogs. But how do your dogs feel about horses? That's the question. Oh, and if your wife doesn't take to 'Eponymy,' we'll saddle up 'Murder the King's English.' What about that for a perfect moniker?"

CHAPTER

12

After all was said and done, Belle and Rosco opted to leave their dogs behind, rather than give them a day in the country at King Wenstarin Farms. Most likely Kit would have gotten along just fine, but given Gabby's penchant for chasing any and all moving objects—regardless of magnitude or temperament—it seemed ill-advised to allow her free range among a few dozen horses fifty times her size. However, in an effort to keep all family members appeased, Rosco took "the girls" out for a three-mile run before breakfast, and by the time the couple snuck out of the house at nine-thirty the dogs were snoozing comfortably on the warm wood floor of Belle's sunny office.

As Todd Collins had predicted, the day was bright and clear, with a temperature climbing into the mid- to upper fifties. A few wispy clouds were floating far out over Buzzards Bay; and although they couldn't actually see the ocean from the house, they felt its presence in a slightly tangy breeze and a wide and open sky. Rosco had yet to put the canvas top and door panels back on the Jeep, so the couple turned up the collars of their jackets and headed out, recognizing that this could well be their last open-air ride until the following spring.

"I'm sorry we couldn't do this yesterday," he said as they pulled away from the city limits, "but I'm glad the weather's held for another day."

Belle reached over and took his hand. "Me, too. I'm looking forward to seeing the Collins farm. I've driven by it so many times that I've been tempted to sign up for riding lessons just to get a peek at what's on the other side of that big gate."

"Grass, horses, and white fencing mostly. And of course, a smattering of road apples."

She laughed and squeezed his hand. "You're such a romantic. But speaking of that, I'm sure happy Sara is seeing Dr. Arthur about her knee and *not* your Dr. Bownes. He doesn't sound like he has a very sympathetic bedside manner."

Rosco shook his head and smiled. "I'm not even going to ask how you jumped from horse manure straight to Sara's knee injury."

"What? It's simple; *A* is for *apple*, and Saul Bownes is an underling with the orthopedic group of Aaron, Abbott, and Arthur—or the 'pedestrian's Triple-A,' as Sara calls them. It's completely logical to make that association. Anybody would."

"Anyone who spends their days counting letters, that is."

But Belle's mind, in typical fashion, was already plunging

ahead. "I told Sara I'd take her to her appointment with Dr. Arthur at three this afternoon, so I guess we should be leaving Wenstarin Farms at two, if that's okay?"

"Sure. If our lunch with Todd and Ryan seems to be lasting longer, we'll just have to excuse ourselves."

Belle leaned her head back and let the cool autumn wind blow her hair. "Oh," she sighed, "this is perfect. I love it when the weather's like this. The sun is warm, but the air is cool. You couldn't ask for a better day."

Rosco angled the Jeep down a long slope and over a small wood-plank bridge that stretched above a narrow stream. He then headed up the opposite hill. When they reached the top they were greeted by a seemingly endless stretch of King Wenstarin Farms' white fencing.

"It sure is a huge operation," Belle said. "Maintenance alone is a mind-boggling concept. It's a good thing I'm not the one responsible for keeping it tidy."

"I'll say."

She gave him a sideways glance. "I'm going to ignore that comment. Besides, I happen to be very handy with a vacuum cleaner."

"When cooking meat loaf."

"Hardy har har. You're just jealous because I can handle a vacuum with surgical skill."

Rosco slowed the Jeep as they neared the King Wenstarin Farms gate. Sitting in the same grassy patch where he'd parked on Saturday was a Newcastle Police cruiser, while a uniformed officer stood beside the guard house. He was a burly man who radiated an air of old-fashioned invincibility and confidence.

"I wonder what he's doing out here?" Rosco said as he

pulled the Jeep alongside the cruiser and set the parking brake.

Belle noticed the frown on her husband's face. "What's wrong? Do you know him?"

"Will Jordan. He's a good cop. Been on the force for fifteen or so years."

"So why the sour look?"

"Al Lever likes to use Will when he needs someone to keep the looky-loos away from crime scenes. Will handles himself very diplomatically for such a big and seemingly tough guy; he's polite but firm and always commands respect, i.e., nobody messes with him." Rosco shrugged. "Maybe I'm wrong. Maybe it's nothing. There's only one way to find out." He stepped from the Jeep and approached Jordan, who was now chatting affably with Pete, the security guard. Rosco extended his hand to the cop. "Good to see you, Will. How've you been?"

"Hangin' in there." He cocked his head toward the long lane of copper beeches. "Are you in on this one?"

"I've been looking into the fire. Is Lieutenant Lever here for some reason?"

"The whole gang's up there; Lever, Carlyle, Jones, police photographer, the print boys, you name it."

"You mean there's been a homicide?"

"Yep. Ryan Collins. Someone ran a hoof pick into the side of her head last night."

Belle approached at this moment and let out a slight gasp as she heard the news. "Oh, no, that's horrible."

"Sorry, ma'am," Will told her. "I didn't see you walking up. That was a little insensitive, the way I said that. Were you friends?"

"No. No, I didn't know her."

"Can we go in?" Rosco asked.

"I'd better check with Lever first. You know how he can get with unexpected guests." Jordan removed his radio from his belt, cleared Rosco's visit, and told Pete to open the gate. When Rosco drove past he added, "You might want to keep your wife away from the actual scene; it's not a pretty picture."

"I guess they haven't removed her body yet," Rosco said as they drove along the long lane, then he added a bleak, "So much for our pleasant day in the country." He turned and faced Belle. "Would you rather wait at the guard house? I'd offer to take you home, but I think I should take a look at this before the crime scene squad packs up. Who knows? The homicide may be connected to the fire in some way."

Belle folded her arms over her chest, suddenly feeling more than just the chill in the air as they passed into the shade of the beech trees. "No, that's okay. But I think I'll take Officer Jordan's advice and stay far away from the crime scene."

When they reached the mansion, Rosco parked beside Al Lever's "unmarked" car, a dark-brown, four-door Chevy sedan that every crook in Newcastle instantly recognized as a police vehicle. Then they silently crossed the lawn, walked up the steps, and entered the house. The foyer in which they found themselves was as grand as the home's exterior: two open, soaring stories with pink marble flooring and peach-colored walls hung with numerous paintings of tranquil horses in bucolic settings. A large crystal chandelier dangled dramatically down, while a circular staircase of the same rosy marble spiraled upward around it. Despite all the hard surfaces, the space was deathly quiet; the only noise was a subdued murmur of voices coming from a room giving onto the foyer and another quiet mumble that seemed to proceed from the second floor.

A uniformed officer stood guard at the foot of the stairway. Against the showy backdrop, he was a disturbing reminder that life wasn't always pretty or pleasing.

Rosco approached the cop. "Hey, Jerry. Lever's expecting me."

"Yeah, I got that."

"Is there somewhere Belle can wait for me?"

The officer pointed toward a door from which the sound of voices rose. "The family's in that living room there. The rest of the house is off-limits to everyone but the maid until the crime scene boys finish up."

"Thanks."

Belle and Rosco turned toward the room, and as they did Todd Collins emerged. His eyes were red and swollen with tears, his face was a waxy white, and his limp also seemed more prominent as though grief were bearing down on his bones.

"Rosco! Thank heavens you're here!" He slapped his bad leg. "I'm sorry I didn't call you, but our get-together slipped my mind completely." He paused and squared his shoulders. "I've been pulling my hair out all morning. These damn detectives! I can't get jack out of them. They won't even let me go back in there to be with Ryan. Do you hold any sway with these clowns?"

"I'm on my way up there now, Mr. Collins," Rosco said. He made no attempt to soften the edginess that had found its way into his voice. "Al Lever's a friend of mine. *Clown* isn't a word I'd use to describe him."

In his distressed state Collins missed the sharpness of Rosco's reply. In fact, his sorrow only served to heighten his inflexibility and resolve. "Good. Consider yourself hired. I want to know what's going on in that room up there. I want the creep who killed Ryan strung up by his fingernails. I don't care what it costs. Friend or no friend, cops don't move fast enough for me. I want answers, and I want them now."

"That's all well and good, Mr. Collins, and I'm more than happy to help uncover your answers, but I'm afraid I can't accept any money from you or be considered under your employment. It would be a conflict of interest."

"What the hell's that supposed to mean?"

"I've been hired by the Dartmouth Group to investigate the stable fire. I can't ethically accept employment from any of the principles in that case—"

"What?" Collins nearly shouted. "You think I burned down my own stable?"

Rosco held up his hands. "I'm not saying that, Mr. Collins."

"Well, you better damn well not be implying anything like it!" A sob wracked his chest and broke up the words.

"I understand how upset you are, sir. And I recognize the fact that you want answers—"

"And pronto!" Todd barked out. "That's my wife who's lying dead up there!"

"Yes, sir. I understand that," Rosco continued. "I can only repeat that this is a sticky situation. However, whether or not I can accept employment from you doesn't mean I won't do everything in my power to help apprehend the person who attacked your wife."

The statement seemed to calm Todd a bit. After a long moment of silence, he gave a decisive nod. "Okay, I see what you're getting at. I appreciate any help you can give me."

"Good . . . I was wondering if Belle might be able to wait in the living room with your family while I take a look around upstairs? I shouldn't be more than ten or fifteen minutes."

A weak smile found its way to his lips. "Oh, of course. I'm sorry. In all of this ugliness I didn't think; here I am standing next to my favorite crossword puzzle person." He offered his hand to Belle. "This was my whole reason in having you out to King Wenstarin Farms—to meet the infallible Annabella Graham."

"I don't know if I'd go that far," Belle said, and followed it with a sympathetic, "This is just horrible, sir. My deepest sympathies."

Todd led Belle into the living room, and Rosco crossed back over to the police officer.

"Pretty gruesome up there?" he asked.

"Oh, yeah, it's a good one."

CHAPTER

13

"Left at the top of the stairs," the uniformed officer told Rosco as he passed. "Then down the hallway. Just follow your nose."

Rosco climbed the long staircase, but when he reached the landing he realized the cop's directions had been immaterial. Outside the entry to one of the bedrooms, the hall was buzzing with activity. A police photographer was in the process of packing up her equipment, a member of Abe Jones's forensics team was lifting fingerprints from the door jamb, and another was moving on his hands and knees toward the far end of the hallway, stopping now and then to retrieve some object from the carpet and then seal it in a containment bag, which was duly labeled.

"Is this clear down here?" Rosco called to the man bent over the carpet.

He cocked his head back toward Rosco and said, "Yeah, we're all done with that end. Knock yourself out."

Rosco walked to the doorway and slid past the fingerprint expert. It was a large bedroom, furnished with what he assumed were valuable French antiques. The dresser, nightstands, armoire, and bed were ornate and gilded. Sky blue, apple leaf green, and powder pink seemed to be the color scheme, and the walls boasted paintings that matched: pastel-colored gardens, soft-faced and amorous couples, fountains, and flowers in full blossom. Rosco guessed they were pricey objects. Against this bowerlike decor, the businesslike humans with their dark and austere clothing were a stark contrast.

He spotted Lever, Jones, and the medical examiner, Herb Carlyle. All had removed their latex gloves, which indicated that forensics had finished with the room; and judging from the bulging ashtray, Lever was already on his eighth or ninth cigarette—meaning things weren't going as smoothly as he wished. But then, with Carlyle on hand, homicide scenes were never easy.

True to form, the ME had plunked himself unceremoniously on the deceased's bed and was scribbling notes on paper attached to a stainless-steel clipboard, while his equally spooky assistant, Estelle, hovered at his side holding a large black plastic zippered bag. Ryan Collins's body was stretched out sideways across the bed only a few inches to Carlyle's left. She was obviously still in the spot where she'd died.

Her corpse was lying face up. She was dressed in dark red satin men's pajamas, and from the neck down it almost appeared as though she were sleeping. From the neck up, however, the story was different. Her head rested in a large pool of blood that had begun to dry; the color now resembled that of her pajamas. Her skin was no longer pink or even a deathly blue; it had become a chalky gray white, and her features were flattened against her facial bones. From Rosco's vantage point he wasn't able to observe the extent of the wounds, but he noted they were centered above her ear on the left side of her head.

Lever and Jones had their backs to Rosco and hadn't yet seen him enter, but Carlyle looked up from his clipboard and uttered a carping, "Polycrates, wonderful, just what we need. The squeaky-clean hero in action." If his words had failed to indicate the disdain he felt for Rosco, his tone made up for them. The edgy relationship dated back to when Rosco had been NPD and had spared no criticism of the ME's sloppy methods. "This guy's like a bad penny," Carlyle continued in his jeering manner. "Is this some unfortunate coincidence, Al, or did you invite him here just to make my life miserable?"

"Alright," Lever grumbled, "I'm not here to play referee between you two children. If you're finished, Herb, let's bag her up and move on out of here." He turned to Rosco. His eyes looked tired. Homicide was Lever's beat, but unlike Carlyle, he didn't enjoy it. "The only reason I let you in here, Poly-crates, is because you've got a relationship with these people."

"Not much, Al."

"Anything's better than nothing."

Estelle placed the plastic body bag on the bed beside Ryan and slid the zipper open. Then she and Carlyle hefted the corpse into the bag and sealed it.

"What happened?" Rosco asked Lever.

But the medical examiner replied with an answer Rosco had heard from him one too many times: "Pretty cut and dried, really."

He waited for Carlyle to say more, and he wasn't disappointed. When it came to lugubrious details, the ME was in his glory. "Somebody slammed a hoof pick into her temple. And, yeah, we got the weapon. Once probably would have been enough to do the job, but our perp really went at it. Six or seven whacks from what I can tell. I'll get a clearer picture once I get her back to the morgue and do some digging around." Estelle smiled at this thought; clearly she was also anxious to get to work.

Rosco, along with Lever and Jones, watched as the pair placed the body on a gurney. As they left the room Lever said, "Let me know if anything unusual turns up, will you, Herb?"

"Sure, Al, but like I said, it's pretty cut and dried. Pun intended. In case you didn't catch it the first time."

When Carlyle was out of earshot Jones said, "For once in his life, he may be right. It didn't take a rocket scientist to determine cause of death on this one."

"Did he pinpoint a time?" Rosco asked.

"He's thinking she's been dead around six or so hours and places it somewhere between two and five A.M.," Al told him. "Before you start dumping on Newcastle's crack medical examiner, a.k.a., *brother to our illustrious mayor*, Abe agrees with that assessment."

"Hey, did I say anything?" Rosco studied the bed linens. "From the looks of these sheets, I'd say she'd gone to bed, then got up for some reason, was attacked, and fell back down, where she died."

"That's how we've put it together," Al said.

"Any sign of a struggle?"

"No," Abe said. "And I don't think she was attacked from behind either. If that had been the case, she would have fallen onto the mattress face-first."

"Someone could have hit her once, then rolled her over and finished the job," Rosco suggested.

"I considered that," Abe continued, "but I don't like it. It's too methodical. My assumption is that the perp was hoppin' mad and just laid into her. If the first blow had come from behind, the others would have, too. I say he, or she, nailed her once and then just went to town. Ryan Collins never knew what hit her."

If Rosco had heard this assessment from Carlyle, he wouldn't have believed a word of it, but since it came from Abe Jones, he was inclined to take it as gospel. He looked around the room once again. "This is a spare bedroom, right? What gives with that?"

"According to Mr. Collins he's been snoring a lot lately. So she packed up and moved over to this room shortly before midnight," Lever answered.

"And he didn't see or hear anything unusual, I take it?"

"Nope. No sign of forced entry. He told me he came in to wake her at seven and found her dead. That's when he called us."

"He was cool enough to recognize the scene for what it was," Abe added. "He didn't touch a thing and sealed off the upstairs until we arrived. As Carlyle said, we have the murder weapon right here." He indicated a clear plastic bag containing the bloody hoof pick. It sat beside his evidence case.

"Any prints?"

"I'll check that when we get downtown. The handle's plastic, so if they're there, they'll be clean."

"Was the door locked?"

"Collins says no," Lever offered. "Even if it had been locked, it's clear to me she must have known her attacker and opened the door. Nothing's been stolen, according to her husband. This has all the makings of a crime of passion. Strangers don't nail each other like this."

"Unless it's *intended* to look like a crime of passion," Rosco observed.

"My money's on choice number one, Poly-crates."

"What about the front door, Al?"

"Collins maintains all security issues are handled at the main gate, so it's seldom that *any* of the buildings on the farm are locked. And all employees are logged in and out by the guard." Lever coughed twice, lit a cigarette, and dropped the match into the ashtray. "Okay, Poly-crates, my turn to ask you; tell me what you know about Collins and the rest of the clan."

Rosco spent the next ten minutes bringing Al up to speed on everything he'd learned about Todd Collins and his children, even Bartholomew Kerr's gossip, and then finished with, "So as far as I'm concerned, any one of them could have done it—including the old man. When you think about it, he was the only one who admits to being in the house at the time."

"There's also Jack Curry, the barn manager; Orlando Polk and his wife, Kelly; the daughters; Heather's husband, Michael Palamountain; Chip and his girlfriend, Angel; they all live within the compound," Abe tossed in.

"Ah, ah, ah, not so fast, Good Doctor," was Rosco's wry response. "Polk's still in the hospital, remember?"

"Hallelujah," Al intoned through his cigarette smoke, "someone with an alibi. My favorite kind of person."

CHAPTER

14

N est of vipers was the term that popped into Belle's brain the moment Todd escorted her into the living room, the two having left Rosco to ascend to the second floor and whatever unpleasantness awaited there. The oddity of the linguistic association, as well as its seemingly self-contradictory words—*nest* and *viper*—made her pause in mid-stride.

Nest, she thought, *a tree home in which birds raise their young, a haven, a retreat . . . as well as clutch of poisonous snakes.* Belle studied the room; it seemed to corroborate the allusion: a peaceable place decorated in pale and tranquil shades and emitting a discernible aura of wealth—as opposed to the glittering and watchful eyes that now regarded her. If she hadn't recognized them as belonging to human faces, she would have imagined viperous tongues flicking out to test the air as she approached. The decibel level also raised; it was the quick bump in sound that occurs when people are caught discussing a secret or a forbidden topic.

"Belle, I'd like you to meet my daughter Fiona. . . . Fee, this is the famous crossword queen, Belle Graham."

The hand that shook Belle's was limp with disinterest, although the eyes narrowed into suspicious slits. *Ryan's gone,* they seemed to protest, *and now Pop's introducing another blondie into our midst. Great! We'll have no end of girlie brides.*

"My husband—" Belle began, sensing it was time to set the record straight, but Heather's booming voice interrupted her.

"He's the PI who's charged with determining whether the barn fire was accidental or a case of arson," she announced to the room as if she were in charge of disseminating all information. Belle decided Rosco's description of Heather fit the woman perfectly. The word *horsy* seemed coined for the Heather Collinses of this world.

Fiona, with her perfect hair and flawless makeup, turned away to begin murmuring to a man Belle could only assume was Jack Curry—at least he looked like the rough and ready trainer Rosco had encountered.

Todd covered his eldest daughter's rudeness by formally introducing Heather and her husband, Michael Palamountain, but any polite exchange was cut short by the roar of Chip's voice as it rose from the other side of the room. "Pop, this isn't some damn social visit . . . or another one of your cherished family reunions! None of us wants to be here, so let's just cut the cute palaver."

"Dear brother sounds as if he's just a wee bit hungover this morning, Daddy," Fiona observed in a voice that oozed both oil and venom.

"Can it, Fee! Like you're Miss Perfect, you who's screwing—"

"Excuse me? Are you talking home repair once again, Chipper?" was the fierce retort. "Because you know I don't have a clue when it comes to—"

"Home repair! That's a laugh. Home *wreck* is more like it." He forced a remembered laugh.

"Oh, how clever of you, Chipper. The bottle of whatever you're currently enjoying certainly elevates your wicked wit. I'm sure your little girlfriend heartily agrees, don't you, Angel, honey?"

But before a much chagrined Angel could reply or even move away from Chip's unsteady shadow, Heather ordered a brusque, "Leave her alone, Fee."

"What? And forsake our habitual, happy-family fun and games just because she's a fish out of water? Oooh, sorry about that. I didn't mean to imply you were as teeny-tiny as an angelfish."

"Leave her out of this," Heather repeated in a growl, and Fiona spun on her.

"Where do you get off, telling me what to do? You with your banker husband and your safe and predictable marriage. No wonder you spend all your time down in the stables—"

"Fiona. Heather." Todd's commanding voice broke in. "Girls. Stop. This isn't an easy time for any of us. Sniping only makes it worse. Now, I want you to apologize to one another. And to Chip and Angel, too."

But the "girls," instead of being mortified by this parental reprimand, simply glared at their father with a sullen rebellion usually reserved for teenagers. *And who's fault is it that we're gathered here while a homicide detective and his prying team take over the house?* their lowering glances seemed to demand. *You're the one who married Ryan in the first place. You're the one who gave us a "stepmom" younger than we are. You're the one who cast us aside.*

"Pop's right," Chip added, a beat too late; then he lurched into Angel and gave her a hearty and wobbly squeeze, which caused her to rock back on her heels and nearly fall.

Out of the corner of her eye, Belle saw Heather share a meaningful look with Fiona; then their heads swiveled in unison toward Angel, both women steadily observing the shoes that had caused their brother's latest squeeze to lose her balance. They were sling-back, fire-engine-red stilettos: footwear woefully inadequate for tromping around a horse farm. The sisters' eyebrows raised in smug disapproval, while Angel—and then a still-swaying Chip—registered their sneers.

"How long do we have to sit around here, anyway?" he groused.

"It's my understanding," was Michael Palamountain's didactic response, "that we're expected to remain in situ until Detective Lever has had the opportunity to speak with all of us."

Chip replied with an elongated groan. "In situ," he muttered, dragging out the letters. "What an insight. May I cite your excellent use of Latin, Michael? And why stop there, old boy? Why not add *intra muros*, between these walls. On *inter nos*, between ourselves. Which we all know is how Daddy likes to keep things."

But before anyone could reply to this barb, another voice broke in. "Anything you need, Mr. C?"

The speaker who'd just entered the room through a nearly

invisible service door had a soft southern drawl and a simi-larly gentle air. "Coffee or juice . . . or some sweet rolls, maybe? Or I could make up a batch of those biscuits you're so fond of."

"Ah, Kelly, I didn't know you were still here," Todd said. "I thought you were going to the hospital to be with your husband." Genuine concern echoed through the tone.

"I couldn't leave you all like this, Mr. C. Not with what's happened. I'll get up there later. Don't you worry. Anyway, Orlando'll understand. I know he will." Kelly gave him an uneasy smile. "Besides, I'm not altogether sure he even rec-ognizes me."

"But he is improving, right?" Fiona asked, although her voice lacked both warmth and compassion.

"He's doing better, thanks. That's what they're all tellin' me, anyway . . . C'mon now, who wants me to fetch some-thing from the kitchen? It's the least I can do, and I sure don't enjoy rattling around out there on my lonesome while the police prowl hither and yon poking their noses into everything. C'mon gang. Speak up. Your wish is my com-mand, as they say. How about it? You Fiona? Or Michael? Heather? Jack? Mr. C.—?"

"I could use a refill on this O.J." Chip held out an empty glass.

"Without the vodka this time," was Fiona's acid addition to the request.

"That's what a *screw*driver is, sister dearest—or maybe you need Mr-Fix-It there to tell you," her brother hissed while Todd's voice thundered out:

"I won't have it, I tell you! All this backbiting and snip-ing . . . My wife is lying up there dead at this very moment.

Attacked. Stabbed! Murdered in this very house! And not one of you has the courtesy to remember that fact, or to consider what my feelings might be." Then his angry speech suddenly faltered, and his shoulders slumped; and Belle watched the commanding and patriarchal figure diminish into that of an old and griefstricken man. *Not vipers,* she thought, *they're too cold-blooded for this lot. Maybe tigers is a more apt analogy. And one of them is a killer.*

CHAPTER

15

"'He who rides a tiger,' as the Chinese proverb so aptly warns us, 'is afraid to dismount.'" The statement was delivered by Bartholomew Kerr as he stood on Belle and Rosco's front steps. "Of course, Sir Winston Churchill applied the same adage to the world's dictators in his sterling work *While England Slept*, and then concluded with a customarily pithy: 'And the tigers are getting hungry.'"

Bartholomew paused in his monologue only long enough to add a peeved, "I simply cannot believe I'm being asked—strike that: *ordered*—to write an obituary on Madame Ryan Collins! An obit, for Heaven's sake, Dear *Bella*! As if I were no more than a snotty-nosed copyboy or a drooling features editor being put out to pasture." He groaned in abundant self-pity. "Aren't you even going to ask me in for a spot of morning sustenance? Sorry, I didn't call in advance, and all that, but the dictator we call our beloved editor in chief is riding my striped and tortured back. Why else would I be up and about at the unholy hour of eight-thirty in the morning?"

Ordinarily, Belle would have happily invited Bartholomew in for a cup of his favorite jasmine tea, but she had a sense that this visit was less social than he was pretending. She'd seen Bartholomew Kerr in story-hunting mode many times before, and this was definitely one of those moments.

"Your darling hubby's not around perchance, is he?"

Belle shook her head as she opened the door—which set off a ferocious amount of yapping from the two dogs, who raced around the corner and threw themselves at their diminutive friend.

"And how are the dear duchesses?" Bartholomew asked them, bending down to pat each in turn. "My Winston sends his fondest regards. At least, I assume he does. Bulldogs are reticent creatures. But then, of course, they're English. Need I say more?" Then in typical Bartholomew fashion, the little man skipped back to his previous subject.

"I'll wager Rosco might be out at King Wenstarin Farms. A return jaunt to supplement yesterday's sojourn?"

"How did you know we were there yesterday?" In a flash, Belle recognized her mistake. If Bartholomew's question were no more than a fishing expedition, she'd obviously taken the bait.

He laughed in reply. "Don't worry, *Bella-bella.* I already knew you were on-site with Big Al et alia. A wee birdie named Estelle blabbed. It seems her confrere is not one of your husband's staunchest admirers. Though dear Estelle seems a bit infatuated with your hubby's body; purely from a medical standpoint, I would hope. So, tea and sympathy for a poor wight consigned to write an obituary of a vapid vamp . . . ? What do you say?"

While Belle prepared Bartholomew's jasmine tea, he rambled on about Ryan Collins: how her marriage to Todd had "wrought enormous changes in the manse," how "she sacked all the live-in help and hired day laborers—for a little *privacy*, or so she stated," and how she'd "insisted that the *brutish* Jack Curry be reinstated in the Wenstarin Stable."

"The conclusion to such activities is quite obvious, I'm afraid, Belle," he observed as he delicately sipped the fragrant brew his hostess had set before him. "Our tragically demised Ryan was having an affair with Jack before she met Daddy Big-Bucks. When she set herself up as mistress of the Collins domain, she forced her besotted bridegroom to reinstall Curry in his former role—while ridding herself of any pesky staff who'd spot any questionable nocturnal comings and goings . . . snoring, indeed!" Bartholomew snorted. "Most likely the guest bedroom was the lovely Mrs. Collins's normal habitation of an eve; and Todd is too proud or too pigheadedly vain to admit his wife had decided to take her charms elsewhere."

As she listened, Belle began to wonder if there were *any* secrets left in Newcastle; and Bartholomew's next question confirmed her suspicions.

"How's Sara faring with Dr. Arthur? Favorably, I hope. I've been told he's a gentle man as well as a gentleman—unlike others of his staff."

This time Belle was better prepared. "I've only met Dr. Arthur; he seems thoroughly professional."

Bartholomew pointed his sharp nose at her, as if he were sniffing for a fib. "Dame Sara will have to undergo physical

therapy, won't she, *Bellisima*? What a bore! All those yaw-
ping types urging one on to greater heights of fitness and
prowess. Of course, Dame Briephs is a New England original. She *enjoys* being hale and hearty—which is precisely
why she found her son's friendship with the Collins gang so
distasteful. Not that they're a sickly crowd, lord knows—
unless you count murder as detrimental to one's health. But
then, robust specimens are not always the most stellar ex-
amples of clean living, are they?"

"More tea?" Belle asked.

Again, Bartholomew gave her curious stare. "Methinks
the lady doth conceal something."

"No, I'm not, Bartholomew. I promise. Rosco and I happened to be invited out to the farm yesterday, that's all. It
was pure coincidence that we arrived to find Ryan Collins
had been killed."

"No signature crossword puzzles tucked under the re-
cumbent body, I take it?"

Belle laughed. "Not a one."

"Tell me about Heather's husband, Michael Palamountain," Bartholomew said.

"You're putting the entire family into the obituary?"

"It's background, *Bella mia.* I like to gather a full spec-
trum of details before I put pen to paper—or fingertips to
keyboard, as the case may be."

"I was in the room for half an hour *tops*, Bartholomew. I
can't possibly tell you what he's like."

"Hmmmm . . ." was the thoughtful reply. "How's this
for a possible scenario? Palamountain is the farm's banker,
which means he handles stud fees, et cetera. High finance,
which as we're all painfully aware, can lure the greedy into

the naughty land of embezzlement—or *mountains* of cash, in this case . . . Thus, the aforementioned Ryan learns that her middle-aged stepson-in-law has his proverbial fingers in the till, threatens to *finger* him herself—which leads to her untimely demise. It was a hoof pick, wasn't it, rather than an ice pick? Or, dare I say, an accountant's red pen? Oh, and wait, you being a word couturier, as it were, would appreciate the allusion: Palamountain employs a device normally used on a Palomino."

Belle crossed her arms and laughed again. "You're too much, Bartholomew! Have you ever considered joining Al's homicide unit at NPD?"

"I don't like doughnuts," was his starchy response. Then he added a pensive, "Of course, if Ryan Collins had the goods on our boy, Michael, why didn't she simply tattle to Toddie?"

"I don't think there's any evidence to suggest Heather's husband was pilfering funds from King Wenstarin Farms, Bartholomew."

"Oh, goodness, *Bella*, I'm a gossip columnist; I don't require evidence!"

CHAPTER

16

After Al Lever had given him the green light to leave King Wenstarin Farms the previous afternoon, Rosco had driven Belle home so that she could keep her appointment with Sara, and then continued to his office. Once there he'd phoned the Avon-Care rehabilitation clinic, claiming to be Dr. Saul Bownes checking on a patient—one Dawn Davis. The clinic had been good enough to inform him that Ms. Davis had not missed any of her appointments thus far, which had been scheduled for Tuesdays, Thursdays, and Saturdays at 10 A.M. So on this Tuesday morning at ten minutes before ten Rosco found himself sitting in his Jeep in the Avon-Care parking lot on Nathaniel Hawthorne Boulevard waiting for the arrival of a twenty-six-year-old woman, five-foot-five with auburn hair, which Walter Gudgeon described as falling midway down her back—a woman both he and the surgeon had seemed to believe was innocence personified.

From Rosco's point of view, however, that word was slated for serious revision.

A woman matching Dawn Davis's physical description pulled into the lot a few minutes later, and Rosco immediately stepped from his Jeep and approached her.

"Excuse me. Are you Ms. Davis?"

She kept her eyes on him as she locked her car with a push of the remote button. The headlights flashed, and the horn sounded two short beeps. The remote remained clutched in her hand with a finger poised on the panic button. "Who are you? What do you want?" The tone was challenging, while the "green gold eyes" that Gudgeon had mentioned were anything but "soft"—or even polite. Rosco would have said they looked angry.

He offered her a business card. "My name is Rosco Polycrates. I'm a private investigator."

Dawn glanced at the card but didn't take it. "Anybody can make those up on a computer." She tossed her head in curt dismissal and began to walk away, although she was careful not to completely turn her back on Rosco.

He pulled his Massachusetts-issued I.D. from his jacket and opened it for her. "I'm licensed by the Commonwealth, Ms. Davis. I have a few questions for you. I can always return with a police officer, but I suspect that wouldn't be in your best interests."

Dawn stopped and faced him fully. "What's this all about? I haven't done anything wrong."

"Really? You're in remarkably good shape for someone who was operated on just four weeks ago."

"The sling came off after two weeks, just like I was promised," was her belligerent response. "I don't know who you are, or what you want." Again, she began to move away, but she continued to keep her eyes on him.

Rosco kept pace with her. "I'm talking about your supposed kidney transplant."

Dawn spun around. "My what?"

"I've been hired by Walter Gudgeon, Ms. Davis." Rosco studied her face as he spoke, but failed to notice even a flickering of her eyelids when he mentioned the name. He also didn't spot any evidence of the supposedly sweet and gentle person either Gudgeon or Bownes had suggested Dawn Davis was.

"I don't know anybody of that name," she said with a hostile shrug.

"Mr. Gudgeon maintains he gave you $250,000 so that you could have a kidney transplant. He claims he dropped you off at Newcastle Memorial Hospital on September sixth for that purpose—the very day you had your shoulder operation."

Dawn stood frozen for fifteen seconds while she glared at Rosco.

"You are Dawn Davis, aren't you? And you did have rotator-cuff surgery performed by Saul Bownes?"

She didn't reply, but her face puckered in wrath. Then she pointed at irate finger. "I know what you're up to, mister, but if you bother me anymore, *I'll* be the one going to the police. And if my hospital records were released without my approval, well that's just plain not legal."

With that she turned and stomped away into the Avon-Care Center.

CHAPTER

17

"She's one tough cookie, Sara. That's all I can say," Rosco offered with a shake of the head. "The charming 'girl' who conned Walter Gudgeon was nowhere in evidence this morning. And if she's a con artist, which I'm convinced she is, she's a genuine pro, because I couldn't trip her up in the slightest."

Sara Crane Briephs might have been confined to a wheelchair, and that contraption might now be resting on a magnificent Persian palace carpet in the midst of other singular antiques collected by generations of Crane family members, but in all other ways the doyenne of White Caps—as well as her domain—remained unchanged: an elegant and venerable residence awash in damasks and chintzes and mahogany furniture so polished it all but sparkled.

"Could you have been a trifle harsh in your approach, Rosco dear? Tipped your hand too soon, as they say?" the doughty lady suggested as she watched his wife pour afternoon tea; while Belle, for her part, forced her hands not to tremble. The proscribed ritual of simultaneously holding aloft both a silver pot and a gold-rimmed porcelain cup set in its saucer was one that Sara had only recently relinquished—and only then to the young woman she considered her surrogate granddaughter. However, Belle was keenly aware of her "apprenticeship" stature. *There's many a slip twixt the cup and the lip,* she quoted the ancient epigram in silence, adding a rueful, *and between the cup and the pot—as well as the activities Sara was hardwired to perform, and the meager hostess-type skills I was taught.*

"I'm not saying you were harsh, mind you, Rosco," Sara continued, gazing philosophically at Belle's unsure labors. "But perhaps, there might have been another means of eliciting information from Ms. Davis—before getting her dander up, that is."

Rosco sat back on the Hepplewhite settee. Unlike his wife, he felt genuine ease in Sara's beloved White Caps, but then he wasn't a gentlewoman-in-training.

"I honestly don't know what to make of the situation," he said. "I guess what I expected was a bunch of phony, sugarcoated responses . . . lies that would have given her away. Avon-Care assured me that Dawn arrived like clockwork for each appointment and was a conscientious and undemanding patient—personality traits that totally jibe with what Saul Bownes suggested."

"I'm certainly glad he's not my physician," Sara piped in. "He sounds like a dreadful person. Sinister, really. Don't you agree, Belle?"

Belle nodded, but kept her focus on the cup she was now transferring to her right hand, while she picked up a plate of lemon slices with her left, proffered both to her hostess, before returning her concentration to pouring herself the third and final cup of tea. *Whew!* her brain rejoiced. *Thank heaven that's over! And I'll just brain Rosco if he asks for a refill.*

While Belle completed her nerve-racking task, Rosco casually grabbed a fluted silver dish filled with homemade macaroons, passed them to Sara, then snagged two for himself. The freedom with which he began chomping away earned another grimace from his wife.

"I know Gudgeon only asked me to locate Dawn," he said between heedless and happy mouthfuls, "but I'd really like to get some hard evidence that would prove she's a crook; something that would convince Walter to go to the police and press charges. If he doesn't, she's free to pull the same stunt elsewhere. And that's why I'd like to have your help with this, Sara."

"My help? But I'm just an old lady confined to quarters for the foreseeable future—"

"Not from here . . . but when you become a patient at the Avon-Care facility," Rosco answered.

Sara cocked her head to one side. Her blue eyes regarded him with birdlike intensity. "You want me to pilfer Dawn Davis's files!"

Rosco chortled. "Not quite. What I want you to do is strike up a conversation with Ms. Davis—"

"And then get the goods on her!" Sara handed Belle her cup, adding a peremptory, "More tea please, dear. And you needn't fill it quite to the top this time."

Belle glowered at Rosco who remained blissfully unaware of his wife's discomfort.

"It's clear that I can't talk to Ms. Davis again, Sara. If she even spots my Jeep at a distance, she's liable to scream for the cops, which, as I said, Mr. Gudgeon wants to avoid. Clearly she knows this." Rosco reached for another macaroon. "And while we're on the subject, you do realize that everything I've told you must be kept in the strictest confidence? In fact, we wouldn't be having this conversation if I didn't need your aid. And I'm still not altogether comfortable sharing a client's name."

Sara nodded, but the expression held a hint of impatience. "You know I'm the soul of discretion, young man." Then she thought for a moment. "Something about this case of yours rings a bell . . . what is it . . . ? What is it? Oh, I remember now. There was a similar situation down in Florida several winters ago: a young woman preying on elderly widowers. I'm not sure the crime was ever resolved." Sara took her refilled teacup. "Just right his time, dear," she said to Belle before returning to Rosco.

"So, you're proposing I cozy up to Ms. Davis, who doesn't know me from Adam. But if she believes her *cover's been blown*—that is the correct term, isn't it?—then who's to say she'll even return to complete her scheduled therapy sessions? I wouldn't. I can tell you that. I'd be on the next plane to Belize—" Sara interrupted herself as she abruptly set aside her cup. "Oh, my goodness! Emma forgot the deviled eggs she made you, Belle dear. They're not on the tray, and I didn't notice the oversight until this very second. That's what age does to one. People forget the simplest of things . . . Hand me the silver bell, will you? Our Emma will be so bitterly disappointed if she can't present you with your favorite treat."

Emma was Sara's maid and alter ego. The two women had been together for half a century, and had weathered so many communal storms that the labels of mistress and servant had become irrelevant, although Emma continued to cling to her traditional taffeta uniforms: pink or gray during the day, black at night—with the requisite starched white apron, of course.

"I can go out to the kitchen, Sara," Belle offered. "There's no need to bother Emma."

"It will do her good, my dear. She gets far too little exercise, and I certainly wouldn't wish my current sedentary state to befall her. Imagine her tooling around in the kitchen in this unwieldy device—"

"You could do the cooking, in that case," Belle tossed in.

"What! And deprive her of the opportunity of lording it over me from her home on the range? What a terrible notion. Emma's the queen of the cuisine. I wouldn't dream of tampering with that title." With that Sara rang the bell, then returned her gaze to Rosco. "The problems I foresee with your suggestion are these: One, I'm not scheduled to begin physical therapy until the swelling in my knee subsides—by which time your Dawn Davis may well have skedaddled. And two, I can't be accompanied by Belle—as I was to Dr. Arthur's office—because she's so instantly recognizable. Anyone with half a brain, and it sounds as though your Ms. Davis has more than that, will make the connection. She may not have realized that you were the private eye to whom the illustrious cruciverbalist, Belle Graham, is wed, but I'll warrant she'd put two and two together if she saw me with your lovely bride. Now, as for the first quandary: I believe I can successfully make a preliminary foray to Avon-Care—under the pretext of examining the place before making a decision about which physical-rehabilitation facility will garner my business. As for the second—"

At that moment, Emma entered. In her hands she bore the promised deviled eggs. "I spotted these on the counter not two seconds ago, madam—before you rang for me."

"Did you now, Emma?" was Sara's wry reply.

"I did." Emma's posture was as commanding as Sara's, notwithstanding the wheelchair and their present difference in height; and there might have been more conversation as to when the bell had rung and when the treasured eggs had been discovered were it not for the fact that Sara suddenly burst out, "Guess what, Emma? You and I are going to become subcontractors of the Polycrates Agency! Think of that! Just like our Belle, here. Rosco has asked us to infiltrate a health-care facility this coming Thursday. But my news is completely hush-hush, of course; *strictest confidence* and all that." She eyed Emma from head to foot. "You may dress as my maid, if you'd like, unless you feel the choice would cause undue suspicion—which is a possibility. Perhaps we should invent a more devious disguise for you."

Rosco shook his head and shot Belle an amused glance. *A pair of "subcontractors" whose combined age is one hundred sixty,* the look said. *Who else will Sara decide to "hire" on my behalf?*

"I believe the choice of a uniform is an excellent one, madam. Which one do you wish me to wear?"

"Oh, I think the gray, don't you, Emma? The time for our rendezvous is ten in the morning, but the pink might appear overly informal. We want to be taken seriously, don't we?"

"And a full or half apron?"

Sara thought. "Half. There won't be any cooking involved. Unless it's someone's goose."

Belle couldn't stop chuckling the entire way home. "Well, how else did you imagine this playing out, Rosco? You know you can't get Sara involved in any scheme without her pulling out all the stops. Just be grateful those two don't want to dress up as Batman and Robin. Besides, you can't have forgotten the situation in Hollywood when she actually believed she'd become a world-class thespian, or the time we took her to that inn in Vermont. Or our wedding, for pete's sake, which she *insisted* be performed on the senator's yacht."

Rosco shook his head. "I don't know . . . The idea of Emma in her uniform, and Sara togged out in a Queen-Elizabeth-type hat . . . I'm not certain they're going to inspire a woman like Dawn Davis to share her deepest and darkest secrets. On the other hand, who could suspect that dynamic duo of trying anything underhanded?"

"They could always shame her into gabbing," Belle shot back. "Ask where her white gloves and lace hanky are, for instance. Besides, you deserve everything you got, sitting there wolfing down cookies while I was trying to keep the tea from sloshing all over the floor."

"You're the neophyte lady of the mansion, not me," was Rosco's serene response. "Anyway, in case you'd forgotten, you're also the one who invented the term *subcontractor to the Polycrates Agency.*"

"And now you have two more," Belle laughed.

"Hooo boy."

"And you'd better hope the three of us never gang up on you and mutiny."

"Or demand union benefits. I'm losing sleep over that scenario already."

CHAPTER

18

The moment the car once again reached the seclusion of the Munnatawket Beach parking lot, the driver glanced down at the blank sheet of quarter-inch graph paper lying on the passenger's lap. "I still don't know why—"

A hand was raised, commanding silence. "How about we play the James Boys tonight, what do you say?"

"Can't you take this seriously? I'm not into games tonight."

"Who do you want to be? Frank or Jesse?"

"I really don't want—"

"Make up your mind," was the brusque reply. "Jesse . . . or Frank. C'mon, this thing only works if you act on instinct; you know that. Besides, when you look at the string of murders those two logged in, I'd say we couldn't get more serious."

"Hooo boy."

"And you'd better hope the three of us never gang up on you and mutiny."

"Or demand union benefits. I'm losing sleep over that scenario already."

CHAPTER

18

The moment the car once again reached the seclusion of the Munnatawket Beach parking lot, the driver glanced down at the blank sheet of quarter-inch graph paper lying on the passenger's lap. "I still don't know why—"

A hand was raised, commanding silence. "How about we play the James Boys tonight, what do you say?"

"Can't you take this seriously? I'm not into games tonight."

"Who do you want to be? Frank or Jesse?"

"I really don't want—"

"Make up your mind," was the brusque reply. "Jesse . . . or Frank. C'mon, this thing only works if you act on instinct; you know that. Besides, when you look at the string of murders those two logged in, I'd say we couldn't get more serious."

"But I—"

"Don't tell me you'd prefer Groucho and Harpo? Or maybe Abbott and Costello?" This was said with a laugh, but the sound was cruel and goading.

The response was a beleaguered sigh. "I liked playing the woman's part last time." Another pause, followed by, "Okay, I'll be Jesse."

"Spell it with an *ie* if it'll help you work through that feminine thing." The suggestion was accompanied by another jeering chuckle.

"Just skip it, okay? But I've gotta tell you, this is getting way, way too harebrained for me."

"Tortoise and the hare . . . You wanna play bunny rabbit instead? And I'll be a big, old snapping turtle—"

"Stop it! I said I'd do Jesse, didn't I? So quit it! I just don't understand why we're going through the trouble of making another stupid puzzle when the first one got no reaction whatsoever."

"Frank's" head shook in frustration. "That's exactly *why* we need to create another one, Jes; clearly, the first attempt failed, or the transmission didn't go through. Who knows? All I can tell you is that no one's approached the guilty party. At least, not that I've heard."

"Parties," "Jesse" corrected acidly. "There's more than one, *brother* dear."

"Right, fine, *parties.* Have it your own way. Anyway, we also made a serious construction mistake with the last one. I checked out the newspaper crosswords. These things need to be symmetrical."

"Well, that sure makes it *easier,*" was the muttered reply. However, Jesse's hands were now trembling so violently that the caustic tone of voice sounded no more threatening than a puff of evening air.

"What's wrong with you all of a sudden? You're not losing your nerve, are you? Look, we agreed on this thing . . . We've got to get information to them; and we need to stay anonymous. And the only way to do that is—"

"Someone was murdered!" Jesse nearly screamed. "In case you've been so busy you haven't noticed."

Even though they'd returned to the deserted parking lot and the darkened beach, Frank swiveled around in the car seat to see if any other cars had approached.

"Will you settle down?" The voice was a snarl. "You're going to blow this, you know that? You're going to blow it for both of us. I'm willing to go out on the limb here, but you have to do your part."

The response was another near-shout. "Why don't you call that damn Polycrates and disguise your voice? You're good at pulling accents. I've seen you do it at parties."

"There's a brilliant idea. Why don't you call him yourself?" When there was no answer, Frank added a cold, "Point made, I take it . . . Which brings me back to our PI's snooping wife. Now, maybe our other attempt failed . . . maybe the fax was screwy, who knows? But we made a mistake. The thing didn't look genuine enough, maybe; and these things get signed, too. Like books. They've got authors' names—"

"Are you nuts? We sign our names?"

"Not our real ones! What do you take me for? And no Bonnie and Clyde, or Frank and Jesse . . . or stupid Ant and Grasshopper, either. Why clue her in to the fact that there are two of us? But we do need a moniker that piques her interest. We want her to do the damn crossword, don't we? Isn't that what we're doing sitting out here all by our lonesome? So, give me a name, any name."

Jesse stifled another groan. "Alfred Hitchcock. You want to play guessing games, be my guest."

"I'm doing this for both of us, remember?" A mini flashlight was flicked on. "And we title our little oeuvre 'To Catch a Thief.'"

" 'Thief' isn't altogether accurate, in case you'd forgotten."

"Just stuff it, will you? Besides, that's your opinion. The point is to get their attention. Accuracy comes later. Okay, let's start to do some work here." A fifteen-square area was marked out on a sheet of graph paper. "All right; give me some movie titles."

"There's that Mel Brooks one. That should attract attention." Jesse's answer was sarcastic and flat, and Frank responded in kind with a short, mean laugh.

"There you go! Now you're getting the hang of it."

"This is the last time I do this, brother dear," was the icy reply.

"Never say never, Jes."

"I'm serious, Frankie. I can't do this any longer. I can't."

Across

1. Brown or Thorpe
4. Govt. consumer agcy.
7. Grocery chain
10. Cut grass
13. Boxing great
14. "Give me some ___!"
15. Atomic energy watchdog; abbr.
16. Baseball stat.
17. With 19-Across, film by 10-Down
19. See 17-Across
21. Summer in France
22. Dry, in Roma
23. Beals hit film
27. Pen tips
31. Mr. Disney
32. Drunkard
33. M.A.S.H. role
34. Surface fish
35. Construction sign
37. Idaho range
38. Classic Romero film
41. Dollars and cents
42. Shakespearian bad guy
43. Collar
45. Ensemble
46. Prescription notation; abbr.
47. Mr. Autry
48. Six-sided state
49. Classic McQueen film
52. Moral element
54. ___ guzzler
55. With 58-Across, classic O'Toole film
58. See 55-Across
62. Some savings; abbr.
63. Diplomat; abbr.
64. Cry of surprise
65. New, prefix
66. Neither's partner
67. Female ruff
68. Pig pen
69. Mr. Beatty

Down

1. Option for 13-Across
2. Not well
3. Ms. Farrow
4. Trust
5. Ate
6. Patagonia's home; abbr.
7. Bee or ant
8. Meal prayer
9. Current option
10. Director, Brooks
11. Mine find
12. Had been
18. Pep
20. Offer up
22. Willy's winter weather wear
23. Send on; abbr.
24. Illustrated
25. Its capital is Tiranë
26. From here on
28. Reaffirm one's vows?
29. Cowboy's cloth
30. Grads
33. Make over
35. Dagger
36. ___ Angeles
37. two-year-old sheep
39. Bound with osiers
40. "If we don't ___ together . . ."
41. Bozeman campus; abbr.
44. Turkish title
46. Ms. Cates
47. Deep cut
49. Cooking herb
50. Shore bird
51. Still wet
53. Ski lift

TO CATCH A THIEF

55. Sloe ___ fizz
56. Spanish gold
57. Crewman
58. Mine in France

59. Rest stop
60. Que preceder
61. Turf

CHAPTER

19

The persistent beep of her home fax machine startled Belle out of a reverie that was far from pleasant. Ryan Collins's brutal murder was weighing heavily on her. Added to the slaying was her memory of Todd Collins and his offspring, their backbiting and jockeying for position, their casual cruelty when dealing with one another. And then there was the media circus currently surrounding the dead woman. Stabbed in a guest bedroom at King Wenstarin Farms, she'd been reduced to the unkindest of boldface slurs. It was enough to make anyone weary of reading a newspaper or watching the local evening news.

Belle released a sigh that was more like a heartfelt groan, pushed back from her desk, where she'd been staring blankly at a piece of graph paper, then rose and walked to the fax. *What now?* she groused. *Some frothy crossword submission naming state flowers or trees, or the world's longest rivers, or tallest mountains? Why don't these people leave me alone? Who cares about word games anyway? We've all got more on our plates than wondering how many types of Halloween candy we can find that contain six letters and end with a* T . . . *It's high time I looked for another job and got as far away from homonyms, synonyms, antonyms—to say nothing of caconyms, eponyms, and poecilonyms!*

With a determined sullenness, she wrenched the new puzzle from the machine. "To Catch a Thief," she read in silence, *constructed by Alfred Hitchcock. Oh, great. Just great. Now I'm getting a word game from a person pretending to be a dead man. And it's sent to me at home, on top of it. Why can't people learn this is strictly off-limits!* If Belle had been Kit or Gabby, she would have growled aloud.

Instead, she dutifully made a copy of the submission, slumped back to the desk, heaved herself into her chair, and took up her lucky red pen. "Okay, Alfred," she muttered under her breath, "let's see what kind of thief you're hunting . . ." Then 17- and 19-Across caught her eye. BLAZING SADDLES, she wrote in firm block letters, sitting suddenly straighter. "Oh, my gosh . . . and the solution to 38-Across is DAWN OF THE DEAD . . ."

Belle's pen was flying by now. It didn't matter that the puzzle constructor hadn't bothered with a clever step-quote or a guiding theme. She was convinced she'd received an obvious message—and that the bogus "Alfred Hitchcock" had private information concerning King Wenstarin Farms.

GOODBYE MR CHIPS, Belle penned at 55- and 58-Across. "Oh, wow!" Then she flew out of her chair. "What did I do with that last submission?" she grumbled. "The one that was faxed on Sunday morning and that made me so cranky . . . c'mon, Gab and Kit . . . you guys are always playing with the sheets of paper I ball up and toss out. Help me find the darn thing."

W hile Belle—with the aid of the two dogs—rifled through her home office, Sara's glowing black Cadillac tootled along Nathaniel Hawthorne Boulevard toward the Avon-Care facility and her "coincidental" meeting with Dawn Davis. At the wheel was Emma; Sara sat regally on the wide rear seat, her wheelchair stowed in the trunk—or as she sometimes referred to it, "the boot." Sara was as fond of her Briticisms as she was this "automobile"—a 1956 model that she steadfastly refused to believe was over a half-century old.

"You'll come in with me, of course, Emma," she now stated in her genteel yet commanding tone, "and then what, I wonder? Should you return to the parking lot and wait for me? Or should you remain at my side? What looks more convincing for our charade, do you imagine?"

"I think both choices are equally appropriate, madam," was Emma's thoughtful response. "Someone in your weakened condition either requires aid from a caregiver or, alternatively, feels a need for greater autonomy."

Sara nodded at Emma's perception, approval that the maid/chauffeur noted while glancing in the rearview mirror.

"On the other hand, madam, I feel I could be of help in watching Ms. Davis's reactions to your queries. Naturally, I won't be speaking to her myself, and so may be able to note behavior that might elude you."

Sara nodded again. "Then that's just how we'll carry out our mission. Two sets of eyes are always better than one."

* * *

The entrance into Avon-Care of the two newest subcon-tractors to the Polycrates Agency was as theatrical as anything else Sara did. Emma, in a staid navy coat above her rustling gray dress and starched apron, pushed the wheel-chair, while Sara surveyed the scene with imperial compla-cency. The old lady might as well have been a pasha perched upon an elephant, gracing the masses with a smile that in-dicated polite acknowledgment of her station. Those await-ing appointments couldn't help but grin in return.

By prior arrangement, Emma pushed her mistress to-ward the reception desk, where Sara duly requested to speak with "someone in a managerial position" so that she could better "ascertain" her "treatment protocols." *Protocol* was a new term for Sara when referring to medical matters. She'd been accustomed to the word being used in relation to diplo-macy or other governmental convention and etiquette, but she liked its formal tone—especially when dealing with something as lowly as a battered joint. Then, knowing the "manager" would take a few minutes to summons, Sara had Emma steer her toward a chair near a young, auburn-haired beauty who was studying what looked like a legal textbook. *Our Ms. Davis is probably trying to figure out how far she can stretch the law,* Sara surmised while fixing her target with an energetic glance.

"You're far too young to have a bum knee!" Sara an-nounced, wincing from a pain she didn't feel. Emma imme-diately began hovering solicitously, but Sara waved her away. "I'm fine, Emma. You toddle off and read a magazine or something while I wait. You've been far too concerned about me these past few days, and you know I'm perfectly capable of caring for myself."

Dawn Davis looked up. Instead of appearing disturbed by the interruption, she also smiled. *She's probably sizing me up as another mark,* Sara decided. *A vulnerable, old bat with a servant in her dotage. I must look as if I'd be as easy pickings as poor Walter Gudgeon.*

"Oh, I'm not here on account of my knee, ma'am," Dawn answered. "It's my shoulder. I tore my rotator cuff."

Ma'am! Sara heard. *Oh, the little minx! She's a good one, all right. Knows just how to be polite to us ancient crones. I wonder if Emma caught* that? Sara cast a surreptitious glance toward the figure in gray taffeta before continuing with an empathetic: "Oh, your shoulder! That must be exceedingly painful. How on earth did you do such a terrible thing? I fell at the hairdresser's—which was very foolish. If I'd been wearing trousers, I probably would have torn a cuff, too." Sara ventured a ladylike giggle, and Dawn also tittered politely. Then her face abruptly clouded.

"I had an accident."

"Well, I should certainly hope you didn't tear your shoulder on purpose!"

Dawn Davis studied Sara, while the older woman gazed back in seeming innocence and friendship.

"What sort of an accident, my dear? No . . . don't tell me. I was impertinent to ask, but aren't we fortunate, given all the ills that could have befallen us, that we have two injuries that are so eminently treatable? You and I could be facing problems with our kidneys, for instance, or our hearts, or—"

Dawn's face grew darker. "Kidneys?"

Sara beamed grandmotherly reassurance all the while thinking: *Bingo! That got her attention!* "Yes, indeed. Or diabetes, or high cholesterol—"

"What do you mean, 'kidneys'?"

"It was just a nasty situation that popped into my mind," Sara continued to lie. "I had a dear friend who had to undergo a kidney transplant. That was an ordeal and a half, I can tell you. I wouldn't wish it on anyone. And it cost the very moon, as you can imagine. So, tell me, my dear—if you don't think I'm being too nosy—what do physicians do with torn rotator cuffs?"

"I had surgery. Arthroscopic. I'm not sure how it works or what he did, but it sure feels a heck of a lot better than it did four weeks ago."

"Ah," Sara said as though she'd never heard of such a procedure. "And what kind of surgeon performs such an operation?"

"An orthopedist."

"I went to one for my wretched knee! Fancy that! Mine is Dr. Arthur. Is that who treated you, by any chance?"

An emotion that looked like regret crossed Dawn Davis's face. It wasn't an expression Sara expected. "Your surgeon's the best—at least that's what I was told. He didn't have time to deal me, so I got Dr. Bownes. He was very good, though. Very pleasant and everything."

Something in this delivery, whether it was Dawn's palpable sorrow or hesitant tone, began to affect Sara in ways she hadn't anticipated. "What do you mean Arthur didn't have time to *deal* with you?" she demanded. "That's what physicians are supposed to do, isn't it? Deal with problems."

Dawn gave a dismissive, one-shoulder shrug. "I guess . . .

but you know, how everything happened . . . the emergency room and all that ugly stuff . . . my boyfriend and his run-in with the cops on account of how bad he hurt me . . . oh, man . . ." The words died in her throat. "I didn't mean to say that. Besides, it was a while ago. Forget I talked about him. Okay, ma'am—?"

"You can call me Sara," was the staunch and surprisingly protective reply.

"Sara? Okay? Just forget what I told you, okay?"

Sara glanced at Emma to see what her assessment of Dawn Davis was, and observed a worried and pensive expression that mirrored her own. "Your boyfriend caused this 'accident'?" she asked.

"I shouldn't talk about it, okay? I shouldn't have blabbed. That was just plain dumb. Water under the bridge, or whatever they say. Ancient history." Dawn looked at her watch. "For pete's sake, what's keeping them? I've gotta get to work. We're running short of staff at Papyrus—that's where I work—and the manager's gonna tan my hide if I don't show up for my shift."

"He can't blame you if your physical therapist kept you waiting."

"Wanna bet? He's as big a jerk as my—" Dawn clapped a hand over her mouth.

"As your boyfriend? Is that what you were about to say?"

Dawn didn't reply, and so Sara took the lead. The conniving subcontractor to the Polycrates Agency was nowhere in evidence. "It sounds to me as if you should walk right out on that good-for-nothing person," she stated. "Mistreating a woman! How low can a man stoop? And you realize, dear, that those types don't stop at a single abusive incident."

"Yes, I know . . ." The words were so muffled Sara could hardly hear them. "Look, Sara . . . ma'am . . . I didn't mean to talk about this. I'm really trying to pull things together. I'm taking night school classes and everything. I mean, I don't want to take home the diddly pay I get at Papyrus forever, you know? I want to be a paralegal and work in a law firm or somewhere fancy like that, and well, Andy—he's my boyfriend—he's not too happy about me, you know, giving away all my time—"

"You're hardly *giving* it away if you're earning a paycheck, dear."

"Well, you know how men like to talk . . . and, anyway, I don't think he likes the paralegal stuff, either. He thinks I'm getting ahead of myself or something."

Before Sara could make another incensed comment, Dawn Davis was called for her appointment. She jumped to her feet with the alacrity of someone anticipating being reprimanded—or slapped. "Gotta go . . . listen, forget what I said, Sara. It's just me running off at the mouth. Oh, I'm Dawn, by the way. Dawn Davis." She shook Sara's hand. "I've never met anyone like you. You know, with a maid and everything. That's pretty cool."

Sara watched as Dawn gathered up her purse and bookbag. "You know, my dear, I'm a lonely old lady. I'd be delighted if you felt like visiting me someday. My *maid* could prepare us a meal."

"Really? That would be so cool. Yeah, I'd like that . . . and we could compare doctors and things."

Or talk about a man named Andy whose girlfriend wound up in the operating room, Sara didn't add; instead she opted for a noncommittal: "How about tomorrow after you finish work?"

Dawn thought for a second. "Darn, I can't. I've got a class. Maybe I could cut it, though—"

"Nonsense. You keep up with your schooling. It's very important."

"I could do Saturday," Dawn offered. "Andy won't be around. Like, maybe supper after my shift at the store?"

"That's a date, my dear. Saturday, it is. I'll leave a note with directions to my home with the receptionist—in case I'm already gone when your appointment concludes."

CHAPTER

20

This wasn't the first time some oddball had sent his wife crosswords that seemed to relate to a case Rosco was investigating; and, as in past situations, a number of familiar dilemmas presented themselves. One: Was the message in the puzzle genuine? Two: If it was, who was sending it? And three: Or, could it be that Belle's growing notoriety as a word-game editor and sometime crime solver was making her the target of a person who got his or her jollies by imitating felons and murderers? It was the couple's experience that there were more than a few warped brains in the world, and would-be copycat criminals who constructed complex crosswords during their spare time definitely made that list.

Pondering the telephone call he'd just received from Belle regarding the newly faxed missive, as well as the seemingly innocent puzzle that had arrived on Sunday morning, Rosco again drove out to King Wenstarin Farms. The afternoon had become gray and ominous, and the canvas top and side curtains had been returned to the Jeep, a fact Pete commented on as Rosco stopped at the front gate.

"I guess this means summer is officially over," he said with a broad smile. "You seemed to be the last holdout. All the BMWs and Benzes put up their tops a month ago."

"Never give up, that's me."

"Does this mean you're wearing socks, too?"

Rosco smiled. "Let's not go overboard; still a little early for anything that drastic."

"Well, Mr. Collins has your name on the list, so I'll open up. Hang on a sec."

"Actually I'm here to speak with the barn manager, Orlando Polk. I gather his brush with amnesia has been remedied, and he's back on the job."

"I'm not sure about 'on the job,' but Kelly brought him home from the hospital yesterday. He seemed fine; remembered my name anyway." Pete chuckled, then added, " 'Course I made a real jerk out of myself."

"How's that?" Rosco asked.

The guard shook his head. "Well, I assumed he'd heard the news about the missus being murdered and all, so I was just makin' small talk, you know? Said something like, 'That's a real shame about Mrs. Collins being killed.' " He sighed. "Anyway, the news seemed to hit Orlando pretty hard . . . which is natural . . . I mean hearin' about it for the first time and all. Stuck my foot in my mouth, that's for dang sure. Yeah, my wife tells me to keep my big yap shut, and I never listen to her. It'll dawn on me someday, I guess."

Rosco thought, *Thank goodness there are people who do talk too much; my job would be a heck of a lot tougher if there weren't.*

What he said, however, was a sympathetic, "I could have fallen into the same trap myself, Pete. I would have assumed his wife would have already broken the bad news."

"Yeah, I guess."

Pete opened the gate, and Rosco drove up the long lane of trees, eventually emerging at the center of the farm. He drove directly to stable B, where the barn manager and his wife had their apartment. Rosco wanted to avoid the main house in hopes that he could speak to Orlando without being *chaperoned* by any Collins family members. Parking the Jeep behind the stable, he entered the barn through the large doors on the west end.

The structure's ground floor was divided in two sections. The western end had six roomy box stalls on either side of a broad central aisle; then came a side entrance with double doors leading to an exercise corral, and beyond that, the building was sealed off into what was obviously the manager's living quarters. The entire upper level in the stable area was covered with a hay loft, and Rosco noted it was already well stocked for the winter ahead. He strolled along the aisle toward the apartment, passing the stalls, each of which was occupied by a sleek and handsome steed, who regarded the stranger with curious and haughty eyes. Small frames screwed to the walls separating the boxes displayed the boarded horses' names as well as those of their owners on removable four-by-six-inch file cards. Rosco silently read as he passed, deciding the animals' names could just as easily pass for the gold-leaf monikers members of the Patriot Yacht Club spread across the aft end of their expensive vessels: *Pricey Lady, Windmill, Hokey-Pokey, Flashdance, To a T, Daddy's Girl, Good Guess, Beautiful Dreamer, Endymion,*

Zephyr, Flight of Fancy, Oh, My Word! He chuckled to himself and tapped three times on Orlando Polk's door.

The man who answered was shorter than Rosco had expected, about five-seven or -eight, with long, jet black hair pulled into a ponytail. His skin was darkened and lined from the sun, and his black eyes shone with a sparkle and intensity that gave him a curiously boyish appearance. He extended his hand to Rosco and smiled; his teeth were a gleaming white in contrast to his swarthy complexion.

"I take it you're Rosco Polycrates?" he said, then looked at his watch. "Right on time. Mr. Collins seems very impressed with you, which is good enough for me. Come on in; take a load off."

The apartment consisted of a main room that served as kitchen, dining area, and living area. Open stairs led to a second-floor loft. The partial cathedral ceiling was crafted of exposed, rough-hewn wood, and the decorations reflected the manager's Native American heritage, giving the place the feel of a hunting lodge hidden far off in the woods. Rosco observed that there seemed to be little evidence of a woman's touch; as the thought passed through his mind, Kelly emerged at the edge of the loft. At that height she seemed taller than she actually was, but her short blond hair gave her a pixielike, Peter Pan appearance, and Rosco half expected her to fly down to the lower level.

"My wife, Kelly," Orlando said.

"Yes," Rosco offered as they shook hands, "I remember you from Monday—at Mr. Collins's house."

"Oh, that was a horrible day," she said with her lilting drawl. "I hope I never, ever have to go through something like that again in my life. That poor family. It seemed to bring out the worst in them, rather than the best. It was so, so sad. I couldn't help but feel all broken up inside."

"It wasn't the best of circumstances."

"No, it sure wasn't. And on top of the fire and all . . . I just hope that old saying about trouble coming in packs of threes isn't right." Kelly shook her head. "Well, I've got some work to do, and you two don't need a nosy woman eavesdropping, so I'm just going to mosey along. It was nice meeting you again, Mr. Polycrates."

After she left, Orlando said, "Love of my life. She certainly turned me around."

"I know what you mean. I feel the same way about my wife," Rosco replied as he sat on a couch covered with a woven blanket striped with orange and earth brown lines. "And I appreciate you putting aside the time to meet with me. I gather it can get hectic around here with the Barrington competition coming up."

"Hey, no problem. My doc says to take it easy for a week, and that's exactly what I'm gonna do—kick back, ride my pony, and make sure none of the stable hands messes up too bad. But as far as the Barrington's concerned, we're out of it. That's dead meat. No way we can replace our tack in time."

"Too bad . . . I gather Mr. Collins told you I was investigating the fire for an insurance company?"

Orlando said, "Yep, sure did," as he dropped himself into a wooden rocker across from Rosco.

"I'd like to start by getting a little background information if I could." Rosco pulled a pad and pen from his jacket.

"Shoot."

"How long have you worked for King Wenstarin Farms?"

"Almost six years now."

Rosco noted the information. "So you and your wife arrived before Jack Curry returned to the farm, is that right?"

"Actually, I met Kelly here, at King Wenstarin. We were married a little over a year ago. She was hired as day help for Mr. C. and Ry—" Orlando stopped and corrected himself. "Mrs. Collins . . . Kelly got her job a few months after Jack got his old gig back. Maybe two years ago? Something like that, anyway. What's all this got to do with the fire?"

"Dates are important for the pencil pushers reading the claims forms," Rosco lied with an easy smile. "It's simple, black-and-white stuff. But I suppose the polite thing to ask would be, how's your head feeling?"

Orlando instinctively rubbed the back of his skull and gave a brief laugh. "I've still got a good knot there, I can tell you that. But it's coming along. I'm just happy whatever beaned me didn't break the skin. I'd hate to have to get a haircut just so the docs could throw in a few stitches."

"Any idea what hit you?"

"You'd have to ask someone else that. I heard the crack more than I felt it. Mr. C. told me I managed to get the sprinkler valve turned on, but I don't recollect doin' it."

"I suppose you're aware that the consensus around the farm is that you started the fire—albeit by mistake?"

Polk diverted his eyes and gritted his white teeth, enough so that his jaw muscles popped out from his cheeks. "That's right. Yeah," he said.

Rosco suppressed a grin. *Orlando should take lying lessons from a pro like Dawn Davis,* he thought. *The guy's rotten at it.* "Maybe you could walk me through the chain of events—what you believe might have happened to trigger the accident."

"Well . . . it's all . . . a little fuzzy in my head," was the hesitant answer. Orlando was still unable to look Rosco in the eye, and he offered no further details.

Rosco tapped his pen on his knee. "Okay, I'm going to cut to the nitty-gritty, here. We've got a major blaze. And we've got a bunch of people who feel you started it. Now, it was either a true accident, or you did it on purpose—which constitutes arson and carries a hefty prison term. Insurance companies aren't inclined to buy 'accident' when there's a half-million-dollar settlement at stake. They're looking for any reason that will let them balk on payment; which I personally don't agree with, but that's how it is. So I'd like you to lay out exactly how this problem transpired—whether it's 'fuzzy in your head' or not."

The barn manager remained quiet for a moment, then stood and walked into the kitchen area. "Do you mind if I light a cigarette?"

Rosco shook his head. "Go for it."

He lit up and inhaled deeply. "It was simple. The phone rang in the tack room. I turned around real quick to answer it and knocked the space heater onto the floor, and the place caught on fire." Orlando looked at Rosco and added an unconvincing, "It sure as hell wasn't done on purpose."

"And the liquor bottle in question? Did it hit the floor and break before or *after* the space heater?"

"Umm . . . before . . . no, after. The cord from the space heater dragged it onto the floor and it smashed."

"I see. And then you tried to put out the fire, is that it?"

"No. No. It happened too fast. I was more concerned about getting the horses into a safe area, so I ran to open the place up."

Rosco leaned forward on the couch. "Mr. Collins said that when he looked out from his house he could see someone swatting at the flames with a horse blanket. So, I gather that wasn't you? Was there someone else in the tack room at the time?"

Orlando shook his head. "The training operation was shut down for the day. Barn managers are always the last to leave the place at the end of a work session, you know, kind of square the place away, make sure the equipment is stored properly, and all . . . come to think of it, I guess I did try to put the fire out first. That would have been a natural thing for me to do, contain it. When it started to spread I gave up and ran to release the horses."

"Did you answer the phone?"

"What?"

"Did you answer the phone? You said the phone rang. That's what caused you to knock over the heater. Did you get a chance to answer it?"

"Umm . . . no. I didn't."

Rosco stood, walked over to the door, and then back to the couch. He paced in that fashion for a few seconds, finally saying, "If you were known to be the only person in the tack room at that time of evening, whoever was calling wanted to talk to you. Do you have any idea who it might have been?"

"No. No. I don't know. Maybe it was Kelly. She was in Kentucky visiting her family. Maybe she tried me here in the apartment, got no answer and then rang the tack room."

Rosco continued to pace. "On the other hand, it's my understanding that the phone in the tack room is on a line that's connected to every building on the farm, so if someone were to call there it would ring elsewhere, even in Mr.

Collins's house. Would your wife, an employee, do that? For a personal call? Dial a number that would risk disturbing Mr. or Mrs. Collins or his children?"

Orlando crushed out his cigarette. "Okay, maybe it wasn't Kelly. I told you I didn't answer the thing. Maybe it wasn't for me at all."

"Here's the problem I'm having with this telephone business: that phone rings all over King Wenstarin Farms, yet no one else—Jack Curry, Mr. Collins, Chip, Fiona, Heather, Michael Palamountain, none of them—has mentioned hearing it shortly before the fire broke out. How do you explain that?"

"Okay, maybe it wasn't the phone, maybe it was the intercom. I told you my mind's real blurry. I only remember little bits and pieces. And then not all the time."

"The intercom is a speaker phone; there's no receiver to reach for."

"There's a button you have to push in order to talk. You hear a voice, but you can't answer without depressing the talk button. Maybe I was reaching for that . . . yeah, I'm sure I was. It wasn't the phone at all."

Rosco stopped by the apartment door and turned toward Orlando. "Okay, now we're getting somewhere. And whose voice was so important that you spun around—triggering the events that produced the fire?"

Polk seemed to freeze. He stood in that awkward posture for a long moment, then finally whispered, "I don't . . . remember."

Rosco reached for the doorknob and flung open the door. Standing there was Heather Collins, who all but tumbled into the room.

"Oh," she said as she recovered her composure, "I was looking for Orlando. Ah . . . that . . . spare saddle of mine? The Crosby? Do you know where it is?"

Rosco smiled and held up his hands. "Don't mind me. I was just leaving."

CHAPTER

21

As Rosco drove home, he left a message on Clint Mize's voice mail indicating he had real suspicions that there were serious irregularities concerning the blaze and suggesting that the Dartmouth Group delay payment until he completed his investigation. As far as Rosco was concerned, Orlando Polk was protecting someone, but he couldn't tell whom, or why, for that matter. He ended the call with, "Give me five more days, max; I'll have some answers."

He walked through his front door shortly before six that evening. Belle emerged from the kitchen and hurried toward him, faxes in hand, although she was no match for Kit and Gabby, who reached him in half the time, jumping and yipping, their short tails wagging out of control. Rosco walked to the center of the living room rug, flopped down on his back, and the two four-legged members of the household and its two-legged male resident began rolling around like tiger cubs freed into the wild.

Belle watched this lunacy for about a minute, then observed a sardonic, "I hate to interrupt your lovefest, but I think you might want to take a look at these crosswords."

Rosco shook himself free of the dogs and stood. The "girls" continued to grapple with one another in his absence, so he walked toward Belle and made an attempt to give her a kiss. She stepped to the side.

"What? What's wrong?" he said.

Belle reached up and brushed a few of Kit's hairs from his eyebrows. "I think I can wait on the smooching for a bit. Is that a new cologne you're wearing? Eau-de-road-apple?"

"Hey, I just came from a horse farm. What do you want?"

"Well, it certainly seems popular with the canine set. Perhaps you could patent it and market it to pet shops?"

He smiled, blew her a kiss, and gave her a rundown of his conversation with Orlando Polk, concluding with, "So, we've got ourselves a lying barn manager and a couple of suspicious crosswords? Do we know where they came from?"

"No. That's the weird thing." She handed him the two sheets of paper. "I thought return phone info was always printed at the top of a fax. It has been with every other one you or I have received."

"That's because they were transmitted by honest folk." Rosco examined the paper and began walking toward Belle's office. She followed him as he added, "The information that appears in the header of most faxes is programmed into the sending machine by the owner—just like we did with ours when we bought it. If you don't enter that data, or if you delete it, nothing appears at the other end." When he reached the machine he lifted the receiver. "Have you called out on this line since the message came in?"

"No."

"And no other fax has arrived since?"

Belle shook her head. "No."

"Good. Then as long as this crossword wasn't sent from an unlisted telephone account, we should still be able to access the source number."

Rosco tapped *69 into the keypad and waited. He then smiled, grabbed a pen from Belle's desk, and jotted down a telephone number dictated by an automated voice. "Bingo," he said as he showed it to Belle. "Recognize it?"

Belle thought for a moment. "No . . . do you?"

Rosco stared at the numbers. "Not that I can recall. We can go on-line and do a reverse lookup. But let's think about this for a minute." He dropped down into a black-and-white canvas deck chair and began scanning the puzzles. "Clearly, both were constructed by the same person; the graph paper is marked out in a similar manner, and the handwriting looks the same. Other than that, I don't see what's gotten you all hot under the collar."

Belle stepped behind him and leaned over his shoulder. Again he tried for a kiss, but she put the kibosh on it. "No way, buddy, not until you hit the showers." Then she pointed at the "Hitchcock" puzzle. "Obviously, the real Alfred Hitchcock went to the *Family Plot* years ago, so our constructor chose the name to get my attention—"

"Which worked."

"Correcto. And it also inspired me to resurrect the first illegitimate crossword . . . which took a bit of searching, because I'd already relegated it to the recycling bin—"

"Proving you shouldn't be too hasty when it comes to cleaning up the house," he said facetiously.

"Hardy har har."

"Hey, did I say I liked the squeaky-clean look? I'm the person covered in dog fur, remember?" Rosco studied the puzzles again. "Okay . . . what else can you tell me about these two word games?"

"Both employ a theme: song titles in the first, movies in the second—"

"Well, that's hardly a big red arrow, saying, 'Solve me! I know who dunnit!' "

"Come on, Rosco, BLAZING SADDLES? How obvious is that? Does someone need to hit you over the head?"

He raised an eyebrow. "As in Mr. Polk's accident?"

"Hmmmm . . ." was Belle musing response while Rosco gave an indulgent chuckle.

"Okay, I'll bite. But the title is 'To Catch a Thief,' not 'To Catch an Arsonist.' And here in the middle, at 38-Across, you've got DAWN OF THE DEAD—which could refer to the same DAWN who's currently cozying up to Sara and has ripped Gudgeon off for a quarter mil. We also have a DEAD Ryan Collins . . . So, how do we know what crime these crosswords apply to—if they're connected to anything other than each other?"

"Todd Collins's wife was killed *after* the first crossword was transmitted, so my hunch is that the puzzles have nothing to do with her death. However, I do believe the constructor is trying to tell us that Chip started the barn fire."

Rosco smiled. "I take it you're drawing that rather far-fetched conclusion from BLAZING SADDLES and GOODBYE MR. CHIPS?"

Belle nodded energetically. "And there's this," she announced as she pointed to the first puzzle. "HORSE WITH NO NAME. When Bartholomew was here he mentioned a country pub called The Horse With No Name. It's not far from King Wenstarin Farms. Supposedly, all the riding set hangs out there."

"Including Chip Collins . . ." was Rosco's slow and pensive response.

"What a smart guy."

"And what about DAWN Davis?"

"I'm assuming the reference is a fluke. Just like MIA being the solution to 3-Down in the second puzzle, or ILSA appearing at 4-Down in the first. Besides, DAWN relates to death in this instance, rather than financial chicanery."

Rosco nodded, but didn't speak for a moment. "I know exactly where Bartholomew's pub is. It might be a good time for me to have a little chat with the Chip off the old block." He glanced up at Belle. "This is all hush-hush, but Al considers young Mr. Collins a prime suspect with regard to his stepmother's murder. He asked me to ostensibly question Chip regarding the fire, but also do some probing of his relationship with Ryan. I think I'll swing by The Horse With No Name tomorrow at lunchtime. If I can catch him with a few beers in his belly, it may loosen his tongue."

"Well, I certainly don't want to be accused of spreading rumors," was Belle's own facetious reply, "but Bartholomew suggested that Chip and Ryan had a little fling—which is pretty darn sleazy."

"This is interesting," Rosco said as he pointed to 23-Across in the Hitchcock puzzle. "One of the horses I saw when I went to interview Orlando today was named FLASHDANCE."

This time, it was Belle who paused in thought. "Do you think the barn manager's our mystery constructor?"

Rosco laughed. "Not unless this fax number turns out to be Newcastle Memorial Hospital, which is where he was when the first crossword appeared. He was also in a semicomatose state."

"Hmmmm," Belle said as she strolled over to her computer and turned it on. "I wonder who is creating these . . . and why he or she won't come forward? Any guesses?"

"Not a one. Although, I did see both Heather and FLASHDANCE in the same barn this morning. And her behavior— the person, not the horse—seemed more than a little flighty."

Belle was about to make a smart-aleck comment about disco queens and equestriennes when her computer screen lit up. "Do you want to do this reverse lookup thing? I'm not sure how it works."

"Sure." Rosco crossed over and sat behind her computer. "What's this backgammon icon?"

"Don't worry about it."

He clicked on the icon.

"Leave it alone, Rosco."

"What? This is what you do all day? Play on-line backgammon?"

"I don't play *all* day. I just gets my mind off crossword puzzles for a little while. This is why I don't let you near my computer. You start snooping around."

"Man . . . just when you think you know someone . . . Backgammon, huh? You know we could play together—in real life, I mean?"

"What, and risk you winning? You know how fiercely competitive I am. This way if I lose, I remain completely anonymous."

Rosco chortled. "Okay . . . here it is; reverse lookup. Read that phone number to me, will you?"

Belle read it, and Rosco entered the numbers on the screen. "Ho, ho, ho," he said as the information came up. "Look what we have here."

Belle leaned over his shoulder. "Wow, you mean these crosswords were faxed from the Dew Drop Inn?"

"It looks that way."

"But the place's latest 'rebirth' into a 'luxury resort and spa' never got off the ground. It's been boarded up for over a year—not that too many 'renovations' were accomplished."

"Well, the telephone line must still be hot." He reached for Belle's desk phone, dialed the number, and let it ring ten times before hanging up. "Interesting; no disconnect message, but no fax squeal either. I guess the investment group that bought the inn is still hoping to accomplish their plans. Although given the fact that the old place has undergone a bunch of failed attempts at rehab over the years, things don't look promising." Rosco paused. "Periwinkle Partners, I think that's the latest group to own it."

"What?" Belle said as she turned to face him.

"Periwinkle Partners. Those are the investment folks who bought the Dew Drop Inn."

"But that's who Michael Palamountain works with when he's not dealing with the horse farm. He's CFO of Periwinkle Partners. Bartholomew told me."

"I imagine it must be true then. Mr. Kerr prides himself on getting his info directly from the horse's mouth."

Belle made a face. "You're unrepentant, you know that?" Then she added a perplexed, "But if Palamountain is the one sending these puzzles, does that make him innocent? Or guilty?"

"And therefore the poor penitent Palamountain of Periwinkle Partners?"

"Just stop right this minute."

"Or Michael, the misguided and misbehaving millionaire?"

"Rosco!"

He was silent for a moment, only. "And where does Heather fit into the scheme?"

CHAPTER

22

In a kill-two-birds-with-one-stone concept, Rosco had originally hoped to take Kit and Gabby for an early morning run in the large park adjacent to the deserted Dew Drop Inn, while at the same time checking the old establishment's phone lines. However, a steady downpour of unpleasantly cold rain greeted the threesome as they stepped out onto their porch. For a full five minutes, human and canines watched the wet stuff tumble from the sky in buckets. The waiting Jeep looked many sodden miles away. Then Rosco adjusted his plans, retrieved an umbrella, and hooked up their leashes.

"Sorry girls, no park today," he said. And the three plodded out into the elements to return eight minutes later drenched to the core. He toweled off the dogs, fed them, wolfed down a bowl of granola, kissed Belle good-bye, and drove over to the Dew Drop Inn alone. If Kit and Gabby intuited where he was heading, they didn't seem to mind. They gave him a *Have fun, big guy* look and curled up in Belle's office.

Because the inn's current owners had forsaken it the previous year, the rambling structure was beginning to again show serious signs of neglect. Several of the new windows had broken panes; the wide veranda facing both the sea and overgrown gardens was piled with the detritus of New England storms: leaves, twigs, and sand blown up from the dunes and bluffs overlooking Buzzard's Bay, while the salt of ocean-splashed spray had turned what paint remained on the woodwork and shutters into a flaking and moldering mess that all but screamed *Dry rot!* and *Save me before I crumble completely!*

Rosco considered the series of investors the romantic old place had inspired over the years: all of them hoping to restore the inn and its spectacular grounds into a viable business—and all of them failing and quietly decamping. Now it was apparently Periwinkle Partners' chance to return the hotel to its former glory; however, leaving the structure to lie fallow hadn't helped their cause.

The locks, like most older hotel locks, weren't sophisticated, and Rosco had little difficulty bypassing them. He'd worn jeans and work boots and had a telephone repairman's tool belt strapped to his waist. He entered the inn by way of the back kitchen door. Worn and dented pots and pans still hung from large iron hooks, and the kitchen utensils appeared undisturbed since the last meal had been prepared circa 1960. A layer of dust covered everything, and a number of window screens had collapsed onto the countertops. He walked through the kitchen and large formal dining room and down a long corridor of guest rooms where he jimmied one of the room locks, entered, and tested the phone line. It was dead.

Rosco repeated the process in a half dozen more rooms, and the same held true: all the lines had been disconnected. He crossed through the main lobby and stepped behind the reception desk. The reservation book was still open to the last day of operations as if awaiting the arrival of a ghostly visitor, and a doorway to the rear was still marked with a sign reading MANAGER. He glanced at the knob. The door had been forced, and the wood splintered at the jamb as though a crowbar had pried it apart. The damage was obviously recent.

He nudged open the door, stepped inside, and tested the phone line. Although it was hot, there was no fax machine in sight, leading Rosco to surmise that whoever had sent Belle the crosswords had provided their own machine. *If it was Michael Palamountain,* his thoughts continued, *he would have had a key. On the other hand, if he wanted to make the situation appear to be an ordinary break-in, this is the ruse he might have chosen.* Rosco stood studying the room. Nothing else seemed disturbed. No desk drawers had been disturbed, no cupboards ransacked. All evidence pointed toward a burglar too disappointed to hunt further.

Rosco returned to his Jeep, but as he left the inn's empty parking lot he noticed Al Lever's "unmarked" brown police cruiser resting on the far side of the dog area. Rosco drove around the park, stopping beside the cruiser so that the two driver-side windows were inches apart. He slid his window open, and Al lowered his. A plume of cigarette smoke escaped into the dripping morning air. Al's dog, Skippy, jumped around in the backseat anxiously.

"Looks like Skippy has some business to attend to," Rosco observed.

"It's raining like hell," was Al's laconic reply. "Where's Kit and Gabby?"

"Hey, I listen to the weather reports," Rosco lied. "Who didn't know it was going to rain all day? I left them at home. As far as I know they're playing backgammon right now."

"Yeah? Then what're you doing all the way out here if you don't have any dogs with you?"

Seeing no need to keep Al in the dark, Rosco briefed him on his reasons for being at the inn, as well as everything else he'd learned during the past few days. Al in turn brought Rosco up to date on his investigation into Ryan Collins's homicide. One: The only fingerprints found on the murder weapon belonged to Orlando Polk, and the hoof pick had a B burned into the handle, indicating it came from stable B. However, as everyone knew, the barn manager was confirmed to have been at Newcastle Memorial at the time of the killing, which provided him with an airtight alibi. And two: According to Abe Jones's report, there were no out-of-place fingerprints at the crime scene. Lever viewed the discoveries as confirmation of his own suspicions—that the killer was probably one of Todd Collins's offspring. "Whoever bludgeoned Ryan Collins was angry as hell," he concluded. "But like they say, being stiffed out of a large inheritance can produce a seriously bad heir day."

Rosco grimaced at the play on words. "Who says that, Al—besides you, I mean?"

"You got a better motive, let me know," was the terse response.

"You're not ruling out Todd as the perpetrator, are you?" Rosco asked.

"I'm not ruling out anyone, Poly-crates. I'm just going with my gut. And right now, it's pointing to the kids."

"If I were you, Al, I'd keep remarks that refer to your waistline at a minimum."

"Ho, ho."

"Well, I'm going to try to catch up with Chip Collins out at The Horse With No Name," Rosco added after a moment. "Apparently he shows up there like clockwork on Friday for the half-priced oysters."

"Yeah, like he needs to count his pennies—or even his one-grand notes." Then Al's caustic tone softened as he looked at Skippy. "Bring us a doggie bag, Poly-crates, but forget the raw bar for my man Skippy, here. Fried oysters he likes . . . Rockefeller, clams Casino, whatever, but he's not big on the sushi-style items."

Rosco didn't bother to ask how his former partner had ascertained the dog's taste in seafood. For all Rosco knew, Lever hand-fed Skippy each and every meal. For such a dyed-in-the-wool curmudgeon and cynic, Al was a notorious pushover when it came to his beloved canine companion.

"You wouldn't be influencing Skippy's choice of cuisine, would you, Al?"

"Keep me posted," was Lever's sole response.

From the inn, Rosco drove directly to his office. He shook the rain from his parka, hung it on the coat rack, then sat at his desk. His answering machine blinked with one message that had been logged in only five minutes earlier. He tapped the play button.

"Yes. Rosco. Todd Collins here. I had a long talk at the club last night with my good friend Hank Farley—that's Dartmouth Group's CEO—but I assume you know who Hank is . . . I tried to persuade him to remove you from this damn fire investigation, because we need to straighten out this *conflict of interest* nonsense and get you working full time on finding Ryan's killer. I'll admit I'm not as confident in Newcastle's Finest as you are." Without the merest pause, Collins's authoritative voice pounded ahead:

"Problem is, Hank's hamstrung by the weenies on Dartmouth's board of directors. He feels it'll send up flags if he bumps you from the case. He told me the only solution is for *you* to remove *yourself* or close out the investigation. Well, there is one other option, which is for me to drop the claim, but we're not going to go there." Collins finally took a breath and added, "So what's it going to be? I'll make it worth your while. Give me a ring. I'm at the farm. You've got the number. I want Ryan's murderer brought to justice, and I want it done yesterday."

Rosco lifted the receiver to return the call, but then let it drop back into the cradle. He had nothing to say to Todd Collins. He would work the case as he saw fit.

By noon Rosco was nursing a draught beer at the long oak bar of The Horse With No Name. The spot had been a roadside tavern for over two centuries. Unlike the Dew Drop Inn, new ownership simply picked up where the former left off. The age-darkened beams of the ceiling didn't undergo a

sunny facelift; the publike atmosphere of the dining room
didn't morph into bistro French or southern Italian; no one
tried a menu that was Asian-fusion or Hispano-Mayan or
Tuscan-Bulgarian. The staples remained traditional American fare. At this point it had been in the same family for over
thirty years, and Friday's half-price oyster special meant that
there wasn't an empty table to be had. This fact worked in
Rosco's favor. Three people had already asked if the bar stool
next to him was available, and he'd managed to send them
on their way with, "Sorry. I'm saving it for a buddy of mine."
Ten minutes later Chip Collins arrived and approached him.

"Hey, how's it goin', Rosco? I didn't know you liked this
joint. You saving this stool for anyone?"

"Nope." Rosco tapped the cell phone on his belt. "I was
supposed to meet an old friend, but he just called and said
he couldn't make it. Have a seat."

Chip sat next to Rosco and gave the bartender a nod.
Without a word, a dark amber ale was placed in front of him.

"Only way to go," Chip said. "The snobs think you've got
to have champagne or some froufrou drink when you sit down
with a plate of oysters. But anyone in the know will tell you a
good beer keeps your taste buds sharp." He pointed to the
chalkboard behind the bar. "Try the ones from Fishers Island,
New York; none better in the country. It's a small-scale farm,
and the owners know their business."

"I'll do that."

"How're you coming with that fire thing? I think the old
man's getting a tad annoyed with the insurance company."
Chip chortled as he spoke. "Pop's not a pleasant man to be
around when things don't go his way . . . or as quickly as
he'd like."

Rosco smiled. "I imagine after all is said and done the Dartmouth Group will pay off. Clint Mize explained that to your father. Unless, of course, the situation proves to be a case of arson."

Chip ignored the inference, turning instead to the bartender and ordering them both a dozen oysters. He was careful to specify the types he wanted served.

"Let me ask you something," Rosco continued as if he were making casual conversation. "Orlando Polk insists he heard the phone, or maybe the intercom, just before the fire started. Did you hear it ring up at your cottage?"

"Not the phone, no. And I keep the damn intercom turned off. Most of the time it's just my sisters knocking each other over something. I get tired of listening to their gab. It starts sounding like talk radio."

Rosco took a sip of his beer. "I know what you mean. I've got sisters, too. *Greek* sisters. When it comes to vendettas, they take the cake." Then he added a seemingly nonchalant, "Can I be up front with you?"

"I hope so."

"I have good reason to believe your barn manager didn't start that blaze. I think he's covering for someone. I can't figure out who, and I can't figure out why. The thing is, I feel the fire marshal's initial assessment is correct: that the blaze was an accident. There are a lot easier ways to start a fire than with a space heater. So I don't get it. What do you think, Chip? Who's Polk covering for, and what's his reason?"

Chip swiveled his stool around so that he was facing Rosco. "What? You think I started that fire? And that I'm paying off Orlando to keep his mouth shut? Because I don't want to get in Dutch with my old man for what I did? Is that it?"

Rosco shrugged and pasted a diffident smile on his face. "Hey, that's not a half-bad scenario . . ." He cocked his head as though weighing the notion and then discarding it. "But my hunch tells me the idea won't hold water. You just don't seem like the kind of guy who'd let someone else take the fall for him. So, if not you, who? Your brother-in-law, Michael? Heather? Fiona?"

"I don't know about my sisters, but I was nowhere near that barn. And Angel can back me up on that," Chip insisted hotly. "Besides, if I *had* inadvertently set the place ablaze, I would have owned up to it and tried like hell to save the building. Sure, the old man and I have had our differences over the years, but I'm not afraid of him. And believe me, Rosco, I've done worse things in my day than burn down a barn, and he hasn't thrown me off the property yet." By now, Chip's tone had become neither confrontational nor defensive; in fact, it carried a certain amount of familial pride. Rosco found himself believing the pronouncement.

"Okay, then what about your sisters? How's their relationship with your father? Or Jack Curry? Could he have started the fire and be afraid of losing his job?"

"I guess . . . but what difference does it make? No matter who did it, it's still an accident, and the insurance has to pay off. Anything else is a Wenstarin Farms's internal problem, right?"

Rosco nodded. "Then let's look at arson as a possibility. I recall Heather stating that your competitors at Holbrooke Farms might have had a motive."

Chip finished off his ale. The bartender arrived with their platters, and another round of beers was ordered.

"I'd love to believe that Holbrooke Farms business

of Heather's, I really would," Chip said between oysters. "They're a bunch of jerks over there. But they wouldn't stoop to that. And logistically it's next to impossible for them to sneak into our compound—or pay someone to do their dirty work for them. Despite Heather's allegations to the contrary, my father commands too much loyalty from his employees. He can smell a rat quicker than a cat can."

"Then we're back to Orlando, and who he's covering for. What can you tell me about his wife, Kelly?"

"Pretty girl. Nice. Quiet. Helpful. Friendly without getting in the way. She was in Kentucky when the fire broke out—and that's a long way to toss a lighted match, let alone a space heater."

"I know. I'm just trying to see how the pieces of the puzzle fit together."

"Kelly serves dinners up at the Big House; cleans and so forth during the day. Her father's ill, so she's been going back and forth to Louisville a lot lately." Chip was quiet for a long moment. Finally he said, "You're convinced Orlando didn't start that fire?"

"Not *convinced*, necessarily. But I do know he's lying about the events of the evening in question."

Chip nodded. "It's an interesting thought . . . an innocent person putting himself at risk because he's determined to protect the guilty party. We could all learn from that model."

Rosco swallowed another oyster and said, "These *are* on the money, thanks for the recommendation." Then feeling that Chip was being honest with him, he opted to move on to Ryan. "I'm sorry about your stepmother. It must be tough. I didn't want to pipe up the other day at the house. It was Lieutenant Lever's show, and I was trying to stay out of the way."

"Good riddance to bad rubbish. That's my position on the situation. She won't be missed."

Rosco raised his eyebrows. "That's kind of cold."

"Hey, that's how it is."

"I wouldn't talk that way around Al Lever if I were you, he's apt to put you at the top of his suspects column."

"Don't make me laugh. As much as I disliked Ryan, I wouldn't kill her. My old man adored her. Just look at him. He's a wreck. I wouldn't put anyone through what he's experiencing right now—and that goes double for my own dad. He married the snake, he must have seen something no one else did."

"What about Heather and Fiona; how did they feel about Ryan?"

Chip let out a long laugh. "If you think I'm going to rat out my sisters, you're crazy. The fact is, I don't care who killed Ryan. It's over. 'Who did it,' is the cops' problem. And if they try to cart one of my sisters off on a murder charge there's going to be more Boston lawyers at Wenstarin Farms than horses. O. J.'s Dream Team will look like public defenders."

Rosco decided to push the edge of the envelope. "I guess you know that some people around Newcastle believe that your relationship to Ryan might have been a little closer than it should have been."

Chip roared with laughter at Rosco's statement. After he'd regained his composure he said, "I haven't heard it phrased that politely before."

"Well?"

"I wouldn't do that to my old man, either. Not in a million years. Besides, I just told you how much I detested her."

He finished his last oyster and ordered a dozen more. "How about you, Rosco? Another round?"

"Why not?"

"Sure, Ryan came on to me; she came on to everyone. Why the hell do you think I despised her so much? Fiona and Heather were well aware of her activities, too. Her behavior made them sick. We tried to warn the old man a few months ago, but he wouldn't believe a word of it. It got dicey for a while there, so we let our accusations drop. The issue became a don't-go-there kind of thing."

"Lever's got this inheritance-money-is-the-root-of-all-evil theory. In cases like this, that's often the first motive homicide detectives jump to. Do you know whether your father was planning to leave everything to Ryan—rather than to you kids?"

Chip swigged his beer, then stared into the half-full glass. "Well, bully for Lever. The fat man got something right," was all he said.

CHAPTER

23

Daylight was waning over the still-soggy grounds of the Dew Drop Inn when Belle's cell phone rang with its distinctive "Brinnnnggg Brinnnnggg." The sound she'd chosen was similar to an old-fashioned rotary phone; and combined with the dusky air and the coal black hulk of the abandoned building, the effect was eerie and unsettling—as if a message from the departed were about to be delivered.

"Hello?"

"Where are you, dear girl?" crackled through into the autumn twilight. Sara simply couldn't get used to the notion that one could receive and transmit calls wire-free and from any location. When Belle lent her elderly friend her cell, Sara stood rooted to one spot while she talked—as if she were speaking into a wall-mounted hand-crank model with a party-line system eager to eavesdrop on the conversation.

"Rosco and I are at the dog park—"

"Oh, of course you are. It's Saturday afternoon. Where else would Newcastle's dog fanciers be other than the grounds of the old inn? I do wish one of those consortia that keeps snapping up the place would finally renovate it to its former glory. It's a shame to allow that marvelous structure to decay. Of course, if anyone ever does return it to its heyday I would guess they would invite all of you dog fanciers to depart—"

At this point, a prodigious amount of barking overpowered Sara's speech. Al Lever's canine buddy, Skippy; Abe Jones's "lab mix," Buster; Martha's Peke, Princess; Stanley Hatch's elderly collie, Ace; and Bartholomew's beloved bulldog, Winston—accompanied by Kit and Gabby—had picked up an unfamiliar scent and were voicing their concern—or their ardent enthusiasm at discovering a new and tantalizing smell.

"Sorry, Sara," Belle said as the pack roared away, "I didn't hear you." She walked a distance from the two-legged throng, as well. Talking to a disembodied voice while in the company of flesh-and-blood companions was something she frowned upon.

"No matter. I was simply rambling on about the Dew Drop Inn during its prime. Actually, I called to tell you that Dawn Davis just phoned to say she was not able to keep our date this evening." Belle's ears perked up. She looked over at Rosco, who caught her glance, and sent back a quizzical look in return. *It's Sara,* Belle mouthed, then turned around and strolled farther off. The elusive Ms. Davis didn't need to become a subject of discussion among those gathered on the inn's sodden lawns.

"Apparently, her odious boyfriend didn't want her 'hobnobbing with the rich' . . ." Sara continued with more than a little ire. "That happens to be a quote, if you can believe such nonsense."

Belle frowned into the air, and the expression grew into a scowl as Sara's voice continued:

"Of course, the poor girl was mortified, and so attempted to pass off his remarks as a jest. But I could detect the ruse. I'm genuinely concerned about her, Belle. I understand the scheme you and Rosco suspect her of orchestrating, and I realize that I was chomping at the bit in my desire to aid you. But I cannot believe that such a sweet young lady would—" More yaps and yips and growls and snarls cut short Sara's remarks again. Belle covered her free ear with her hand.

"But Sara," was her response once the hullabaloo had died down, "these are precisely the characteristics Ms. Davis presented to Walter Gudgeon: an innocent and helpless victim who only wanted a friend—"

"And so she does," Sara swiftly interjected. "Remember, Dawn all but stated that her boyfriend physically abuses her."

"That's what she told *you*," Belle persisted. "She gave Gudgeon another story: an ex-boyfriend who wouldn't help when she most needed it."

"She should have kept him confined to a list of *former* friends," was Sara's swift retort. "Instead of taking him back, or whatever she did. We women can be so foolish where our hearts are concerned—"

"But you don't know what she said is true . . . whether he's a current lover or not. You haven't seen him; you don't know if he even really exists—"

"I know what I heard in her voice, and that's good enough for me."

Belle stifled an anxious sigh. "And did you extend a second invitation to your home?" she asked in as reasonable tone as she could muster. Sara's sudden and staunch defense of Dawn Davis was beginning to worry Belle. The pattern seemed uncomfortably similar to the ploy she'd used on Gudgeon.

"Well, no. She told me she'd call when she learned her new work schedule—which apparently is changing."

"I gather Ms. Davis didn't provide her telephone number," Belle prompted.

"Her boyfriend doesn't like her receiving calls from people he doesn't know—"

"In other words you didn't get it."

The silence on the other end of the phone was excruciating. Holding the machine close to her ear, Belle could almost visualize Sara's proud and defiant face, and she squinted in nervous anticipation of the old lady's patronizing response.

"I did not choose to pry any further, Belle. To do so would only have added to her discomfort."

Belle did her best to conceal her exasperation. "But don't you see, Sara, this is the same approach she used on Mr. Gudgeon—"

"What the young lady is alleged to have done in the past, and what my present experience of her is, are two very different things—"

"But they're not! This is precisely how Dawn Davis works her con—"

"Well, she hasn't asked me for a dime!" was Sara's irritable reply. "And I assure you she doesn't intend to." Then the old lady did something Belle could never have imagined. She hung up without a single word of farewell.

Returning to her friends who were now trying to corral the excited dogs, Belle's expression was troubled.

"Is Sara okay?" Rosco asked.

"Oh, sure," Belle lied, and everyone there immediately recognized the fib—if not its motivation.

"Oh dear," Martha tossed in, "I hope that tumble she took in Maxi's shop isn't the sign of more serious problems to come." She released a lengthy sigh. "Don't feel bad, Belle, honey, your face is like an open book." Martha sighed anew. "It's a tough business getting old. My dad became real cantankerous when his health started to fail . . . forgot simple facts, couldn't remember where he was sometimes or with whom. It got so bad, I had to take his checkbook away from him; and if that didn't cause a ruckus, my name isn't Leonetti. But Dad was giving his money away to any supposed charity that knocked on the door. Not that he had lucre to burn . . . but you write ten checks for ten dollars a pop, and it adds up."

Belle couldn't think what to answer. Savvy Martha was closer to the truth than she realized. "Oh, I'm sure Sara's simply feeling a bit constrained and homebound," Belle finally announced, attempting a nonchalance she didn't feel. "After all, she's not accustomed to depending on others to propel her around."

"Sara Crane Briephs under house arrest," piped up Bartholomew with an empathetic chuckle, but that single word *arrest* only heightened Belle's sense of gloom. As far as she could determine, the infamous Dawn Davis was softening up another potential mark, and unless Rosco could prove the Gudgeon case, no criminal charges would be made. She glanced at Rosco, who shared her look of worry while he offered an overly robust:

"Looks like its getting too dark for Frisbees and ball-chasing. I guess we'd better pack it in."

Abe Jones's Buster was the last of the canines to be rounded up, and then only because Abe walked up onto the inn's veranda and leashed him. "Looks like someone was walking around the old place," Abe remarked as he returned to the group. "Recently. The footprints are fresh."

"Really?" both Rosco and Al Lever responded too quickly and in near-perfect unison.

Abe chortled. "You two wouldn't happen to have already heard about this, would you? The lock on the office door? No one needs to be a forensics expert to recognize a little B and E when the perp whacks away at a door like that," he added facetiously.

Neither man answered, so Abe shook his head. "Not that I want to know what the situation entails. But you remember what they say about friends keeping secrets from their buddies?"

It was Belle who responded. In the evening light, her face looked wan and worried. "No. What do they say?"

"If you can't trust your pals, who are you gonna confide in? The police department?" He laughed again, then studied Belle. "Hey, puzzle lady. Lighten up."

But she'd taken the comment too much to heart to bother producing a smile.

CHAPTER

24

"But it's terrible, Rosco," Belle was insisting as they drove home from the dog park. Twilight was now gone, and the sky looked like darkest night. "Sara has never hung up on me like that. And I doubt she's done it to anyone else, either. She's far too ladylike and self-controlled to slam down the phone. This is a side of her I've never seen."

"Maybe she simply dropped it," Rosco suggested as he maneuvered the Jeep around a four-legged shadow that darted across the country lane. "Or your cell-phone reception went on the fritz. We know how often that happens."

"Was that a black cat running across the road?" Belle asked as she spun around in her seat and peered through the rear window.

"It wasn't a dog," Rosco answered. "And it especially wasn't one of those two sacks of snooze lying prone on the backseat."

"That's a terrible omen, a black cat," Belle continued as she stared into the jet-colored trees lining the roadway. Where the Jeep's headlights sheered past them, the trunks appeared gray and lifeless; left without illumination, they reverted to an even more inhospitable sight. "What do you think it means?"

"That some poor creature isn't as fortunate as the spoiled pooches who grudgingly allow us to share their home?"

"I'm being serious, Rosco!"

"You're not attempting to equate a lost or feral feline with Sara's odd behavior, are you?" was his amused response. "That might be considered a catty remark—"

"Rosco, I'm not making a joke!"

He reached over and rested his hand on her thigh lovingly. "I know you're not. And I realize that you're worried about your aborted conversation with Sara, and with her weird defense of the highly questionable Ms. Davis. But I also don't think you should start imagining dire circumstances, or peering into tea leaves, or having your palm read just because a stray cat skedaddled across the pavement. If it had been a deer, you would have been thrilled to catch sight of it."

"That's true," was the pensive answer. "I guess it's the Bambi connection."

"And I would have been thrilled it didn't end up as a hood ornament."

Belle shivered at the thought and let out a long and perturbed sigh. And Rosco understood that his wife was far from convinced that the abrupt culmination of her phone call to Sara call might have a logical explanation.

"Why don't you phone from our landline as soon as we

get home? You can use the excuse that your cell reception broke up, and you couldn't hear everything she said. After all, maybe she's imagining you hung up on *her* rather than vice versa."

Belle considered the suggestion, wrapping her arms around herself as if the cold were bothering her instead of her troubled thoughts. "I don't think that's the case, Rosco. Sara was really, really cranky. But I'll give it a try." She sighed again. "And that was odd how Martha intuited the problem, wasn't it?"

"She was talking about her father, Belle," was the gentle answer. "You know Sara's not in the same boat."

"I know. But the two cases struck me as being painfully alike—"

"Except that Sara Briephs isn't losing her marbles."

"Mr. Sensitive."

"Okay, she's not undergoing *memory-loss issues.* Is that better?" Rosco swerved to avoid another darting critter—this one had the bushy tail of a fox—and when it gained the safety of the underbrush bordering the lane it turned red and baleful eyes on the passing car. "No problems with foxes streaking by us, are there? No Celtic myths or Norse legends?"

Belle shook her head, and Rosco continued. "But we have to bear in mind Sara's age, and that she took a serious tumble. She may not be firing on all cylinders as a result, albeit a temporary condition. She has been given pain medication, remember."

"Which is all the more reason to worry about Dawn Davis's potential ploys."

"The cunning vixen, as it were." Rosco chuckled briefly.

"You're not allowed to speak for the rest of the ride home," Belle told him, although she was smiling as she spoke.

"Not even to remark about *playing possum* if we happen to pass one of them scurrying into the weeds?"

"Absolutely not."

"Kit and Gab are going to be awfully disappointed," Rosco laughed.

"They're exhausted and asleep. And besides, all they hear when we're yakking is blah . . . blah . . . blah . . . walk . . . blah . . . blah . . . treat."

"I wouldn't be too sure. Remember they live in an erudite household." Then he patted his wife's leg again. "Don't worry, Belle. Sara's a smart lady. No one has ever pulled the wool over her eyes, and no one ever will."

"You're getting dangerously close to the forbidden *critter* terrain, buddy."

"I didn't say anything about wolves in sheep's clothing, did I?"

"Just stop right there." But she couldn't help smiling.

Returned to their cozy abode, however, Belle's concerns about her friend increased when she called White Caps and was informed by Emma that "Mrs. Briephs has already retired for the evening."

"But it's only seven, Emma," Belle asserted while the response was an implacable, or so it seemed, "Madam has been feeling poorly. Possibly you could try again tomorrow?"

Frustrated and unhappy, Belle hung up and turned to Rosco. "Emma's lying; I'm sure she is. I'll bet Sara's right there in the room and refusing to speak to me."

"You don't know that—"

"Yes, I do!" Then Belle did something she seldom allowed herself to do; she began to cry.

Concerned but not altogether surprised by his wife's reaction, Rosco put his arms around her. "Sara's an old lady," he said gently. "No matter how much she dislikes admitting the fact. As I said before—and as Martha also suggested— maybe that spill did more than damage Sara's knee. Maybe it genuinely scared her, gave her a frightening glimpse of her own mortality. It makes sense that she's emotionally as well as physically shaken. And it also seems logical that she could have a delayed reaction . . . and even that her anger over her own failings could find a scapegoat in you."

But Belle was not to be consoled. "That awful Dawn Davis!" she railed. "This is all her fault!"

Rosco continued to hold his wife while the sleepy dogs roused themselves from their torpor and ambled close to lend their own furry support. Belle felt their two wet noses nudging her. "Two . . ." she mumbled. "Two . . . two—" Her words abruptly ceased, and she stood straighter until her eyes looked into Rosco's face. "When I spoke with Sara, she insisted *her* experience of Dawn and the allegations against her were '*two* very different things.' That was the phrase she used." Belle reached into her pocket to retrieve a tissue, then blew her nose and frowned in concentration. "What if—just *if*—Sara's Dawn Davis isn't the same person as Walter Gudgeon's Dawn Davis? What if they're two different *people,* rather than two different *things*!"

Rosco started to reply, but Belle stopped him. "Which means we could be dealing with a case of identity theft . . . More than that; personality theft."

"Whoa . . . whoa . . . That seems pretty far-fetched—"

"But it's possible, isn't it?"

"Well, sure, yeah, I guess. *Anything's* possible. The Bay Area could have a snow-free winter, for instance, or our health insurance premiums could be cut in half; gas prices could tumble to fifty cents per gallon—"

But Belle paid no attention to the facetious tone. "What if another woman met Dawn, *Sara's* Dawn, that is . . . then befriended her, heard the story about the abusive boyfriend who'd landed her in the emergency room, and the resulting need for surgery, as well as the genuine date of the hospital stay, et cetera. Then this phony Dawn sets her greedy sights on Mr. Gudgeon and invents a far more expensive procedure to con him out of a quarter of a million dollars . . . She doesn't even have to look like the original woman, because Gudgeon has never met her. All he's asked to do is hand over the dough and then drive the bogus Ms. Davis to the hospital on the right day."

"That doesn't fly; both Gudgeon and Bownes described Dawn the same way. I had no trouble recognizing her."

"Okay, okay, so our fake does some makeup work. Descriptions are very general, they aren't conclusive like photographs or face-to-face meetings."

"Belle, I know how much you love Sara, and that you're incredibly loyal; but just because she believes this woman is innocent doesn't make it so."

"Hear me out, Rosco. I know this sounds crazy. But if it's true, it's an amazing con . . . because it means that our phony Ms. Davis had two marks: Walter Gudgeon and the real Dawn, and worked it all out brilliantly."

"Was Bownes in on the scam?" was the skeptical reply. "I grant that he's no sweetheart, but a con artist? I'm not sure."

Belle ignored her husband's dubious tone, although she considered the idea, and then shook her head. "I doubt it . . . a surgeon who's part of a prestigious practice. Besides, what would his motive be? Cash? No, these guys make a bundle anyway." Then her gray eyes opened wide, growing charcoal dark in her excitement. "But our con artist would have to be someone who either worked at the hospital or in the orthopods' office—"

"Or had a snitch on the inside."

"Now you're with me—"

"If Dawn isn't, in fact, *Dawn*."

"Right."

"Let me call Gudgeon. Time for a little Dawn Patrol."

CHAPTER

25

Nine A.M. on a Sunday morning isn't an hour most folks choose to resupply their home offices, or have important paperwork copied, or order business cards, or hunt for a new desk lamp or ergonomic chair, but Papyrus had a small line waiting for the doors to unlock when Rosco and Belle drove into the parking lot. The vehicle they'd picked for this excursion was Belle's gray sedan. It looked as bland and unremarkable as the office superstore's facade, as the new shopping mall across the street, or the interstate highway that separated the two mega "retail parks." The term was one Belle might have commented upon if she and Rosco weren't engaged in this mission. "Retail park," she would have huffed. "There's a modern-day oxymoron if I've ever heard one. Who dreamed up a loopy title like that? Commerce doesn't occur in grassy knolls and bosky glens."

As it was, she said nothing; instead, she adjusted the

brown wig and scholarly tortoise-shell glasses she'd donned in order to mask her identity. Since a byline photo always appeared in the *Crier* with her puzzles, she didn't want to take any chances that Dawn might recognize her and connect her to Rosco. In a matter of moments, Papyrus's door was unlocked by the manager. The couple watched the customers begin filing inside and sat tight, waiting for Walter Gudgeon to appear.

When his navy blue Lincoln Town Car arrived ten minutes later, Rosco and Belle hurried across the macadam to speak with him before he had a chance to exit his car.

"What's all this?" was Gudgeon's irascible question. "I thought you and I were going in there on our own, Polycrates. You didn't mention bringing a woman."

"My junior assistant, Lexi," Rosco told him with a slight but firm smile. "She works undercover for the agency. Ms. Davis will recognize me the minute you and I approach her. That's why I thought it better if Lex here accompanies you."

Gudgeon fidgeted. "I don't like this . . ." he admitted in a dull half-whisper. "It seems like harassment. I'd rather just let the kid have the damn dough." He stared through his windshield at Papyrus's uninspired shopfront. "She has to work in a place like this, and on a Sunday morning? Maybe it's better she just holds on to the money. Besides, like I told you, Polycrates, I want this mess kept on the Q.T. My kids would—"

"Lexi's discreet," Rosco interrupted as he opened the door for Gudgeon and watched him step out. "I'll follow you as far as the entrance. In case Dawn recognizes you and things turn ugly, Lex and I have wireless communication. I can be with you in a second."

Gudgeon flinched and seemed about to retreat to his car,

but Belle, a.k.a. Lexi or Lex, soothed him with a warm, encouraging smile. "Mr. Polycrates and I have reason to believe this may not be the same woman who conned you, sir; that we may, in fact, be looking at a case of identity theft, and a seriously criminal confidence game that goes beyond your exposure to it." Then she added a quiet, "Either way, if this is the Ms. Davis you tried to help, we're still concerned she may be attempting to work the ruse a second time."

Gudgeon heaved a reluctant sigh, but allowed himself to follow Belle. Rosco waited until they reached Papyrus's entrance before trailing behind.

The harried young woman working the Xerox machines matched Gudgeon's description to a tee. Belle strode toward the copy center desk, pushing her way past a number of clamoring patrons—all of whom needed their jobs done ASAP and all of whom were impatient and shrill. "Miss!" they shouted, "Miss! I just need a . . ." The person who called herself Dawn Davis twirled around like a crooked top, tearing open reams of neon-bright paper, matching a photographic reproduction to the black-and-white original, and unjamming a recalcitrant machine while an irate voice screamed, "That better not be my only copy you left crumpled up in there! That's an important legal document."

Belle propelled Gudgeon into the shouting throng, but he kept his eyes on the floor. "Is that her?" Belle prompted in a sotto voce tone as she positioned herself with her back to Dawn so that Gudgeon could look over her shoulder. He finally glanced up, staring goggle-eyed at the woman in the center of the copy meltdown.

"Sir? We need you to make a positive I.D. Whether you

choose to pursue this or not, we need to be certain we're on the right track." Belle again whispered.

"No," he murmured.

An expression Belle interpreted as utter confusion now covered his face.

"I . . . It's not . . . It's not her," he added. "I'm sure of it."

At that point, Dawn Davis caught sight of them. "What do you need? If it's not photocopying, please go to the information desk for assistance." The tone was both brusque and weary. In the midst of a busy morning, she had no time for confused customers taking up space.

"Mr. Gudgeon?" Belle pressed. "Can you positively state that this woman is *not* the Dawn Davis to whom you——?"

"I'm Dawn," was the curt interruption. "What is it you want?" She instinctively glanced at her name tag, which only read *Dawn*. "How do you know my last name?"

Walt Gudgeon shook his head. "But you're not the same young woman who——"

"Who what?" Dawn demanded.

Belle turned to face her. "Sorry, we have a friend named Dawn Davis . . . Just a coincidence."

"Look, folks, I don't want to be rude, but I've got work piling up here. I don't know what you two want." She paused for a second, studying them. "I'm guessing you're not goons sent by the landlord. Ditto social services. My credit card's paid up. The same for that heap of rusting metal the car dealer fobbed off on me." Then Dawn leaned hard against the counter, oblivious to the howls for service surrounding her. "So state your business, or get in line with whatever copy order you've got. And if you're looking for another lady named Davis, just move along, because it ain't me."

Noting her aggressive stance, and suspecting that the cat was out of the bag, Rosco quit his hiding place and came forward; while Dawn, at the same moment, spotted him. Her eyes narrowed, and she glared at Gudgeon and Belle. "What is this, pops?" she snarled at Gudgeon. "Are you in cahoots with this loony tune? I already warned him not to annoy me."

At that, Gudgeon spun away and began striding briskly toward the exit. Belle and Rosco were a step behind him, and Dawn's voice, calling loudly for the manager, followed a second later.

"It's not her," Gudgeon swore under his breath. "I'm going home. I never should have agreed to this ridiculous scheme. We did the electrical work on this building. There's bound to be someone in here who'll recognize me, and if my son . . ." He tore through the door and out into the parking lot, then turned on Rosco and Belle. "I want you to drop this investigation, Polycrates. Pretend you never met me. I don't know where you dug up that woman in there, but as far as being a private investigator, I find you seriously lacking. And don't waste any postage sending me a bill."

"Her name is Dawn Davis," was Rosco deliberate reply. "She had legitimate surgery for a damaged rotator cuff on September sixth, the same day you took your Dawn to the hospital for a kidney transplant."

"Well, she's not the young woman I know." Gudgeon yanked open his car door.

"Does she at least resemble the person to whom you gave money?" Belle asked in her best "good cop" attitude.

"Hair and eyes are the same," was the truculent response as Gudgeon climbed into his car. "And probably height and weight, too. Yeah, and age, I guess." Then he turned the key in the ignition. "But that wasn't Dawn. It's not her face, and I'm insisting you get off this case," were his parting words before he drove away.

Belle and Rosco watched the car speed off. "Actually, he can't order me to abandon the investigation because he never paid me a nickel. I didn't even get an advance from the guy," Rosco observed after a moment.

Belle nodded although it was clear that her thoughts weren't on her husband's missing fees. "You know what's bothering me about this? Other than the potential stolen identity problem, I mean . . . it's a Dr. Jekyll and Mr. Hyde sensation I'm getting about this Davis woman. It's almost as if she's two people herself, and then the counterfeit who duped Gudgeon is a third. Sara swears up and down that Dawn's gentle and sweet, but that hasn't been your experience—or mine."

Rosco didn't speak for a moment. "You realize that we're both accepting the fact that Walter Gudgeon was telling us the truth about the woman in Papyrus not being the person he helped?"

"Right, but it's a two-way street, Rosco. Dawn didn't recognize him either."

"These con people can be very slick."

Belle cocked her head and looked at her husband. "And your point is?"

"Like I said, he could be lying."

"But why would he do that?"

"Blackmail? Fear of being exposed for being a foolish guy who was conned by a pretty girl? Which would make the scene we just witnessed seem a heck of a lot more plausible. Gudgeon had cold feet before we went in there, remember? And Dawn played her part perfectly."

Belle squinted in concentration. "He definitely didn't want to look at her. I had to urge him to do so, and his reaction was closer to that of a kid caught stealing candy than a grown man confronting a woman who resembles someone he has more than a passing acquaintance with."

"And then there's the darker possibility that Gudgeon wanted to find Dawn because he plans to do her harm, either in retribution or for some even more sinister motive. We actually only have his word that he really gave her the $250,000. In other words, it's possible that Dawn Davis isn't the baddie in this; Gudgeon is. Either way, if we walk back in there, she'll deny ever receiving the money, no matter what the truth is."

Belle released a long and frustrated breath. "If you're right, then we're back to square one. And Sara's still in danger . . . Any suggestions, *Mister* Polycrates?"

Rosco remained silent for another moment. "Maybe I need to explain the situation to Sara—"

"As opposed to your *junior* assistant?" was the needling response, but the feeling was more hurt than teasing.

Rosco's tone when he answered was tender. "Sara's relationship with you began on rocky ground, remember—?"

"That's because she thought you were such a cute, young hunk," Belle shot back. "And I was just an interfering word maven as well as a rival to her son in the crossword-puzzle wars."

"I'm simply suggesting that you two may need to cool off for a bit. You're incredibly close to Sara—as she is to you. Maybe your relationship is verging on a mother-daughter scenario, which in the Polycrates family can spell F-I-R-E-W-O-R-K-S. And I know from experience that those conflagrations can require—"

"A guy to put out the flames?" Belle asked.

"Let's just say, a disinterested party is helpful to have on hand. And lots of water."

Belle sighed anew. "Perhaps you're right. Besides, women her age were raised to accept the fact that men called the shots. Maybe you can persuade her that Dawn Davis isn't the guileless person she seems."

"All I can do is try."

"And apply a bit of the Polycrates charm," Belle added with a small smile.

"The good thing is, the pressure is now on Dawn. If she's guilty, she bolts, and we never see hide nor hair of her again. If she's not the person who conned Gudgeon, she'll show up at the Avon-Care center on Tuesday for her therapy."

"Good point . . . I like the way you think."

He put his arm around her waist. "Anything else?"

"I'll let you know." They began to walk to her car, and she added, "I meant to ask you, what was with the name Lexi?"

"I had to call you something, didn't I?"

"And that was what you chose on the spur of the moment? Lex? You've been reading too many Batman comic books."

"It's from *lexicographomaniacal*, your 'crazy about cross-words' word. I thought you'd like it."

"Oh," was Belle crestfallen reply, "I was actually hoping your explanation would be that it rhymed with sexy."

"Huh, I wish I'd thought of that . . . I guess it's too late to change my answer, isn't it?"

"What do you think?"

"If I answered yes, would I be correct?"

"One hundred percent, Mr. Disinterested-Party."

CHAPTER

26

The kitchen at Tulip House was a galley-type affair, seven feet long with beige countertops and matching cabinets on either side of a central walkway floored with ceramic tiles—a utilitarian work space that perfectly suited Jack Curry. Although he was a big man, he found the confined area much to his liking. Probably it was the horse trainer in him that enjoyed the total control he exerted over the room; nothing was more than a short step or an arm's length away: stove, dishwasher, fridge, microwave, pots and pans, mixing bowls, knives, cutting board, sink; and he planned his meals as if arranging hurdles for a show, intermingling simpler tasks with those that required more concentration as though he were piquing a horse's interest and enthusiasm.

At the moment he heard the knock on his front door, Jack was in the process of using a new chef's knife to dice a sweet green pepper destined for the western omelette he'd planned for dinner. Within easy reach were an onion, a late-season tomato, and chunk of yellow Vermont cheese, all of which would soon fall to the blade.

"Come on in," he shouted. "The door's unlocked."

He returned to his work and looked up only when his visitor's form appeared in the kitchen doorway. He shook his head slowly and gave a disapproving glance. "Not a good idea, *my partner in crime*. If we're seen together alone too often, people might begin to talk."

"As in, 'What would the neighbors say?' Is that it?"

Jack didn't bother to respond; instead, he pushed aside the pepper and began to deftly peel the tomato.

"It's dark. No one saw me."

"Quite the stealthy critter, aren't you?" He glanced at his visitor's hands. "What's with the gloves? Playing doctor tonight, are we?"

His unexpected guest also looked down at the gloves. "Blisters. They're killing me. I guess I've been working too hard—"

"Blisters from overwork, there's a joke. I didn't think you knew what the phrase meant." He gave a snide laugh and waved the tip of the knife in the air. "Come on over here. Let me show you how to make an omelette, Jack Curry style." With his free hand, he reached up and lowered the window shade, while his guest walked over and leaned on the counter next to the stove.

"That's the knife I gave you for your birthday . . ." The tone was suddenly wistful.

"Yep. It's a beauty," Jack replied. "And you know something? You're the only one who remembered the big day."

"The only one?"

"Surprising, ain't it? Hell of a world we live in when *family* doesn't care for its own."

The response to this was an abrupt, "We've got to talk, Jack."

He shrugged. "So, talk. Who do you want to be? Cleopatra? Ghengis Khan? Jack the Ripper . . . ? No, sorry. I forgot. That part's always reserved for me."

"Can that stuff, alright? Last night I woke up at three in the morning. I could see that damn puzzle in my head clear as day. And you know what, Jack? I didn't like what I saw."

His casual, "Which one?" had a disingenuous tone. He returned his concentration to the cutting board.

"Don't get cute. It doesn't become you."

"Okay, so fine, we don't make any more word games. You told me the last one was the end for you, anyway. So be it."

"It's a little late for that, Jacko. The cat's out of the bag— as you well know. Did you think I was too stupid to discover what you laid out in those dumb black and white squares? You don't think I noticed that you were straddling both sides of the fence?"

"I don't know what you're talking about. You helped make the puzzles, right? You drew 'em out with your own fingers."

"Don't double-cross me, Jack. I know a lot more than you think I do."

"Goody for you."

"Like who killed Ryan, for one thing."

Jack's response to this statement was to open the refrigerator door. There was no indication he'd heard a word that was said. "I know there's cilantro in here somewhere," he muttered to himself. "Nothing better than fresh cilantro for a nice, fresh tang . . . found it . . . good . . . Well, so, enlighten me. Who killed the lovely Ryan? Was it you? Should I be shaking in my boots?"

"Is that part of your plan? To set me up as her murderer? You'd be better off killing me, too—"

Jack reached out and pulled his guest so close their faces nearly touched. "If you don't know what you're talking about, you'd be well advised to keep your mouth shut."

"I saw you, Jack. I was there."

"Saw me? Saw me what?"

"Let me go. I can't breathe—"

"I thought that was how you liked it."

"Well, I don't anymore."

Curry released his grip; the gesture was both defiant and all-powerful. " 'Don't hurt me, Jacko. I don't like it anymore,' " he mimicked as he returned to his task, but his guest's hurried words ignored the insult.

"Sunday night. I saw you slip out the back door of the Big House. It didn't take a brain trust to put two and two together the next morning when Ryan turned up dead."

Jack placed the knife on the cutting board. "You're suggesting I *killed* Ryan? Is that it?"

"I'm not *suggesting* anything. I know you did. But I don't care. She's gone, and we're all happier because of it. But you'd better not buck me, or I'll go to that Lever jerk with everything I know."

Jack laughed. It was a hearty, self-satisfied sound. "You're crazy. You've got no proof. It's your word against mine, and we all know how much Pop C. admires me. Besides, if you saw me leave—or *think* you saw me leave—that places you at the murder scene, too, doesn't it?"

"I was outside."

"So you say. And you just admitted to being there—which I don't."

"You're as low as they come—"

"Two peas out of the same pod, *Jessie* with an *ie.*" He slid the pepper into a frying pan and turned to the cilantro, holding it under running water while he grabbed a fistful of paper towel to dry it. "So, you figured out that puzzle, huh? Good for you. Very bright. But, you see, I've been busy, too. Doing some solo work. Working on a little *insurance policy* in the form of another couple of crosswords—"

"What do you mean 'insurance policy'?"

"That's for me to know and you to find out. It's amazing how similar our handwriting is, especially our printing. Have you noticed that? That'll keep Ms. Graham guessing when she sees my latest creation. But I'm an easy-goin' guy: I'll give you a helpful hint about what I've been up to: The nice people at the post office are involved."

The response to this was a snarling, "Well, if that Graham woman figures out what you wrote in that other puzzle, I'm going straight to the cops with everything I know about your involvement."

"Oh, I sincerely doubt that. Besides, like I said, if you turn me in, you might as well be jumping straight into this frying pan here. And I'll throw in the olive oil free of charge." Jack grabbed the onion, cut it in half, then nicked the tip of his finger as he began dicing. He emitted a crude curse, followed by a tight-lipped, "Damn, that smarts. New knives, they're like horses and women: ya gotta break 'em in." He stuck his finger into his mouth and licked at the drop of blood that had formed on the end. "Hand me a bandage, will you? There's some in that top drawer there."

His visitor pulled the box of bandages from the drawer and tossed it to him. "Where'd you learn how to chop onions anyway? You do it like a scared old lady. Here, give me that knife. I'll show you why I bought it for you."

"So it's kiss and make up? We're back to Bonnie and Clyde again? Boy, you sure do like bein' unpredictable."

"This time I'll be Clyde."

"Gonna get kinky, are we? Well, take off your gloves. How clean are they?"

"They're clean. I don't want to get onion juice in my blisters. It'll sting like crazy. Do you want me to dice up that thing for you or not?"

"Does this mean you're sticking around for supper? That would surely get certain people talking, wouldn't it?" He chuckled, handed over the knife and proceeded to open the bandage and fold it over his fingertip. He then opened a second bandage to hold the first in place. Another laugh escaped from his lips. "It's a good thing I trust you. All of a sudden that knife looks awfully big in your hands."

"Never trust anyone, Bonnie," was the terse reply as the knife was plunged through Curry's ribcage and into his heart.

Jack Curry only had time to create a surprised and quizzical glance before he sank in a heap onto the ceramic floor. His killer regarded the bulky, inert form for a second, then stepped over it in order to rinse the blood from the gloves and knife before walking into the living room and dropping the blade on the floor. There, Clyde stood for a long moment, pondering what the dead man had meant by "insurance policy." Opting not to take any chances, Clyde began a search of Tulip House in earnest. But it only lasted for a few minutes, because a knock at the door and another voice calling Curry's name brought the pursuit to an immediate halt. At that point nothing had been found.

Across

1. Tempe campus; abbr.
4. Existed
7. That guy's
10. Question
13. Shadow
14. Malady
16. Middle grade
17. M for M thought, part 1
19. Jerry Lewis link?
20. ___ Na-Na
21. Taxi
22. Gravy problem
23. M for M thought, part 3
27. Marshal of Napoleon, and family
29. Exist
30. Calif. neighbor
31. Turkeys
35. Storage box
36. Music man, Coward
39. Following
40. ___ de Pascua
42. Vitamin jar letters
43. Singer, Turner
44. M for M thought, part 4
49. 7-Across, in Paris
50. Morning drop
51. Donkeys
53. Salty
55. M for M thought, part 5
58. Buck tail?
59. Turf
62. June honorees
64. Scooted
65. M for M thought, part 6
69. Stare at
70. California road
71. Maker of 68-Down
72. NASDAQ competitor
73. Explosive letters
74. Comedian, Louis
75. Absolutely

Down

1. "Much ___ About Nothing"
2. Scatter seed
3. Sound of disgust
4. M for M thought, part 2
5. Wine label
6. Hearst grp.
7. Bodybuilder
8. Port ___, TX
9. Tax form info
10. Watchdog agcy.
11. Appear
12. Hold on to
15. Manhattan; abbr.
18. Bat wood
22. Letters on a Lucky pack
23. Rote
24. Notre Dame
25. ___ Park, CA
26. Portuguese city
28. Cheer
32. Elevator company
33. Hawaiian bird
34. Spanish women; abbr.
37. Author, Millay
38. Drops back
41. Sound track
45. Mil. rank
46. 70-Across; abbr.
47. Inner; comb.
48. Author, Deighton
52. Norms; abbr.
53. Chatter from 51-Across
54. Actress, Blakely
56. "The ___ Ape"
57. Singer, Fisher
58. Space

MEASURE FOR MEASURE

59. Editor's mark
60. Be in debt
61. Time for 50-Across
63. Tennis segments

65. Many times, for M for M penner
66. Coffeepot
67. Singer, Charles
68. Coloring agent

CHAPTER

27

"I'll tell ya, they surely do like their puncture wounds up there at Wenstarin Farms," Lieutenant Lever observed with his customarily dry delivery. "It doesn't make life easy for their cleaning woman." He leaned back in his battered swivel chair as he spoke and would have hoisted his big feet onto his desktop if it weren't for Belle's presence. Abe and Rosco, who were also in the homicide detective's office, shared a look. *The next thing you know,* the glance said, *Lever's going to push aside his overfull ashtray and pretend lighting up never entered his mind.*

"At least this victim only got punched once," Al continued with a grumbling sigh. "I must say Curry looked pretty peaceful lying there. Surprised, of course, and not real happy that someone had taken a major poke at him with a kitchen knife . . ." Lever moved the ashtray an inch, then slid it back to its original spot as though he were pondering a chess move. Behind the closed door to his office, the station house was humming with the noise of early morning and the start of a new day trying to safeguard the citizens of Newcastle—which made the almost chilly stillness of Al Lever's office that much more noticeable.

"Of course, from my point of view," he continued, "the guy was supremely lucky he couldn't hear the hysterics going on around him after his untimely demise: Fiona screeching that Heather had murdered the love of her life out of jealousy; then Heather belting her big sis; hubby Michael getting in a huge 'I sincerely hope you weren't cheating on me' lather; Dad trying to intervene and getting cocked in the head by both his loving daughters—accidentally it would have seemed, although Dr. Freud might have decided otherwise. And last but not least, Chip's girlfriend, Angel, fainting dead away the second she arrived on the scene." Al fiddled with his ashtray once again and shook his head.

"If that's what having tons of moolah does for 'ya, I sure don't want it. Give me the grief-stricken next of kin any time—unless, of course, that sad sack is the murderer. Anyway, besides the crossword that turned up, the reason I wanted our little pow-wow is this: I've got our Miss Heather locked up down in the hole, while the DA works up a murder-one charge, but the situation just seems too pat for me. Something else is in the air, and I can't put my finger on it." Lever paused briefly to gaze longingly at the mangled butts lying heaped in front of him, and Belle took advantage of the intervening silence.

"And where did you find the crossword, Al?" She was seated at the far end of the room, bent over a copy of the puzzle that had been retrieved from the crime scene.

It was Jones who answered. "Curry had it on him. It was folded in eighths in the rear left-hand pocket of his jeans— hanky-size. The place was torn apart, so consensus is that Heather was searching the house when she was interrupted by her husband. Was she looking for the puzzle? Who knows. But she was ticked off big-time; and that's how we pieced together the scenario for the DA. However, I'm with Al; something's fishy out there."

"Has Heather admitted to the charge?" Rosco asked.

"She ain't admittin' to nothin'," Lever said. "As soon as all fingers were pointed in her direction, the call went out to the family lawyer. She hasn't made a peep since. The attorney's on his way down from Boston now. Like we don't have enough of them in Newcastle?"

Abe stood, positioned himself behind Belle and looked over her shoulder. "So, what's the puzzle telling us? Anything?"

"I'm getting there," Belle told him as she went back to work. "One thing I can surmise is that the constructor is a brainy individual. The step-quote's from Shakespeare, and it's cleverly worked into the scheme."

"Or *was* 'brainy,'" Rosco added, "if Curry created it."

"Which we can't automatically assume, Poly-crates," Lever interjected. "Even if his fingerprints are the only ones we I.D. on the paper, the thing could still be a plant, or it could have been handed to him earlier in the day. Heather could have even transferred his prints, then hidden the crossword on him after she knifed him—"

"*If* she's the guilty party," Abe interrupted. "We'd love to believe that; it sure would make life simple, but the woman swore up and down that she *found* Curry already dead, the knife on the floor, and the house half ransacked—"

"While Palamountain insisted he discovered his wife alone with the body." Al laughed. The sound was more like a bark. "Real loving duo, those two. Michael phones us, fingers his missus, summons the rest of the charming clan, then watches the fireworks explode while she gets the tender-loving-handcuff treatment and is stuffed into the back of a patrol car and genteelly 'escorted' off to my jail." Lever shook his head. The chair creaked under his weight, while Rosco, in his own equally nicked and timeworn metal chair, hunched forward.

"Okay," he said at length. "Give me the scene again: Fiona's railing at her sister and accusing her of having an affair with Curry—which causes Heather to take a whack at her?"

"The only word Fiona used was *jealousy*, Poly-crates. I won't venture a guess as to what she meant by that, but Palamountain apparently assumed *affair* is what his sis-in-law was referring to, because that's when he joined in the shouting match."

"But if Heather and Curry were romantically involved, why would she kill him?" Rosco continued. "The husband would have the stronger motive."

"There's the rub," Al mumbled.

"And who's to say Palamountain won't prove to be our guilty party?" Abe tossed in. "Just because he claims he found his wife with the knife in her hand doesn't mean she'll wind up being guilty of murder one. It won't be the first time NPD nabbed the wrong person."

"And what about Orlando and Kelly?" Rosco asked. "Did they show up at Tulip House, as well?"

"No, but I had one of my officers bring them up. They didn't have much to say. I think they were in a state of shock."

Belle glanced up at this point. "And Angel fainted when she and Chip appeared at the scene?"

"Yup," Al said. "Dropped like a stone. Her boyfriend didn't even have time to catch her. Of course, he seemed half-crocked at the time. Why do you ask?"

"ᴀɴɢᴇʟ is in this puzzle," was Belle's quiet reply. "And ᴄʜɪᴘ was in an earlier one I received. That crossword was well executed and symmetrical; but this one isn't, nor was the one that was faxed to me at home the day before Ryan Collins was found dead. They were all constructed by the same person . . . or so I assume, as the handwriting seems to match. Or at least it's very close. Do you have any samples of Curry's?"

"My team is working on that," Abe answered. "Mr. Collins has promised to get me some of Jack's endorsed paychecks, so I can make a comparison. But I'm not completely convinced that the handwriting on this puzzle matches the other two. And for a *brainy* wordsmith, Curry doesn't seem to have put much else down on paper."

"But these clues are printed," she said. "Can you still make a match from a signature?"

Jones gave her one of his patented smiles. "I can do anything, my dear." Then after a slight pause he added, "But you're right; because everything's printed, it makes the job a little tougher. Collins said that Curry might have drawn up some barn invoices, which would be printed."

Belle returned his smile then tilted her head and stared at the completed puzzle. She read the step-quote aloud. "ᴏ, ᴡʜᴀᴛ ᴍᴀʏ ᴍᴀɴ ᴡɪᴛʜɪɴ ʜɪᴍ ʜɪᴅᴇ ᴛʜᴏᴜɢʜ ᴀɴɢᴇʟ ᴏɴ

THE OUTWARD SIDE. . . . Pretty creepy when found on a corpse, wouldn't you say?" She looked at Rosco. "The word DAWN is here, too."

Rosco nodded, but he didn't look happy about the revelation. "*Dawn* and *Angel* aren't unusual words. But if we're looking for a bogus Dawn in the Gudgeon case, Angel certainly fits the bill size-wise. Give her a wig and some high heels . . . Then again, the appearance of both names could be coincidental."

"I thought you told me that the boys in blue didn't believe in coincidence when it came to criminal investigations," was her amused reply.

"We don't," Al blustered. "On the other hand—"

"On the other hand," Belle continued in the same easy tone, "when a dead man is discovered with a crossword stuffed in his pocket, it's not a bad idea to pick apart each solution and clue. Of course," she added, "this puzzle can't possibly refer to Curry's murder."

"How do you figure that?" Al asked her. "The simple fact that it was found on his body is good enough for me."

"But if he were the constructor, that would mean he knew who was going to kill him—which makes no sense. And I'm also wondering why would he have permitted a relatively small woman like Angel to stick a knife in his chest—if, in fact, she's the guilty party? With no signs of struggle anywhere? That's what you said, Al, isn't it? Even Heather would have had a difficult time attacking someone Curry's size."

Abe raised his hands and shook his head. "Let's get away from worrying about how big or small our killer is. This was a straight shot to the heart. The perp was facing Jack. There were no signs of forced entry, which means he recognized the person. They were in the kitchen together, supper was on the way, he had no reason to fear for his life. The knife went in. It was over before Curry knew it. So, no, there was no struggle involved. The way I see it, he was caught totally off guard."

"And let's not forget that this puzzle could be a plant," Al observed. "And that our murderer could be Michael Palamountain . . . who might be purposely trying to stymie the investigation by verbally blaming his wife, whom he knows will be found innocent—and relatively painlessly, too, given daddy's bucks and a fleet of high-end lawyers. So, Michael plants the puzzle and tosses in Angel's name, simply to add to the confusion."

"Also, Palamountain definitely knew that the phone lines at the Dew Drop Inn were still operational. *Someone* had to fax that puzzle to Belle," Rosco said in quiet agreement.

"Yeeeshh," Al groaned. "From where I sit, it looks like a bunch of people have an awful lot to hide—not just Heather."

Additional silence enveloped the foursome with each escaping into their private thoughts. Belle used the time to retrieve the crosswords she'd previously received, pulling them from a file folder and walking across to Al's desk to spread them across the surface. "'Submission,'" she read, "'To Catch a Thief,' and now 'Measure for Measure.' If I'm missing a hidden message, I don't know what it is."

"Unless you've got to *submit* to the *thief* in order *measure* your *catch*," Lever wisecracked while Abe gave a stagy groan.

"Stick with police work, Big Al. You make a better detective than a linguist. Whatever you just said made absolutely no sense."

Belle rearranged the puzzles, then studied them again.

"Okay . . . my initial take on this situation was that the word games referred to the case of arson—which seems pretty obvious: BLAZING SADDLES, and so on. But now I'm wondering if that wasn't just a big curveball, or something to pique my interest, which it ultimately did. We've got DAWN as the answer to 61-Down in 'Measure for Measure,' while WALT, or *Mr. Disney*, appears at 31-Across in 'To Catch a Thief.' So here's my suggestion: I think it's possible, in fact likely, that these crosswords refer to the Dawn Davis con job. That they've been connected to that situation from the start." The three men looked at her; they didn't speak. "And . . . is it possible the fire and Gudgeon's quarter-of-a-million-dollar swindle are somehow intertwined?"

It was Lever who finally spoke. "Okay, Belle, I'll bite. What's the link? And if you can tie together the Curry and Ryan Collins murders, and come up with a guilty party, I'm making you a full-fledged member of the force. I don't care what your lovin' hubby says."

Belle chortled. "Hey, I'm just a cruciverbalist, Al. Like Abe said, you're the cop. You tell me."

CHAPTER

28

The upshot of the Lever, Jones, Belle, and Rosco confab at NPD was the conclusion that two murders at the same location and only a week apart had to be connected. And the fact that the anonymous crosswords might have been created by one of the victims, and that they seemed to bear a link to the Gudgeon situation, meant that one scenario remained out in left field waiting to be resolved: the barn fire. It was for this reason that Rosco decided to clean up the mystery of the stable blaze once and for all by making a return visit to the Collins spread, where he intended to have a second face-to-face with the stonewalling Orlando Polk. This time, Rosco wasn't planning any polite, I'm-your-best-pal-in-the-world approach.

When he braked the Jeep in front of the King Wenstarin Farms main gate, Pete swung it open without delay, simply noting a pragmatic, "You're becoming quite the regular around here, aren't you, Polycrates? Next thing you know, you'll be taking riding lessons." He forced a jovial laugh, but it quickly turned into a pensive frown. "These folks are going through some real hard times. I sure hope you and your police buddies can get it straightened out for them."

"We're working on it, Pete. We're working on it."

Rosco drove up the long lane and parked his Jeep behind one of the horse barns, out of sight of both stable B and Todd Collins's residence. He then walked directly to Polk's apartment and entered without knocking. The barn manager was sitting on his couch watching a midmorning talk show on the TV. When he saw Rosco he reached for the remote, silenced the set, and stood.

Rosco glanced up at the loft area. "Is Kelly here? I need to have a word with you in private."

"No," was the tenuous answer. Orlando appeared both confused and irritated, although his eyes bore a wary watchfulness. He shook his long black ponytail in a poor attempt at indifference. "I took her to the airport early this morning. She's flying back to Louisville."

"So soon?"

"She beamed in with her mother after we came back from Tulip House last night. Her mom was at the hospital. The doctors don't think her father's going to make it through the week."

Rosco eased off his tough-guy routine momentarily. "Oh. Well, I'm sorry hear that. That's not easy."

"We've been expecting it. He's been ill for some time now. Kelly seems ready to handle it—at least, she says she is. But it's still going to be hard. It's a shame I never met the guy. There seems to be no point at this late date with him not able to recognize much . . . And then, of course, there's this whole awful mess with Jack." Polk shook his head. "What did Kelly say the other day? About trouble coming in packs of threes? Well, boy, that sure seems right."

Rosco pointed to the couch. "Why don't you sit back down?" When Orlando did, Rosco continued to speak from his standing position. He folded his arms across his chest in case the barn manager misinterpreted his stance or the reason for his presence. "I came here to get some answers; and I'm sorry that this is a difficult time for you and Kelly, and I'm sorry I'm going to be playing hardball, but I'm not leaving here until you come clean with me about this barn fire. You didn't start it; I know that. So who did?"

Orlando began to protest, but Rosco stopped him.

"Don't. Don't try to make a fool of me. I've been around too long. We've had two murders on this property in the last week. You were in the hospital for the first, but your alibi for last night is weak. You say you were with your wife, but where is she now? How do we know she hasn't just headed for the hills, and you'll be the next one to fly the coop?"

Polk stood, his black eyebrows pinched in rage. "You have no right to come in here and point fingers at Kelly. Go visit her family if you don't believe me. Go to Louisville. Go to that hospital and talk to her. We have nothing to hide."

"Yes, you do," Rosco pressed. "You didn't start that fire. Kelly didn't either, because she was in Kentucky. So who are you protecting, if it's not your wife? If this is a case of arson, you're an accessory to the fact by not divulging the truth. You'll pull just as much time as the perpetrator."

"I don't know," Orlando almost thundered. "I don't know who it was."

"But it wasn't you." Rosco posed this as a statement, not a question, but the answer was a low and stifled:

"No. It wasn't me."

"How could you not know who started the blaze? You admit you were there in the stable when it began. Todd found you there. So, who are you protecting? It makes no sense for you to take the fall for this unless you're saving someone else's hide. So who is it?"

Orlando flopped back into the couch and shook his head. "Why can't you leave well enough alone, Polycrates?"

"Because I can't!" Rosco raised his voice and pointed an accusatory finger. "You were in that tack room with someone else, and that person started the fire—either accidentally or intentionally. Now, who was it?"

The two men remained motionless for a long time, Rosco studying Orlando, and the barn manager glaring accusingly back. Finally, sensing a change in Rosco's mood, Orlando shifted on the couch, slumping forward and staring at the floor. "You have to go," he mumbled. "I have nothing more to say."

"No. No," Rosco said, his lips forming a private smile. "I get it . . . I get it now. You really don't know who started the fire, do you?"

"That's what I've been saying all along."

"But you *are* protecting someone, aren't you? I mean besides yourself?"

Orlando didn't answer, and Rosco pushed ahead.

"Half of that stable still stands. Something tells me that

if I go over there right now and climb up into the hay loft I might just find a cozy little nest built for two. And I don't mean something made by a couple of turtle doves. Am I right?"

The barn manager remained stony faced.

"So when the fire broke out you were having yourself a roll in the hay, as it were, with some secret honey. All this while your wife is back in Louisville looking after her dying father. What a charmer, you are. Of course, you need to take the fall for the fire, rather than have Kelly find out what you were up to."

Polk placed his head in his hands, but still made no reply.

"But you know something, my friend? What you were doing—and with whom—doesn't change a thing. Because if we determine that the blaze was a torch job, you're still an accessory to the fact. Unless, of course, you care to come clean with what you know." Rosco walked toward the door, then turned back. "It doesn't make any difference to me who you were shacked up with, but believe me it's going to come out sooner or later. I gather it was either Fiona or Heather, which obviously compounds your prob—" Rosco stopped himself midword.

Orlando lifted his head and made eye contact with Rosco for the first time in minutes, then he glanced away again. It was clear he knew that the detective had made the necessary leap to the truth. He shook his head, his ponytail swaying in defeat. "It was real stupid. I don't know what I could have been thinking. Kelly probably would have understood, after a while, but not—"

"But not Mr. Collins." Rosco took in a large breath and let the air out slowly. "You were up there in that loft with the boss's wife. Of course, you couldn't blab." He moved over and sat on the couch's armrest. "So Ryan Collins sneaks out the back of the barn and runs up to the Big House just in time to tell Todd she's returning from her evening ride; how very ironic." The barn manager failed to acknowledge the dig, so Rosco added, "And you don't have any idea who was in the tack room?"

Polk shook his head.

"How about the whack on the back of your head? Falling timber? Or did someone come after you? Because if you were intentionally hit and then left to die in the blaze, that's a murder attempt, and it doesn't make for a pretty picture."

"I can't answer that, either. All I can tell you is that something hit me. Hard."

"Well, Ryan Collins's death was no accident, and you're the only person in the world with an ironclad alibi. Do you think your boss had any knowledge of this sordid business between you and his wife?"

"I guess you'd have to ask him that."

CHAPTER

29

Although it wasn't yet noon, Todd Collins was perched at the wet bar in his study, drink in hand, when Rosco knocked on the open door. Orlando Polk's surly comment, "I guess you'd have to ask him," was still fresh in Rosco's mind, and his hurried pace and determined expression reflected the encounter. If the owner of King Wenstarin Farms was surprised at the intrusion, or by the steely look in Rosco's eye, he didn't reveal it; instead, he waved his visitor in, the ice cubes clacking in the crystal rocks glass.

"I don't suppose I can interest you in a libation, Polycrates?" Collins asked, then gazed briefly at the tawny liquid. "For someone who's gotten rich on selling high-end hooch, I'm not much of a drinker—at least I wasn't until now. Just 'shows to go ya' that you *can* teach an old dog new tricks . . ." The words trailed off. "What brings you out here? If you're the bearer of more bad tidings, I'm not sure I want to hear what you've got to say." But before his unexpected guest could answer, Todd continued with a dejected and bitter, "I guess your wife never figured out the name of the farm—the name of the whiskey, too. I thought she would have by now. Oh, we put a picture of some bogus Irish chieftain on the label, but that's part of the inside joke . . ." When Rosco returned a blank stare, Todd added an apologetic, "King Wenstarin is an anagram for Winning Streak. So, your 'Anna Graham' didn't pick up on that, huh? I must say, I'm disappointed. I was absolutely certain she would . . ."

He swirled the whiskey in his hand again and stared into the glass as though expecting to see either angels or demons. "But maybe that's because our family's been on such a *losing* streak recently. Winning would have been a long way from her lexicon." He released a heartfelt sigh, then sank down into one of two leather club chairs that bracketed the fireplace. The hide was a dark, subtly mottled green; contrasted with the flickering orange flames in the hearth, the polished brass of the fender rail and the crisp white paint of the walls, the picture should have been one of affluence and serenity. Instead, it was somber and cheerless.

"Take a seat, Polycrates. I'm not going to bite. What's the problem this time?"

Again, Rosco saw no reason for beating around the bush, but he also had no wish to hit Collins with more bad news if he could help it. "I just came from talking to your barn manager about the stable fire—"

"Don't tell me Orlando's finally figured it out?" Todd grumbled. "Sure he did. Of course, he did. The guy's no dummy . . . I have to admit, I took a certain amount of perverse joy in watching him squirm and fess up to doing something he didn't. But I guess he was bound to learn how the blaze began sooner or later. Heather never was able to keep her mouth shut." When Rosco made no reply, the patriarch's heavy voice continued. "This is not a family that keeps secrets from each other. I'm well aware that Heather started that damn fire, and I also know precisely how—and why. She admitted the whole thing just as soon as the emergency crews left. She felt awful about the situation. Naturally, she would. Anyone would. She sure as hell hadn't planned to instigate that kind of conflagration when she followed my wife to the stable . . ." Collins permitted himself the briefest of pauses before plunging ahead. It was almost as though he'd forgotten Rosco was in the room and was speaking out of his own deep need for confession.

"Heather told me she and Michael had strong suspicions Ryan was sleeping with Orlando—among others. A lot of different men, according to them. So Heather decided to spy on Ryan and catch her redhanded—which is how the whole mess started. Heather was trying to get me down there to confront my wife, discover her in a compromising position. My daughter was the one who was reaching for the damn tack room telephone to call the Big House, not Polk. The rest of the story you've already heard: the booze bottle, the damn space heater; it was an accident waiting to happen. Unfortunately, it was an accident that seems to have been the first in a tragic chain of events. Ironic, isn't it, that a bottle of whiskey could cause such ruin?" Todd paused again. His craggy face was covered in a dark and angry frown.

"What about Orlando's crack on the head? Some folks

would suggest that a jealous husband might have left him there to die?"

Todd shook his head. "No, that's not me; I don't favor the death penalty. I'd rather sit and watch people rot and pay for their sins for the rest of their lives, day in and day out. Death is too easy for some people. I saw how the beam hit Orlando, so did Jack. Don't forget we were the ones who pulled him out."

"Your witness is dead, Mr. Collins."

"That he is; but Orlando's alive . . . I know what you're thinking, Polycrates: 'Why did we let him take the fall for the fire?' Well, let me just say that it was easier than airing all this dirty laundry in public. And like I said, I took some enjoyment in watching him sweat bullets. I think he owes me one, wouldn't you agree? And being blamed for causing an accidental fire isn't necessarily a career-breaker. Not everywhere, at least."

Rosco didn't speak for a second or two. He intuited that expressing any surprise over Collins's admission of Heather's guilt, as well as his prior knowledge of his wife's unfaithfulness, might force the man to clam up. Instead, Rosco ventured a soothing, "Your daughter must love you a good deal, Mr. Collins. Both your daughters."

"Yeah, and I was the dope who tossed them aside. Married a woman who couldn't hold a candle to either of them . . . didn't listen to them saying that Ryan wasn't worthy of my affection. I cut them off, turned my back on them—and Chip, too. Why do us old dogs do stupid things like that? Why do we let pretty young women flatter us into thinking they care? And then why do we ignore our true families, our own flesh and blood, as a result?"

Rosco considered the question. For a weird moment, he almost imagined he was talking to Walter Gudgeon. "Mr. Collins, let me ask you something—"

"Go ahead. It feels good to finally get this stuff off my chest."

"You said your daughters made other attempts to expose your wife—"

"And Chip, too. In their own way, each of my kids tried to tell me she was cheating. Hell, Chip went so far as to call her a tramp, and I slapped him across the face."

"Is it possible that one of them killed her? You know the police love to play the inheritance card. I understand you intended to leave the farm, pretty much everything, to your wife?"

Collins shook his head slowly. "I don't believe they would do that. Not because they're not capable of rage, or keeping their eyes on a buck. My kids are definitely a chip off the old block—no pun intended—and they're damned used to getting their own way, and can be ferocious when they don't. But I believe their concern over me would have prevented them from killing Ryan out of spite. Oh, sure, they wanted to prove her to be the trollop she was and hoped and prayed that I'd toss her out . . . but bashing her head like that, and letting me find the body? No, that's not their style. Ryan would have to do something pretty abhorrent to push them over the top." Collins smiled a weary smile. "And that's saying a lot, because they surely must have hated the woman. But I didn't raise any murderers, Polycrates."

Again, Rosco was silent. He was aware of a clock ticking on the mantelpiece, of the distant whir of a vacuum cleaner moving through the second floor, of a leaf blower working the far end of the garden: all homey and comforting sounds intruding into a space that was far from peaceable. "So you must not believe that Heather killed Jack Curry."

Todd Collins didn't immediately answer. "I've been struggling and struggling with that one. I know Fee went off the deep end last night, accused Heather of all sorts of nasty things . . . but I simply can't see her shacking up with Curry when she knew her sister was about to marry him again . . . let alone murder him."

"Would Curry have cheated on Fiona in that fashion?" Rosco prompted.

"Well, that's another story. I don't hold with speaking ill of the dead, but I don't believe I'm doing so when I say that Jack was a diamond in the rough. He had flaws that no amount of polishing was going to remove. Fee knew that. Hell, she'd been married to the guy once, and she'd also spent a sizable amount of time on the show circuit with him. There's a lot of testosterone flying around out in those pony rings—and, believe me, it's not just the stallions. People who engage in that type of winner-take-all experience need to put their pent-up energy somewhere. And let me tell you, the women trainers and riders are just as wild as the men."

Rosco nodded while Collins continued, "I'm going to miss Jack Curry, I'll tell you that much. I'm going to miss the heck out of him. He was one fine trainer, and a good friend. And he was also the only man who could keep Fiona in line. It was the one good thing Ryan did, insisting I bring him back here, and I never regretted my decision for a minute."

Rosco made a mental note of the fact. "How long ago was that, again? That you rehired him?"

"Shortly after we were married. Ryan thought it would be good for the stable, as well as for Fiona—even though Fee was already hitched to that jackass Whitney Applegate. Of course, I never explained to my daughter that her love life had played a part in my decision. I just said I was damn glad to have Curry back working the Wenstarin horses. And if you have a child who's unhappy with a spouse, a parent has an obligation to shake things up a little, get them back on the right track."

"So your wife was interested in making your daughters happy?"

Collins didn't immediately respond. "I don't know about other occasions, but she was then, yes. And, yes, I also realize people suspected that she and Jack had been an item when they were both kicking around in the smaller southern circuits a few years back. But I hadn't met her then, and I never asked about her history. Call me blind, if you want. One thing I do know: Orlando may have been shagging my wife, but Jack was too loyal to pull a stunt like that. And too grateful that I'd brought him back into the big time. I guess you could say I rescued him. I sure as hell saved him from himself. He'd had money problems and so forth when he and Fee were first hitched, but from what I'd heard he'd finally gotten himself in debt big-time, and was starting to hit the sauce in earnest. But he cleaned himself up before he came back to Wenstarin Farms, and that was good enough for me."

Again, Rosco nodded in thought. "I appreciate your talking to me so candidly, Mr. Collins. And I also realize that this isn't an easy conversation for you to have."

Collins allowed himself another wan smile. "I told you, Polycrates, I'm glad to unburden myself. It's kind of odd, but I haven't had a soul to talk to since Ryan died. Oh, my kids, sure, but . . ." He took a deep breath. "It hasn't been easy knowing how, and why, that damn fire started. And what happened afterwards . . ." Tears choked his voice. He leaned back in his chair and seemed to visibly force himself into self-control again. Then he released a hollow laugh. "I guess this interview means that you're going to help me find my wife's killer. Now that your concerns about arson are re-solved, I mean."

Rosco hedged his response with a noncommittal, "If your son and daughters knew about the situation with your barn manager and your wife, did Kelly know as well?"

Collins thought. His frown deepened. "You're not sug-gesting Kelly killed Ryan, are you?"

"Jealousy's a powerful motive, Mr. Collins." Knowing that the emotion worked both ways, Rosco closely watched Todd's face, hoping the statement would bring on some re-action, but it didn't.

"Little Kelly? Kill Ryan? Why, Ryan was a good three inches taller than Kelly . . ." He shook his head from side to side. "No . . . that's just not possible. Kelly's like a doll. Scurries around here like a tiny mouse. She wouldn't have it in her. Besides, she was thankful as all get-out when my wife hired her. They were more like best buddies than em-ployee and employer."

"Which would only add to a sense of betrayal if she dis-covered her friend was moving in on her husband," Rosco observed.

"I don't buy that. No, you're barking up the wrong tree with Kelly. She doesn't have a mean bone in her body."

Collins drained what was left of his drink, appeared to

consider pouring himself another, then put the glass firmly on a nearby table. "I've got to lay off of this stuff," he muttered, then added a reasoned, "Maybe I can imagine Kelly getting angry with her husband for cheating on her, but never Ryan. Not in a million years. Those women were really close. Of course, Kelly would have a tough time beating up on Orlando. She's too petite, and he's pure muscle. She'd move out if she knew, but I can't see her trying to resort to physical violence."

"But your daughter's not a big woman, and yet she's in custody for killing Jack Curry."

Collins covered his face with his hands. "Oh, my poor Heather . . . I told you I've been wrestling with this . . . I simply can't believe there's any truth to that, either."

Rosco gave him a moment to calm down. "Tell me about Michael Palamountain, Mr. Collins."

He released a long sigh and looked up. "Not much to tell. He's an investment guy. Quiet, reserved—at least, I believed he was until last night." Collins thought for a moment. "But then, those were highly unusual circumstances, and no one was behaving well." He paused again. "Michael handles the farm's financial transactions."

"And you trust him?" The statement was more question than comment.

"I'm a businessman, Polycrates. A fancier of good horseflesh, absolutely, but I couldn't indulge this very, *very* expensive habit if I didn't also run a lucrative corporation—and then try to make the farm into a moneymaker as well. Yes, I trust Michael not to cook the books, if that's what you mean." He let out a small chuckle. "But don't think I'm not looking over his shoulder every minute."

"Palamountain also sent your daughter—his own wife—to jail, sir. It was his word that put her there."

Collins groaned again and again stared at his empty glass.

"Heather insists that she found Curry already dead and his house in disarray," Rosco continued with a little more force. "Michael, on the other hand, claims that he discovered his wife holding the murder weapon, and, I gather, looking pretty darn guilty, having already washed the knife. What kind of a husband would cause his wife to be arrested, Mr. Collins?"

Todd made no response other than to lower his head in thought again.

"Is there a possibility, sir, that Michael Palamountain's convinced she'll be found innocent? That, in fact, he knows who the guilty party is and realizes that a good lawyer can easily get your daughter acquitted—?"

"Wait. Wait up there. You're suggesting Michael killed Jack? Or Ryan? Or even both?" Disbelief echoed through Collins's voice. "He's a money manager and venture capitalist, not a thug. Even if he knew for a fact that his wife was cheating on him, no way would he resort to killing one of the best damn horse trainers in the country!"

"Somebody did, sir. And if you want to be absolutely certain your daughter didn't kill Curry, maybe you need to figure out who else did."

Rosco stood. As Al had said, the situation at King Wenstarin Farms was looking both far too simple and way too complicated—which was what happened when a bunch of people started lying to protect one another. And no matter how disgusted Todd's kids might have been at the introduction of Ryan into the household, the Collinses were still a family; and families, as Rosco knew, could go to desperate measures to save one of their own.

"I'm sorry Belle didn't figure out your anagram for King Wenstarin, Mr. Collins. Truthfully, she wasn't looking for a word game like that, even though you shared the clever names of some of your horses. She's been kind of preoccupied with several peculiar crossword puzzles she received—which, until now, she assumed were connected to the stable fire."

Collins sat up straighter. His cautious eyes grew brighter. "You don't say."

"The name Chip was in one of them, as was that nearby pub, The Horse With No Name."

If Rosco was hoping for a reaction other than a careworn disinterest, Collins didn't provide it. The relaxed face of an experienced businessman or seasoned poker player is all that Rosco observed, and "Crossword puzzles, huh?" was all that Collins said.

"That's right. And the last one had *Angel* in it."

"You mean Chipper's new girlfriend?" He shrugged. "But what does she have to do with anything?"

"Your guess is as good as mine, sir."

Across

1. Rocker's equip.
4. And so on; abbr.
7. Switch positions
10. Guy's date
13. ___ Lanka
14. Gone, in Scotland
15. Army bed
16. Persian Gulf grp.
17. Hoity-toity set
20. Gun grp.
21. Canadian capital
22. ___ about
23. With 47-Across, Sandy Dennis film
26. Slugger, Tony
27. Pyle portrayer
28. Pub offering
29. Hurler, Warren
30. Buddy
33. French salt
36. Architect, Saarinen
37. Confuse
38. Whine
39. Reading and B & O
40. Arab leader
41. Star of 17-Across
42. Green or brown tack-on
43. Yogurt option
44. Sparkle
47. See 23-Across
50. Star of 53-Across
51. Student often
52. Tone or metric lead-in
53. Wanted poster request
58. Help wanted letters
59. Equip
60. Relative
61. Mr. Charles
62. Biochem. prefix
63. Travel aid
64. Disease fighting org.
65. Took in

Down

1. Cigar residue
2. Medical scan; abbr.
3. Oinker
4. Toward the dawn
5. 12 pts., in football
6. Chocolate source
7. Indian or Arctic
8. "Ask ___ . . ."
9. Home for 3-Down
10. USMC NCO
11. Slugger, Hank
12. Study
18. Santa's laugh
19. Wobbly grp.
22. In debt
23. Racing family
24. Pulp product
25. Some ski lifts
26. Day-___
28. Ripen
30. Summer drink
31. MMMI I ÷ II
32. Type
33. ___ drug
34. Namesakes of Ms. Fitzgerald
35. Philippine island
37. Sigh of relief
38. Flag on a lance
40. Bygone flyer; abbr.
41. Japanese neighbors
42. Stopover spot
43. Oxide or acid lead-in
44. Composer, Edvard
45. Popular cleaner
46. Vowel jumble
47. Proof of postage payment

SOCIAL CLIMBER

1	2	3		4	5	6		7	8	9		10	11	12
13				14				15				16		
17			18				19					20		
			21								22			
23	24	25								26				
27									28					
29						30	31	32				33	34	35
36					37						38			
39				40						41				
			42						43					
44	45	46				47	48	49						
50						51								
52				53	54						55	56	57	
58				59				60				61		
62				63				64				65		

48. Slugger, Williams
49. Buddhist king
53. Block
54. Pitcher's stat

55. Retirement acct.
56. Barrel
57. Stare down

CHAPTER

30

Because of the poor cell phone connection Belle couldn't quite determine if the quavering she heard in Bartholomew Kerr's voice was the result of excitement, anticipation, or plain old-fashioned fear. Whatever the cause, his insistence that she drop *everything* she was doing *posthaste* and drive *directly* to the *Crier's* offices possessed more than a touch of panic. His request resembled an order, so she did as he asked. The fact that she was five blocks from the building made it difficult for her to rationalize fabricating any lame excuses.

When she stepped off the elevator on the third floor she was embraced by the same afternoon hysteria that existed on any given day, but since this was a Monday, and not her routine Friday stopover, many employees stood dead in their tracks the moment they spied her. And as she walked down the hallway toward Kerr's corner office her astonished coworkers greeted her with a collection of sarcastic comments like: "Is the world coming to an end?" or, "Now I've seen everything," or, "Is the week over already?" or, "That's not Belle Graham, is it?" while others simply shook their watches questioning whether their timepieces were suffering a communal malfunction. She graced all these antics with a knowing smile then tapped on the frosted-glass panel of Kerr's door.

The door was flung open as if the tiny man had been lying in wait on the other side since the moment she'd agreed to see him.

"Finally," he gushed. "What in blazes took you so long? I feel as though I was about to go into cardiac arrest."

"Seven minutes, Bartholomew. That's how much time has elapsed since you called. What's all the excitement about?"

"Seven minutes? The *Hindenburg* went up in seven seconds!"

She laughed. "The *Crier* building seems to be in one piece."

"Hah! That's a debatable issue, but beside the point. The reason I positively, absolutely needed you here on the QT is because I have received a crossword puzzle, and it's entitled 'Social Climber'!"

"Well, you are the society editor." Belle sat in the chair opposite Kerr's desk as she spoke. "Possibly someone is suggesting a combination of our two sections of the newspaper? Although I think I might have entitled it 'Words in Boldface,' or 'Clues for the Parvenu'... or maybe one of your gossip-loving spies is pulling your leg." She looked at Bartholomew's intent and worried face and forced herself not to smile. "Does the puzzle have a theme, perchance? What are some of the solutions?"

Kerr sighed mightily. "Oh please, dear *Bella*, I have no patience for these word games. This is why I phoned you the second the mail boy tossed the thing on my desk. And I do mean *tossed.* One would think that child believes he's handling Frisbees rather than serious journalistic correspondence."

"So you haven't completed the crossword, then?"

"*Mais, non.* I can only suspect that it has something to do with the horrible situation out at King Wenstarin Farms. Situations in the plural, I should say."

Belle nodded although she had her doubts. The world of "Biz-y-Buzz" was a long way from the homicide division of NPD. "Well, let's have a look at it." This time she did smile, but the expression was indulgent.

Kerr opened the center drawer of his desk as though he expected it to be booby-trapped. With tense fingers he removed a piece of graph paper and walked it over to Belle who perused it, sat bolt upright, and dropped her fatuous grin.

"Well, I have to admit, it does look like the same handwriting as the other three . . ."

"Ah-ha, I thought I was on to something!"

"We'll need to get this copied, Bartholomew. If I'm correct and it's the same constructor who did the others, then it may fall into the category of evidence."

"I anticipated as much, *mia Bella.*" He reached into the drawer again, retrieved a Xerox of the original, and with a smug and seraphic smile handed it to Belle.

She didn't respond; instead, she leaned toward Kerr's jar of pens, grabbed one, and began filling in the grid. When she was almost half finished she said, "Do you have Abe Jones's telephone number at the NPD forensics lab?"

"Oh, please dear girl, I have everyone's phone number."

"Silly me. Of course you do. Abe has the three previous puzzles on file. Could you ask him to fax them over? And while you have him on the line, see if he's authenticated the handwriting of the constructor. The last one was found in Jack Curry's pocket."

"Oooohhh . . . *The Case of the Puzzling Corpse.*"

"There's no evidence he created it, however. And besides, you just received this."

"A plant, then! I amend my offering to *The Case of the Killer Creator.*"

"Do you want me to solve the clues or gab?" Belle chuckled.

"Oh, solve, solve . . . resolve, absolve, dissolve . . . I will turn mum as a mummy. I need to *curry* favor with you, after all, *Bellisima.*"

"You're incorrigible, Bartholomew." Belle laughed again and went back to work. By the time she'd completed the puzzle the fax had arrived with a note reading, *Handwriting as yet unconfirmed. Keep us posted. We're here late today. Surprise. Surprise.*

"Jack Curry . . ." Kerr uttered as he paced the room. "One would not have thought he had the brains required for these lexical leaps, but if he *is* your mystery constructor—or *was*—then I'll be forced to eat my inky words." Bartholomew peered at the puzzle.

"There's a structural problem with this one, too," she said. "But I guess this is no time to nitpick over details."

"What problem?"

Belle pointed at the paper. "Well, you see how the cross-word is broken into three sections . . . and there are no in-terconnecting words that flow from the center section to this part in the upper left, or to lower right? That type of flaw is a big no-no in the puzzle world."

"Perhaps the mistake was done on purpose?"

"Not likely. The other puzzles had problems, as well. But what's interesting is that the constructor dropped the Chip and Angel business favored in the other puzzles and is now focusing on Ryan and Kelly; albeit Robert RYAN and Grace KELLY . . . but the fact that the film titles associated with each actor are DEAD OR ALIVE and HIGH SOCIETY seems more than a simple coincidence." Belle stood and spread the crosswords across Kerr's desk. He positioned himself beside her.

"Well, we know RYAN certainly didn't murder anyone," he said. "Unless she did it from the grave. Which, given her personality, seems entirely possible."

"No, no, Rosco and I believe these cryptics may have nothing to do with King Wenstarin Farms. We think they could be related to another case Rosco's been working on that might have involved Chip Collins and his girlfriend, Angel."

Kerr's ears instinctively perked up. "And what *case* might that be? It's not polite to keep secrets from your close friends, dear one."

"You know I can't tell you about any of Rosco's investi-gations, Bartholomew," Belle said with a smile. "So don't even ask."

"Well, you have all the evidence spread out before me, in

my own office, and on my own desk, I might add. I can hardly see any purpose in keeping me in the dark."

Belle attempted to backtrack by saying, "I'm afraid to disappoint you, but it has nothing to do with the society set."

"Really? Well, if Grace KELLY wasn't HIGH SOCIETY, I don't know who was. And Chip Collins is as social as you're going to get in Newcastle. So let's go, lady, out with it."

Belle scanned the four puzzles quickly; other than the single mention of WALT Disney in the "To Catch a Thief" puzzle, there were no other possible references to Walter Gudgeon.

"Okay," she said, "I'll fill you in on what we've been working on, but I can't mention the name of Rosco's client. Understood?"

"Please, do go on, my dear. And out of respect to that fine man you're married to, I promise not to mention a word of what you say, even if 'Biz-y-Buzz' figures out who's at the center of it all . . . my lips are sealed."

Belle proceeded to tell Kerr the entire Gudgeon story, being extra careful to omit his name. When she'd finished he observed a pragmatic, "Well. There's no fool like an old fool. A terrible tale, but one that occurs more often than you might think—and all across the country." He removed his enormous glasses and wiped them with a linen handkerchief that was as large as one of the formal dinner napkins favored at Sara's showy table.

"You'd be surprised, *Bellisima*, how often this sordid sort of thing happens within the social set. After all, who has an excess of lucre? And who is most afraid of having the nasty tales displayed on the front pages of their local rags? Which is why these con *artistes* so often amble away scot-free. What's a quarter of a million dollars if it keeps your name from being bandied about in coarse and malicious whispers?"

Belle sat up in her seat. "Are you saying this has happened before in Newcastle? Because I'm afraid this Dawn person is setting her sights on Sara."

Kerr raised his hands high over his head. "I confess I know of no other similar confidence games being perpetrated on the Newcastle uppercrust. Although when I was vacationing in Palm Beach three years ago all the hubbub revolved around a mess that was nearly the carbon copy of the one you have described. Right down to the supposed kidney transplant. In fact, the mark was a horse person, and the dollar figure was the same: $250,000."

"But Rosco's client isn't a horse person—"

"I was merely looking for parallels, dearest." Kerr sighed. "This elderly gent in Florida—unlike your nameless pal— was more than anxious to see justice done. I suppose it was because he had no children to embarrass. He was an irascible old-timer set on revenge with a capital *R*, and he could have cared less who knew it. Stuart Stewart. What a name. He made quite a cause célèbre of his missteps. Alas, it seems that in Florida the con-gal assumed the identity of an innocent local; when the authorities untangled the muddle and chased after the true perpetrator, they vanished into thin air. Naturally, before an arrest could be made. Apparently, she'd worked the scheme in other locales across the country."

"They?"

"Yes, I believe the coppers discovered that it was some type of a gang." He plopped his glasses back onto the bridge of his nose. "Wouldn't it be an absolute howl if your *Dawn of the Kidneys* was the same person who'd used her magic tricks down in Florida three years ago?"

Belle thought for a moment. "Well, if that's what happened here, I'll bet the puzzle constructor, Jack Curry or not, knew who had assumed the true Dawn's persona and had conned Mr. Gud—Rosco's client."

"Ah, ah, ah, be careful with that tongue of yours. You almost let the cat out of the bag. What I can't understand, however, is why your ghostly wordsmith didn't simply come forward and state his or her case? Why play this game with the puzzles?"

"Fear of reprisal?" Belle guessed. "Or perhaps, whoever is making these is playing his or her own weird game."

"And I gather with good reason. Look what happened to Jack Curry, if he turns out to be your man . . . well, we do have two dandy murders." Kerr glanced at the puzzles once again. "It's interesting that the constructor mentions Grace KELLY in this latest puzzle, but in the 'To Catch a Thief' puzzle, when the word GRACE appears at 8-Down, the clue is *Meal prayer.* Odd, especially when you consider that Grace Kelly was the star of Hitchcock's *To Catch a Thief.*" Bartholomew lifted the graph paper and pointed to 31-Across. "And there's WALT. See what I mean?"

Belle sighed. "I was afraid you'd recognize Mr. Gudgeon's name."

A confused look swept Kerr's face. "Walt's Wire Wagons? That Gudgeon? What's he got to do with this?"

"Oh. Oh, nothing at all . . . er, he was just doing some electrical work on our house," Belle lied, inadequately attempting to cover her gaffe.

But Kerr saw right through her. "Ahh, my dear, that seems thoroughly unlikely, since he retired a dozen years ago. So he's your old fool. Is that it? Well, not to worry, sweetest, as I said, your secret is safe with me. It's not the first juicy tidbit I've kept under my proverbial hat."

"Thank you, Bartholomew. You're an angel."

"Harumph, not like your killer ANGEL I hope?" he turned back to the puzzle. "No, the WALT I was thinking of is WALT Kelly, the cartoonist. If Kelly were the name he—or she—desired our crucicriminologist, i.e., you, to discover, there were other opportunities—"

But the gossip columnist didn't have the time to complete the thought, because Belle interrupted, raising her voice in excitement as she pointed to 47-Across. "Look at this! GENE . . . which is another Kelly placed in asymmetrically opposite position from WALT . . . And similarly, opposite GRACE, we have THYME, which is a kelly green herb."

"*Timely*, perhaps, dearheart, but a bit of a stretch . . . However, I do believe we're on to something. Because here at 1-Across there's JIM—which could easily become JIM Kelly the football player rather than *Brown or Thorpe*, which is what the clue currently reads. While opposite that on the bottom at 69-Across we have NED, which instead of being the solution to *Mr. Beatty* could easily be NED Kelly, the notorious Australian outlaw—"

"And right down the center is SNOW TIRES. Who hasn't heard of Kelly tires? Oh, Bartholomew! Do you think we've discovered a secret message?"

"Well, Kelly does seem to be a theme."

Belle stared and stared at the crossword, while Bartholomew continued to speak.

"Could it be, *Bellisima*, that Orlando's wife was masquerading as Dawn Davis? And that this newfound friend of Sara's is innocent of any wrongdoing? Just like the woman in Florida?"

When Belle didn't answer, he added a teasing, "Well?"

"I'm thinking, I'm thinking . . ." Belle's eyes crinkled in concentration. "But if someone suspected that Kelly was pretending to be Dawn, why did they design these puzzles to make it appear as if Angel and Chip were the guilty parties?"

Bartholomew also thought. "Well, perhaps Angel and Chip are culpable—of something. This Kelly situation could refer to another matter." He picked up the crossword he'd received. "Do you know, if you look at this 'Social Climber' puzzle the black squares resemble a set of stairs that one might actually climb, landings and all . . . and since we have the title of the film UP THE DOWN STAIRCASE as a solution to 23- and 47-Across . . . and if you follow the steps up . . ."

Belle looked over his shoulder. "Starting at the bottom at 62-Across and climbing to 12-Down—" Her words ceased. She gasped, then gazed at Bartholomew in wonderment. "Wow! That's all I can say: simply, wow!"

"I'm sure you can invent fancier speech than that, Lady Lexicon."

She kissed him on the cheek. "You're a genius. An absolute genius. Did anyone ever tell you that?"

"All the time, honey lamb." He marched his fingers up the puzzle's diagonal line and read the message aloud, "GO ON THE DIAGONAL. What do you think that means?"

Belle began skimming the previous crosswords, starting with the first she'd received as she searched for other sentences that might be hidden on the diagonal. When she reached the third grid she exclaimed, "Ah-ha! Here it is. In the 'Measure for Measure' submission. Going down the staircase this time . . . read from 12-Down to 72-Across. What does it say?"

Bartholomew took the paper from her. "KELLY'LL DAWN ON YA."

CHAPTER

31

"Well, that's all well and good, Belle," Lever said as he reached for his pack of Camels. "And I've already got the bunko boys going after Kelly Polk. As soon as she gets back from Kentucky, they'll pick her up; but right now I've got two murders to solve." He lit his cigarette and looked around the room. "Sorry folks, my office, my rules." Rosco and Abe simply rolled their eyes.

"But isn't it possible that it was Kelly who killed Jack because he'd discovered she was a con artist and was threatening to expose her?" Belle protested. "You just told me his handwriting was confirmed in the 'Measure for Measure' crossword found on his body, as well as in 'Social Climber'—"

"I'm afraid that theory doesn't hold water," Abe Jones interrupted as he fanned cigarette smoke from in front of his face with his hand. "Because we've also confirmed that the two previous puzzles you received were constructed by another person. The style is similar, yes, but not the same. Meaning the 'To Catch a Thief' grid that references your KELLYs wasn't created by Curry. If Ms. Polk intended to kill *anyone* it would've been the person who constructed *that* crossword rather than Jack—"

"But KELLY'LL DAWN ON YA is right there in the puzzle you retrieved from the murder scene," Belle persisted.

"Right," Rosco said, "but that crossword has only been examined by the people in this room—and Bartholomew Kerr. The same can be said of the 'Social Climber' puzzle. Basically, meaning that nobody else has seen a Jack Curry puzzle."

"That's just an assumption, Rosco," Belle stated.

"You're right. It is. But it seems a fairly safe one. We know Curry's cottage was searched, so I'm suggesting that a crossword might well have been the object of the hunt. If it had been found, it wouldn't be in this room right now."

No one spoke for a moment, but smoke continued to plume through the air.

At last, Belle sighed heavily. "I don't know, maybe Heather has been the killer all along, and I'm trying to make too much of these word games. Maybe they were simply designed to expose Kelly as a con artist. But then why two different handwriting samples? And who's the second constructor?"

"And who's my murderer?" Al said, his voice burdened with the same amount of frustration.

"Unless," Belle continued, seeming not to have heard Al's question. "Unless Jack Curry had—"

She was interrupted by a tap on the door. Without waiting for a response from Lever, a man entered. He was in his late fifties, tall and slim with a neatly groomed, graying mustache. His slacks and shirt were perfectly pressed; he also wore a stain-free tie—all of which made him the visual antithesis of Al. A gold detective's badge clipped to his belt indicated that he was Nick Simpson, head of the Newcastle P.D. Fraud Unit. Belle had met him at at a few PAL fund-raisers, so any introductions would have been superfluous. And Simpson was pure business.

"Sorry to bust in," he said, "but I've picked up a few items of interest that I think you folks should be aware of." He then coughed and added, "How can you people stand all this damn cigarette smoke?"

Lever grumbled and smashed his Camel into the ashtray. "Just out with it, okay, Nick? We don't need any lectures on clean living."

"Maybe the rest of them don't, but I'm not sure you fall into that category." Simpson walked over and stood beside a bookcase in the corner of the office so that he could face everyone. "Okay, I just finished up a lengthy conference call with the Louisville Police Department. It seems—"

"Hold it right there, Nick," Lever said holding up his hand, "we've been through this. You've got a case of fraud on your hands, fine, but I've got to concentrate on these homicides."

"Hear me out, Al, we've got a connection. I'm not sure what to make of it, but it's there."

Again Lever groaned, but acquiesced. "All right, shoot."

"We know Kelly Polk decamped to Louisville, so I figured why not have the folks down there pick her up, just in case she's feeling the heat and opts not to return to Newcastle. Louisville offered to put an APB out on her and send a team to the airport. I passed along a description of both her real appearance, and what she might look like in a red wig that falls halfway down her back. And that's when they took some serious notice."

"What do you mean?" Belle asked.

"Suddenly, they were genuinely interested in the details of our case. After I broke it down for them, they said they had a duplicate situation brewing out there. An old guy, a horse breeder, hooked up with a young woman needing a kidney transplant. Same dollar figure—$250,000—the works. The description matches Kelly Polk—this time with a short brunette wig. Only the name in Kentucky is Sue Reynolds, which happens to be the same name as a local woman who recently had minor surgery. I'll add that this Sue Reynolds is also a brunette—as if anyone couldn't have surmised as much."

"So, were still talking con job," Al tossed in. "Where's the connection?"

"You'll never guess who this guy's barn manager was a while back."

"Orlando Polk?" Lever said, making no attempt to hide the fact that he considered this entire line a complete waste of time.

Simpson shook his head and smiled. "Guess again. It was Jack Curry . . . your dead man."

"I wonder . . ." Belle mused.

"What?" Rosco and Abe said together.

"Bartholomew Kerr told me about a similar case in Florida several years ago. I wonder if it's related? That man was also part of the horse-show world."

"This is Bartholomew Kerr over at the *Crier*?" Simpson asked. "I'll give him a call. I'd like to follow up on that."

"It was three years ago in Palm Beach, and the mark was Stuart Stewart. The police in Florida believed it might have been of gang of con artists—one that possibly moved around the country."

"I'll see what I can find out," Simpson said before leaving.

Al watched the door close. "I'm guessing, and let me know how this sounds . . . because I'd still like to find my murderer . . . Okay, here goes: Curry worked at the farm in Kentucky. Quite possibly he remained in touch with the owner . . . who, maybe, told him about this pretty little gal and her medical woes. Jack then began to suspect that Kelly's trips out there weren't to visit an ailing father . . . About the same time, he noticed the same situation developing with Gudgeon, which led him to create the incriminating puzzles, and Kelly stabbed him when she found out."

Rosco chuckled. "Who wants to be the first to shoot Al's theory full of holes?" He then counted off his objections on his fingers. "One: Why wouldn't Curry have simply confronted Kelly with his suspicions? That would have been more his style. Two: There's no indication he knew Gudgeon. They weren't part of the same circle. And three: Who made the first two puzzles?"

Lever threw up his hands. "Well, would someone please give me a solid motive that Heather might have for killing Jack? Because I don't have one."

"Let's go back to something Belle said," Abe tossed in. "Bartholomew mentioned a movable gang in Florida. What if it's the same people? Florida, Kentucky, and now Massachusetts? And if that's the case, who are they? Certainly not any of the Collins clan."

"Kelly, we know is up to no good," Belle said.

"Right, so if she's part of a ring, who are the others?"

"Orlando?" Al suggested.

"No. He's been working for Collins for six years," Rosco said. "He only married Kelly a short while ago. That's not to say he didn't kill Jack, but I'd guess he knew nothing about his wife's con of Gudgeon, or her previous history—if she is a con person."

"There's Michael Palamountain," Belle offered, "but again, he's been at King Wenstarin Farms forever; and he's hardly in need of cash. Which would clear him of being involved in any scam, although not the murder of Curry . . . or Ryan, for that matter." She grumbled aloud and then said, "What about Angel, Al? Do you know anything about her?"

"She's lived in Newcastle all her life. She's not off my list of murder suspects yet, but I'm willing to bet she's never been to Palm Beach *or* Louisville. She doesn't inhabit that kind of universe. At least, she didn't until she hooked up with Chip." He reached for another cigarette, but was greeted by a chorus of groans, so he removed his hand.

"Which means that whoever created the puzzles was trying to frame Angel as the woman who conned Gudgeon," Belle said. "But the Angel/Chip smokescreen is in Jack's 'Measure for Measure' grid as well as our mystery constructor's 'To Catch a Thief' grid." She shook her head. "Arrgh, I'm going through severe mental meltdown here!"

Rosco stood and began to pace Al's office. "Meltdown . . . Meltdown . . . I think maybe you've hit on something, my love. Try this on for size, Al: What we have here might be the *meltdown* of a confidence team. Who are the members of the group? Who could have been in Palm Beach three years ago? Three people, the way I see it."

"Obviously, one is Kelly," Al said.

"And Jack Curry," Belle said excitedly. "We know he was in Louisville, so why couldn't he have been part of the Florida show circuit, too? It's a close-knit community—isn't that what we've been told? Maybe Jack even selected Kelly's marks in the first place, rather than simply discovering that she was up to no good. But who's the third person?"

A knowing chuckle escaped Abe lips. "Ryan. Of course. It makes perfect sense. She's new enough on the Wenstarin Farms scene. And if that's the case, then quite possibly she was the woman Stuart Stewart—"

He was interrupted as Nick Simpson stuck his head back in the door and said, "I just got off the horn with a detective down in Palm Beach. It turns out Jack Curry worked for Stuart Stewart. As a trainer, that time. But the woman on the con was larger than Kelly. I hate to say it, but the description sounded a lot like Ryan Collins."

"Tell us something we didn't know," Lever said with a smile.

Rosco continued with his speculation. "So . . . Jack Curry picks the marks, and then either Kelly or Ryan move in." He started pacing again. "But they reach Newcastle and begin to suffer serious confidence team meltdown. Ryan discovers she has a good thing going with Todd and wants out. Then she shafts them both by becoming Mrs. Collins—and therefore the big, bad boss-lady. Jack hooks up with his ex-wife and realizes he's also staring a gift horse in the mouth. All of which leaves Kelly out in the cold, saddled with the lowly barn manager."

"So she decides to branch out on her own," Abe Jones said, advancing the theory. "She hooks up with Gudgeon . . . Then Curry recognizes that she's about to ruin everything he has going and opts to blow the whistle on her in the form of some ultra-sneaky crosswords. Kelly gets wise and whacks him."

"Lovely," Lever grumbled. "I can buy all that, but who killed Ryan?"

"And we're back to—who made the first two puzzles?" Belle asked. "That's who Kelly should have killed!"

Rosco replied, "Well, if we take into consideration that the crosswords were intended to frame Chip and Angel and that Jack and Kelly had been partners, why couldn't they have made them *together*? Maybe the first two grids are in Kelly's handwriting, and Jack slipped in references to her name without her being aware of it. If Belle never caught on, why would *she*?" He looked at Jones. "Do we have any samples of Kelly Polk's handwriting?"

"I'll get someone on that. I like this. It works for me."

Al raised his voice and said, for what seemed like the hundredth time, "Yes, but who killed Ryan Collins?"

CHAPTER

32

After their meeting in Al's office, Abe Jones returned to his forensics lab and instructed an assistant to drive out to King Wenstarin Farms and obtain a sample of Kelly Polk's handwriting from her husband, Orlando. Rosco returned to his office and reread his entire Gudgeon file. He then phoned Gudgeon, hoping that he might be able to persuade him to identify Kelly from a lineup once she'd resurfaced in Newcastle. Walt was either not home or not picking up, so Rosco left him a message. If Kelly couldn't be proven to have killed Jack Curry, and if Gudgeon refused to press charges against her, she'd be free as a bird, although not very welcome in Kentucky. And probably Florida, as well.

Belle made two stops on her way home. The first was to a trendy boutique pet shop where she picked up a small collection of treats for the girls, and the second was to Papyrus. Her curiosity had gotten the better of her, and she wanted to get some answers from Dawn Davis. Dawn had been unwilling to talk to her at first, but after Belle had explained everything they'd discovered about Kelly Polk, she loosened up a great deal. She admitted that someone matching Kelly's description had stopped by for copy work several months earlier. It was soon after Dawn's shoulder injury; the discomfort had made work difficult, and she'd been complaining about the fact. Over the next several weeks Kelly had returned with other duplication orders and had always been friendly and sympathetic. In fact, the two women had really hit it off, and during the course of the visits, Dawn had found herself confiding many details of her life—as well as information about her upcoming surgery.

The conversation ended with a slack-jawed Dawn observing, "I guess she just walked in the front door of the hospital and straight out the back, leaving poor Mr. Gudgeon in the dust. It's amazing I didn't run into her that day. I felt as though we'd become friends. But it all makes sense now that I know what she was doing . . . I just thought she was being nice, you know, concerned about what I was going through. There's a laugh."

As Belle left Papyrus and drove home to Captain's Walk, she wondered if the Louisville police had found and arrested Kelly yet, and if they had, if they would release her to Massachusetts, or hold her in Kentucky for prosecution. She parked her car at the curb and stepped out. On the porch was a young woman with pale blond hair. She'd removed the mail from the box and was sifting through it as though she hadn't a care in the world on this pleasant autumn day. To any of the neighbors the person would have looked like Belle; but Newcastle's crossword sleuth knew differently. So did Kit and Gabby. They were making so much racket they sounded like a pack of dogs instead of only two. And angry ones, at that.

Belle approached the woman and said, "It's not there, Kelly. Jack mailed it to the *Crier.* All the squares have been filled in."

Kelly tossed the letters on a table and turned. Her right hand held a small revolver that was almost entirely concealed by a tan canvas jacket, while the expression on her face was attentive and polite as though she were a new neighbor stopping by for a chat.

"Just like you never checked into the hospital, you never got on the airplane, did you?" Belle continued. "You're a smart woman, Kelly, if that's your real name. There's a warrant out for your arrest in Louisville. And probably also in Florida by now. You're not going to get away with this, you know."

Kelly waved the gun. "Open the door. Let's go inside. I don't like public places."

"There are three Doberman pinschers in there. In case you didn't happen to hear them snarling. They're trained as attack dogs. They're big, and they're dangerous. They'll rip you apart." If it weren't for the gun being pointed at her, Belle would have smiled at this fantasy. Nonetheless she was surprised at how calm she was, given that she was being confronted by a likely murderer. Belle wondered whether it was the fact that Kelly had made herself up to resemble her intended quarry that robbed the scene of its sense of menace. It's hard to feel threatened by someone whose hairstyle and clothing so flawlessly replicate your own—unless, of course, the mirror image produces anxiety rather than peace of mind.

"Alright," Kelly said, "out to my car. It's that Dodge out there. The green one." She handed Belle the keys. "You're driving. And don't try anything stupid, either. I'm in this too deep. I have no problem with killing another person."

"So you did kill Jack." It was a statement and not a question.

"No, the Man in the Moon did." She laughed. "Of course I killed him. He was a double-crossing weasel. Shacking up with Ryan, right under Todd's nose . . . he had no morals whatsoever. He was a worm looking out for himself."

Belle refrained from mentioning that murder could be considered immoral, as well. "Ryan was also having an affair with your husband . . . is that why you killed her?"

She laughed again. "Boy, I sure wish I had, I can tell you that much. It's crazy, but I felt more betrayed by Ryan than by Orlando. But the truth is, I didn't find out about that junk until after she was dead."

"You're going to have a hard time persuading the police to believe you. They're convinced that Ryan's and Jack's killer are one in the same." Belle decided to confirm Rosco's theory by adding, "And since the three of you had been running a confidence game, and you're the only one left, I'd say the police are on the right track."

"Go on, get in the car. Enough chat out here in the open."

Belle walked down the path, crossed the street, and slid in behind the wheel of an aging Dodge, while Kelly tossed the keys at her. She considered starting the engine and making a run for it, but Kelly was in the passenger's seat as quickly as the thought had entered her mind.

"Where to?" Belle asked.

"I don't know. I've got to think. We'll just sit here for a bit."

"Not a good idea . . . Rosco will be home in a minute. Plus the police patrol this block on a regular basis; it's a tourist attraction."

"Don't try to bluff me, honey, you're no good at it. You're too honest. Sorry, but that's the way it is. You're too easy to read."

Belle put the keys in the ignition, but didn't immediately start the car. "If you didn't kill Ryan, who did? Was it Jack?"

"Oh, you'd like that, wouldn't you? That would make a nice little picture. Three grifters swing into Newcastle and try to take advantage of its fair citizens. But you do-gooders ferret them out and save the day. You'd like to blame this all on the trailer trash of the world, ain't that right?"

Belle fastened her seat belt, and Kelly glared at her and shook her head. "You people are too much, I swear . . . puts her seat belt on like a real angel. What's the matter, afraid you're going to get a ticket? We certainly don't want to break the law now, do we?"

Belle ignored the dig. "Well, if Jack didn't kill Ryan, and Orlando was in the hospital, the only people left are the Collins family."

"What the hell do you think I've been talking about, honey? You think because those people are a bunch of blue bloods they don't get fired up enough to kill someone, is that it? I've seen horse people do awful things to their animals in the hopes of winning a blue. Real painful stuff to make them step higher and hold their tails up straight. And they break the legs of prize horses with baseball bats just to collect the insurance money. That's the truth. Those folks have no control over their emotions or their tempers. They're cutthroat, and they don't consider the consequences of their actions. And then when things don't go their way, they run like rabbits for fear that their names will appear in the newspaper. That's what makes them such easy marks."

"So you're saying that Todd killed Ryan because she was unfaithful with Orlando?"

Kelly shook her head and chuckled. "It's a dirty little cesspool out there at King Wenstarin Farms. But the old man is the only one with any backbone as far as I'm concerned. Don't forget he's already divorced two women. Why wouldn't he divorce the third? He'd never kill Ryan; it's not his style. He would have hung her out to dry without a nickel if he'd known what she'd been up to and then smile like the Cheshire Cat as he watched her *walk* down that long lane and off the farm—wouldn't even call a cab for her. Oh, yeah, Ryan was killed by a jealous lover, but it sure as hell wasn't Mr. C."

"Well, who's left, besides you?" Kelly only smiled, and Belle added, "Unless . . . Ryan was having an affair with someone else?"

"Like I said—a dirty little cesspool."

"Palamountain? Chip?"

"Not hardly. Those boys don't like to live that dangerously. Cross the old man? I doubt it. Guess again."

"Fiona killed Ryan . . ." Belle said slowly, finding the concept bewildering, but also very plausible. "Because Ryan was . . . she and Jack were . . ."

"Now you're cookin', girlie." Kelly waved her gun at Belle. "Start the car. We're going to the beach. I was leaving late that night, when I saw Jack slip in. I knew what he was up to. Him and Ryan had been on-again-off-again for years, but I wanted to be certain I had my information straight, so I stuck around till he left. I sat in Mr. C.'s Bentley and watched the whole thing take shape. Ryan came down and saw him out, gave him a big smooch. That's how I know he didn't kill her."

"And then you saw Fiona go in?"

"You got it. I guess she was out lookin' for him. But she saw that big, fat kiss just as sure as I did."

"Which beach are we going to?"

"Munnatawket. Drive slow."

"You don't need to keep pointing that gun at me, Kelly. I'm not going to try anything."

"Yeah, right, like I trust you."

Belle glanced into the rearview mirror and began to maneuver the car out of the parking place. But she hit the brakes when she saw another car coming her way. The driver stopped and waved her on. "Why didn't you tell the police what you saw?"

Kelly laughed at her. "You really don't get the life do you? You don't get the grift. I don't talk to cops; never have, never will. No matter what. We have our own society; you have yours. If anyone out there hears I talked to a cop, my name's mud. Besides, I had Fiona right where I wanted her."

"You were going to blackmail her," Belle stated.

"Hey, you're a bright girl," Kelly said facetiously. "I was sittin' pretty. We'd all found ourselves a nice comfy home. Ryan had the old man, Jack had half of Fiona, and I had the other half, money-wise, that is."

"But he found out you were conning Walter Gudgeon."

"Yeah. He thought I was putting the whole operation at risk. That's when he got the bright idea to start making those puzzles and set Angel up as being the one on the grift. I didn't like it; I thought it was real stupid, but he kept sayin' it was what the 'smart-set' liked . . . little games of what person's got the goods on another. And besides, Angel was easy to waste. She wasn't family. And Chip would never have stood up to his pop if Todd had told him to dump her." Kelly shook her head in anger and disbelief. "There I was drawin' out these damn grids and writing clues, and Jack's feeding me words that all but shout *Kelly,* and I don't see a thing. Not a thing! And it's not like I trusted the creep, either. Well, he got what he deserved. Both of them did."

Belle slowed for the stop sign at the corner and glanced again into the rearview mirror. It was obvious that the driver of the car behind her either didn't see her stop, or didn't see the sign, or was dialing a cell phone, or was distracted in some manner, but whatever the case, he was going to rear-end her. She pushed her foot firmly down on the brake pedal to avoid being catapulted into the intersection and braced her body as she waited for the impact. Kelly gave her a strange look; it all happened in the blink of an eye.

It wasn't a light tap; it was a forceful collision. Belle's seat belt held her in place, but Kelly lurched forward, her forehead colliding with the hard dashboard. She was knocked unconscious immediately and slumped forward in the seat. A small trickle of blood rolled across her face, as Belle straightened her body and took the gun from her lap.

"I can take that pistol if you'd like," the voice said from outside the car. "I know how to use it." It was Walter Gudgeon.

"I was coming to your house to apologize for being so hard on your husband," he said, "and saw her marching you out to the car. That's the Dawn I knew. That blond hair and outfit didn't disguise her for a second."

Belle unhooked her seat belt and stepped from the car. She rolled her head from side to side to loosen her neck and back muscles.

"Sorry about rear-ending you like that. I didn't know what else to do. I saw you put your seat belt on, so I was hoping it would work."

"It sure made a mess of your nice car."

He shrugged. "It's only a car. I called the police on my cell phone. Do you want to call Rosco?"

"No, he should be on his way home. Thank you, Mr. Gudgeon. It appears as if you saved my life."

"I guess it's all in how you see it, how you look at life. As I was about to plow into you, do you know what I was thinking?"

"No."

"I was thinking that this old Dodge is the exact same color green Young Walt wants to paint the fleet of Walt's Wire Wagons."

"And . . . ?"

"I'm beginning to think it's not a half-bad idea."

Across

1. Grp. for those with 2-Down
4. Fort Worth campus; abbr.
7. Belief
10. Fib
13. Dupe
15. British singer, Chris
16. Coach, Parseghian
17. Horse sense, part 1
20. Talent of 47-Across
21. Some towns
22. Computer key
23. Doctor
26. "___ Rider," Eastwood film
27. Outlaw, Kelly
28. 63-Across task
31. Swan's former coworkers?
35. 50 plus grp.
36. Horse sense, part 2
40. Irish nobleman
41. Pirate gallows?
42. Hosp. workers
43. 43-Down locale
46. Mister in Munich
47. Author of horse sense quote
49. Be in charge; abbr.
52. Aiming
55. Tierney role
56. Horse sense, part 3
60. Grassland
61. MMMC ÷ II
62. Gin cocktail
63. Ambulance workers; abbr.
64. Ship's heading
65. Extra work for 31-Across; abbr.
66. ___ Moines

Down

1. Wide open
2. Sedans and wagons
3. Specific
4. Cash drawer item
5. Gear tooth
6. Spanish article
7. Certain patch
8. Peaceful
9. Potato option
10. Lion portrayer
11. Some savings accts.
12. Comfort
14. Coach, Hodges
18. Horseshoe peg
19. Greek goddess
23. Vaccine developer, Jonas
24. Away from the wind
25. Had been
26. Pistol ___
28. Author, Caleb
29. Spring dance
30. Tach readouts
31. Headliner
32. Skinny
33. ". . . lend me your ___"
34. Mole
35. Way off
37. Comedian, Mort
38. Annoyed
39. Certain satellite; abbr.
43. Stage backdrops
44. Internet discoveries?
45. Prickle
47. Talent of 47-Across
48. Type of trip

HORSE SENSE

49. Amor
50. Pooh creator
51. Don
52. Ready and willing follower
53. Appear
54. School grps.
55. Tiny particle; abbr.
57. Sgt. or Cpl.
58. Grass
59. Chicago trains

The Answers

OFF TO THE RACES

1 M	2 A	3 S	4 O	5 N	■	6 T	7 H	8 R	9 O	10 W	■	11 E	12 S	13 P
14 A	G	I	L	E	■	15 R	E	I	N	A	■	16 L	A	I
17 C	A	R	D	S	■	18 I	N	F	E	R	■	19 L	G	E
20 A	P	B	■	21 S	22 E	C	R	E	T	A	23 R	I	A	T
24 W	E	A	■	■	25 F	R	Y	■	26 O	D	E	S	S	A
■	■	27 R	28 I	29 G	T	O	■	30 C	O	M	B	■	■	■
31 A	32 E	T	N	A	■	33 W	34 T	O	■	35 I	R	36 W	37 I	38 N
39 S	T	O	O	L	■	40 N	Y	U	■	41 R	A	H	A	B
42 U	S	N	R	L	■	43 E	E	N	■	44 A	V	I	L	A
■	■	■	45 B	A	46 N	D	■	47 T	48 I	L	E	R	■	■
49 E	50 N	51 C	I	N	O	■	52 A	F	C	■	■	53 L	54 T	55 A
56 S	E	A	T	T	L	57 E	S	L	E	58 W	■	59 A	I	R
60 S	A	P	■	61 F	E	S	T	E	■	62 H	63 O	W	T	O
64 E	T	O	■	65 O	S	S	I	E	■	66 O	M	A	H	A
67 N	O	T	■	68 X	S	O	U	T	■	69 S	A	Y	E	R

SUBMISSION

1 A	**2** S	**3** P		**4** I	**5** C	**6** A		**7** S	**8** P	**9** A		**10** S	**11** O	**12** S
13 U	T	A		**14** L	I	L	**15** Y	P	A	D		**16** A	N	A
17 D	A	N		**18** S	T	L	O	U	I	S		**19** L	A	D
20 I	G	E	**21** T	A	R	O	U	N	D		**22** A	S	I	A
	23 G	E	O		**24** O	U	D		**25** C	A	R	T
	26 B	O	**27** R	N	T	O	**28** L	**29** O	**30** S	E
31 A	**32** D	U	L	T		**33** N	A	O	H		**34** E	**35** A	**36** R
37 H	O	R	S	E	**38** W	**39** I	T	H	N	O	**40** N	A	M	E
41 S	U	R		**42** A	C	K		**43** E	E	R	I	E
	44 G	O	**45** I	**46** N	G	I	N	**47** C	**48** I	R	C	L	E	S
		49 W	O	E		**50** O	A	R		**51** E	S	E
52 G	**53** O	**54** Y	O	U	R	**55** O	W	N	W	**56** A	**57** Y
58 A	G	E		**59** G	E	T	M	E		**60** R	**61** O	**62** P	**63** E	S
64 S	R	A		**65** A	R	T	E	S		**66** C	R	O	S	S
67 H	E	R		**68** T	S	O			**69** S	K	I	P	S

TO CATCH A THIEF

1 J	2 I	3 M	■	4 F	5 D	6 A	■	7 I	8 G	9 A	■	10 M	11 O	12 W
13 A	L	I	■	14 A	I	R	■	15 N	R	C	■	16 E	R	A
17 B	L	A	18 Z	I	N	G	■	19 S	A	D	20 D	L	E	S
■	■	■	21 E	T	E	■	22 S	E	C	C	O	■	■	■
23 F	24 L	25 A	S	H	D	26 A	N	C	E	■	27 N	28 I	29 B	30 S
31 W	A	L	T	■	■	32 S	O	T	■	33 R	A	D	A	R
34 D	I	B	■	35 S	36 L	O	W	■	37 T	E	T	O	N	S
■	38 D	A	39 W	N	O	F	T	40 H	E	D	E	A	D	■
41 M	O	N	I	E	S	■	42 I	A	G	O	■	43 N	A	44 B
45 S	U	I	T	E	■	46 P	R	N	■	47 G	E	N	E	
48 U	T	A	H	■	49 T	H	E	G	50 E	51 T	A	W	A	Y
■	■	■	52 E	53 T	H	O	S	■	54 G	A	S	■	■	■
55 G	56 O	57 O	D	B	Y	E	■	58 M	R	C	H	59 I	60 P	61 S
62 I	R	A	■	63 A	M	B	■	64 E	E	K	■	65 N	E	O
66 N	O	R	■	67 R	E	E	■	68 S	T	Y	■	69 N	E	D

MEASURE FOR MEASURE

A¹	S²	U³		W⁴	A⁵	S⁶		H⁷	I⁸	S⁹		A¹⁰	S¹¹	K¹²
D¹³	O	G		I¹⁴	L	L¹⁵	N	E	S	S		C¹⁶	E	E
O¹⁷	W	H	A¹⁸	T	M	A	Y	M	A	N		L¹⁹	E	E
			S²⁰	H	A		C²¹	A	B		L²²	U	M	P
H²³	I²⁴	M²⁵	H	I	D	E²⁶		N²⁷	E	Y²⁸	S			
A²⁹	R	E		N³⁰	E	V			L³¹	E	M	O³²	N³³	S³⁴
B³⁵	I	N			N³⁶	O	E³⁷	L³⁸		A³⁹	F	T	E	R
I⁴⁰	S	L	A⁴¹		R⁴²	D	A			T⁴³	I	N	A
T⁴⁴	H	O	U	G⁴⁵	A⁴⁶	N	G	E⁴⁷	L⁴⁸		S⁴⁹	E	S
		D⁵⁰	E	W		A⁵¹	S	S	E	S⁵²				
	B⁵³	R⁵⁴	I	N	Y			O⁵⁵	N	T	H⁵⁶	E⁵⁷		
A⁵⁸	R	O	O		S⁵⁹	O⁶⁰	D⁶¹			D⁶²	A	D	S⁶³
R⁶⁴	A	N		O⁶⁵	U⁶⁶	T	W	A	R⁶⁷	D⁶⁸	S	I	D	E
E⁶⁹	Y	E		F⁷⁰	R	E	E	W	A	Y		R⁷¹	I	T
A⁷²	S	E		T⁷³	N	T		N⁷⁴	Y	E		Y⁷⁵	E	S